Francis Bede writes and lives in Tasmania.

Bede, Francis
Bad Clergy
ISBN: 978-0-9806289-1-3
Copyright © 2018 Francis Bede
First Published Niche Press 2018.
Copyright © 2020 Francis Bede, 2nd edition revised.

For information contact the Copyright Agency Limited.

Bad Clergy

- A question in five fantasies

by Francis Bede

Bad Clergy - A question in five fantasies

Fantasy 1 – Eucharist
1. Matinee Idol
2. Thanksgiving
3. Fly the Milky Way
4. Introducing Placates the Persecutor
5. Dooble, Ooble, Looble or the Family's Higher Consciousness
6. Out Under the Through Door
7. Byway to Salvation
8. The Method of Indream
9. Hero Worship
10. Repast for Enlightenment
11. Stone the Crow
12. Holy Orders

Fantasy 2 – Purgatory
1. The Pub Grip
2. Mon Amour De Brawl
3. His Stigmata
4. The Goosey Two and the Ride
5. A Theme for Syndey
6. Evil or Live
7. Anthrax Blues
8. Forward Passes
9. Rhyme Time
10. Prayers To The Good
11. Doin' it His Way
12. Doin' it Her Way

Fantasy 3 - Resurrection
1. Kings Cross Panorama
2. Why is it So?
3. Ode to the Infamous Non
4. Sex
5. Chastity
6. Stripperama
7. Mary Magdalene the Stripper

8. Crippled Inside
9. Yes They're Going to a Party Party
10. Extracting the Catholic Bits
11. A Hole in the Sky
12. The Dead Conversation

Fantasy 4 - Penance
1. In the Garden of Earthly Delights
2. This Flight Tonight
3. Spirits of The Night
4. Commercial Break
5. What, Another Bloody Commercial Break!
6. Editions Of Her
7. May the Force Be with You
8. Veni, Vidi, Vici
9. Fridee Night Fever
10. The Jeanne Genie Speaks
11. The Ramp Up
12. Before on The Road Again

Fantasy 5 - Divinity
1. On The Road Again
2. Three Persons in a Tub
3. At The Jesus Transubstantiation Centre For Lost Souls - With Tonight's Guest Lecturer the Very Rev. Rev. Luther J Kramer
4. Something About Mary
5. Sympathy for the Beast
6. Blazwaorden
7. After the Sun
8. Once there were No Facts
9. Living After Death
10. A Single Motor Vehicle Accident
11. Sky Riot
12. Sleep Nevertheless

Bad Clergy Slang

Act the gammon/gammoning - priestly insincerity

Back-slang - to enter or come out of a house by the back door

Back-slum - a back room

Brisket beaters - Catholic congregation

Daisy coat - straightjacket

Drops some whid - inadvertently letting words fall

Family - priests who make their living 'upon the cross'

Flash - the cant language of the Family

Flash men - the Bad Clergy

Flash panny - a public house used by the Family

Galloot - fool, idiot

Goosey - sexual abuser

Granville crib - the Bad Clergy's half way house

His-Nibs - the Pope

Knapping dues - what the Family get when they go out together on the night

Lag Motor - the Family vehicle

Lentil - a dollar

Nuts upon himself - self satisfied

Oliver is out of town - when moonshine is masked by clouds

Out and outer - the goosey two

Pulpit's Jerry - sermon fog

Quim - vagina

Shiminy - a sad story

Shiner - eye glasses

Spliff - marijuana rolled into a cigarette, aka joint

Syndey Town - Sydney

Tickle a Marilyn - a shy and clumsy method of mating with a female

To the ruffian - to the extreme, superlative

Toby Men - the Bad Clergy

Wax the candles - share with female company

FANTASY 1

EUCHARIST

1. Matinee Idol

For dry lips, a ceremonial joint funereally passed around. A big
spliff, rolled, tasty, dealer divinity driven
Stuffed.
Tight, twisted, cigarette papered, triple layered, roach ready
Queenslander Head, aromatic, sacristy grown, Golden Wattle
kitchen table, lovingly assembled like holy pastry
Roughed.
From Muldoon to Kelly to Mahone to Clancy, the wet roaches for the
goosey two.
In these hot, meaty
Apparitionist, miraculous, melanoma hours, no patience no quest
When the moon is cloudily clothed on this Fridee night
When the boys'll be out and about to poke around and prize a fancy.

Muldoon the pinked-up whale-headed falsifier used to the gear penance
percolated and sly lentils can buy when he passes the joint from his
kissing hand to the kissing hand of Mahone no less pink but the head of a
buffalo and not used to the fancy comforts of brethren him being from
the back way out and all that shiminy and he laughs as he passes the
weed to Kelly who is like the bare arse of Errol Flynn when he's looking
at girls and the footy and loose change when he takes his toke and
shoves the weed smoke deep into his passionfruity lungs and coughs and
spittle flies across the room to where Clancy sits and soon his kissing
hand grasps the Cuban and puffs like he's the real king of belief and with
a moose head and why should he not think of the punters as gullible
vermin but the mood takes him into sincerity and he's relaxed and over
reaches the roach to two members of the Family to give their lungs a
taste who shall remain anonymous to protect the innocent children
they've left to Father violated.

The Crimes of De Sade lay on the open page where sweet Eugenie
was given to educations
Studied and stained with coffee and dried semen from dedications.
There upon a venereal table propped by broken chairs anchored in a
desolate room;
The supper table under a flickering florescent tube which stabs at the
gloom the sinful Family sit at.
The Family do not alter the atmosphere. For now, the gloom and

smoke generates in them new inspirations. For the silence of past
nights locked into prayerful nothings failed to inspire. Brethren by
day soothing the worried brows of believers: about their perverted
souls condemned to burn in timeless furnaces: repentant, repent, yet
within sight of the Holy God, they are disappointed in themselves.
No-one says a prayer for them. And how the sun's rays pierce the
Bad Clergy's priestly disguises in such an eye spanking way. How
easily do they forget about their obligations and holy orders when the
faithful need them so.

In nomine Patris et Filii et Spiritus Sancti, Amen. To bless and to
give unction. They are Family; from good seminary clergy they stem.
Who like to say an irreverent prayer or two. They speak in flash,
these brothers. The weed's power is to loosen tongues. Much like the
born agains who speak in tongues. The highs'll wear off deep into the
night. Then back to speaking like a Catholic toff. Their clergy alter
egos they put away for tomorrow time. For relief's sake, for some
clergy crime. God ordained them and declared them Heaven's swine.
Of course they'll return to what they were ordained for. They are
nothing except priests who know what they are good for.

And now dear reader, for your entertainment these Clergy turned
Flashmen have put aside their vestments and beads, confirmations
and confessions for some Fridee night mirth and scrumptious
fooly mayhem. When they go out its mostly quiet; occasionally
it's visionary, if their substances be friendly and good. A band of
merry kidders who like to polish their big gig crosses with lemons
and spit and filthy rags, and put them to early nightbed tucked in
pink plastic. They walk away, these locum priests, walk away from
priestly acts and join together as the Family. Tonight, in the year
1980, they can neither stand their priestly selves, nor labour at their
private callings. Saturday might be OK for mugs, and wax head
toolboxes, but they can't get enough of Friday's mind crackers that
are infant, so reckoned the Easybeats. After the long week of prayers
and pressure, after all, fraudulence needs a break. These bad brethren
gambole unarguable words of hope and faith, and afterwards coldly
count the Sunday worship's takings. Their acts of ministry feels like
they're pacing solitary confinement cells; recurring, the scenery's
always the bleedin' same. And so they grind together whinge words

and blow them out of their gas boxes with the sweet smoke of the
heavenly weed. And they think ever so flash and fancy, for anyone
in the maelstrom who dares to look. The Gag 'n Throttle Pub is
running tonight. The Dog 'n Bone Boogie Blues Band plays there
every starless night. They play in a place down under the back
of a freeway beneath the traffic. Alleyways into alleyways and
corners turning left off right and disappearing. Roots songs smash
synthesisers, and smash those who sing along to seven minute radio
rock anthems. None of that American Pie. None of them rocking away
the night. The Family shy away from them tastes. And to the Family,
there are too many music punters whose mental rusts accumulate
in unforced magnitudes who, driven to suicide by country music
which seductively sways in AM breezes, leave this Earth spiritually
unclean. Punk smashes disco and love is a disease worse than a dose
of Anthrax. The Dog 'n Bone Band is OK, but best when stoned.
Clancy hates them, but then again Clancy is Clancy all out of shape
in a restaurant, foreign names, menus, and public toilets.

Miniature upturned replica crosses point the way, which the Bad
Clergy hide underneath mullet singlets placing them just above their
hairy ledge:
They have to keep it on
They have to keep their badge
They have to bear the bloody cross
They have to wear it close to their flesh
They hope the nails will evaporate into air
They hope the loin clothed rider will slip away
They hope to be the revolution which sows a few rude seeds.

Nah! Hope is the final evil, said Nietzsche. For nothing protracts
torment like hope, like hope, dear hope which dangles at the end of a
long, long rope.

The spliffs are coming! The spliffs are coming! One to try, two to
mellow, three to get stoned, four to make sure, five to make sure
again, six to stop them coming.

These males are called by God and bleat in the voice of Family.
Unhappy scrotes. Going to extremes fiercer than Hells Angels.

4

Toby-men. Highway Men. 0.0001% men. Family Men. And two who
are out and outer men. Them who use their clean nostrils to find the
where-abouts of policemen's kennels. Them who've got a week of
odour and stench to keep the Holy Spirit away.

Would they like to take to the pulpit and skite
About the pain that enlightens them?
The pain from clearing out black phlegm
Just before a homily's deliverance
When passions suffer with severance
Essential when blessing the saviour's blood
Muscles cramp when the mass is a dud
Like their profanity, unblessed by the One.
They might seem evil in the light of the sun
Caused by doubt which plagues them at night.

2. Thanksgiving

Fridee night's the night when children begin their futures by searching for the imaginative plays of their untarnished childhood---the night the hungry law finds what it is looking for---the night a satyr boy and nymph girl play up ahead of Saturday nuptials---the night the dead Jesus was laid to rest and then dies again---the night conversations are held between moving car windows---the night the moon might change its mind and retreats---the night for lonely people who fear an unrepeatable life will go unrecorded when death takes their life away---the night the boogie isn't blamed for mass destruction---the night babies are abandoned---the night boredom takes a break---the night as old as decay---the night of shame that is to become street legend---the night the matrons of etiquette never go out---the night the imagination leaves the mind and tries the Earth out for size---the night when chunder enters the official lexicon---the night when suburban heathens worship the object in their hands---the night tragedy moves in for the kill---the night as promising as the first furtive kisses of romantic sensuality ---the night of love that lasts---the night when abstract Hell rumbles at the doorstep of urban patience---the night when curly-headed police politely look upon those who search for adventure and fun when danger flirts with comic relief---the night when teenagers stay at home and learn what discipline really means--- the night when nightclub ceilings shine brighter than the Milky Way-- the night ending a week which shouldn't have to return as it was---the night disaster has a silver lining---the night the Family are closer to each other.

Let them blaspheme with prayer before they go out.

Family Prayer:
We the Family make believe in a God, the patriarch, the Almighty
Maker of Heaven on Earth, of all that is seen and obscene.
We make believe in the Lord, Jesus Christ, the only Son of God
Unconsciously begotten of the Father
God from God, Light from Light, true God from true God,
Begotten, made one in Being with the Father.
Through faith all things are unmade.
Through pastoral work doubt is given its daily rest.
For men and for salvation he fell out from Heaven:

By the jizz of the Holy Father
He was born of the Virgin Mary, and became a somebody.
For tragedy's sake he was crucified under Pontius Pilate;
He suffered, died, and was buried.
On the third day he deceptively arose blurring the witness's vision;
He ascended into Heaven and got seated at the wrong hand of the
Father.
He might come again in glory to judge the living and the dead
His kingdom and its back end.
We make believe in the Holy Spirit, the Lord, the giver of life
Who proceeds from the Father and the Son.
With the Father and the Son he is worshipped and petrified.
He has spoken through the Prophets.
We make believe in one holy Catholic and apostolic Church.
We unacknowledge one baptism for the forgiveness of sins.
We look for the resurrection of the zombie
And the life of the world to come. Alrighty!

Hypocrisy wafts with the smoke
Belief is just an in-house joke
Security is their nether yoke
From the spell they can't awake
The piss they greedily take
The Church for the Family's sake.

The words come forth fast
Stoned and hallucinogenic
The Family join hands in a séance
Beanbags elevate for when Heaven comes a'knocking.

Family Prayer:
It is truly right to give you thanks
It is fitting that we smoke in your glory
Father of infinite goodness.
Through the gospel proclaimed by your Son
You have brought us together in a crumbling Church
Peoples of every nation, culture, and tongue.
Into us you breathe the power of your Spirit
That in every age your children may crumble as one.

Your Church bears steadfast witness to your love.
It nourishes for the coming of your kingdom
And is a sure sign of the wasteful covenant
Which you promised us in Jesus Christ our Lord.
Therefore Heaven and Earth sing forth your praise
While we, with all the Church, proclaim
For our discomfort, we offer you our thanks.

They sit about in a revolving room. The spliffs go about in this early
evening, and their belief is calling out for its doom.

Family Prayer:
Renew by the light of the gospel our Angst
Strengthen the bonds of unity between heretics
And their leaders, who together with your people
May stand forth in a world torn by strife,
And discord is a sign of oneness and peace
To unite us in love, holy and truthful Angst.

Dribbly, fiddly
Sanctifying grace they poach
La la kipper
That's a winking great fat roach!

Family Prayer:
Open our eyes to the needs of all; inspire us with words and deeds
to comfort those who labour and are burdened; keep our service of
others faithful to the example and command of Christ.
Unite us in love, holy and unfaithful God.
Let your Church witness truth and freedom, justice and peace that all
people may be lifted up by the hope of a bad world made new.
Let it not be persecuted for its sins.
Unite us in love, holy and unfaithful God, we challenge you.

When thought's a crime think of God's revenge like a headache,
And when one is deaf to God, the brain throws up a bloody earache.

Tonight they are going out wide and far. Gaits borrowed from
Buster Keaton. Flash suits and black Panama hats. Stunts for a

beautiful dark night. Uneven and fashionably crushed. For confessors
they'll be rushed. In black shoes and off white spats. Family men
remarkably normal. Ironic before their humble state. No forks, knives
or dinner plate. Tastes vary, yet spontaneously ensue. By which the
right hands grasp, and left blesses. It's going to be pizza time. Then
each hand will caress the cheese they call the Cloying Pitch. That
which overwhelms the crusty base as God does with redemption.
Their trouser pits dark and twisted. That's melancholy like the blues
man insisted. Demands for a far potent lace creep in. Ornaments in
shop spaces have become too cheap. They do little to inspire this
pack. Who in tomfoolery, they've got the knack. The Lord's memory
of them must surely jar.

From mouths like dankest caves
Come the babble of crying babes
Come the slang of convict slaves
The Clergy borrow 'em
The Family four and the goosey two
A most conspicuous clerical crew
Opening the night up to their ways
Of indreaming nights and troubled days
And the Devil lets 'em.

3. Fly the Milky Way

The '67 Falcon, the Lag Motor, is ready to fly. Parked outside,
camouflaged by rubbish and paper strewn around it. Ratted bench
seats, rusted pipes, tyres parsed, and black duco. A white Z across its
breast. Radium roof, tinted windows. The shell sparse. Four handle
bars. Headlights, undressed bulbs. An exhaust like a punctured lung.
A rumble to make big bad bikies cry. Sometimes it has a free will of
its own.

Kelly, the coachman, will test his hand; and drives stoned to the local
Shop:
Watching, weaving, clutching, gearing, indicating and then he'll stop.
That'll do, couldn't kill a roo, even if it was stunned by a head light
Even if the blood lust was strong, even if he was full of spite
Caution is the stoned man's cop, and when the green light flashes go
Behind the wheel is a wise man, tyres chainless, driving over snow.

What the Family undo:
The minds of stoned Bad Clergy are spiritually bent. Penitent, scornful
and paradoxically lame. Offering burnt leaves in plastic cups to the
inaugural saviour, bleeding ever since in their pictures, icons, their stolen
reliquary. Catholic icons lay as rubbish around the room. Their prayer
room is like a teenager's. Sad Jesus is posted like a Martin Sharp rock
star. Huge rivets pierce his limbs, nailing his limp body to a purple cross.
His package modestly covered by a mere slip of loincloth. His head
bears a sticking crown of thorns. Above his head stand the psychedelic
letters floating INRI mocking his state of regal death. Hanging on the
ceiling overlooking them. Is there a hint of a mocking smile? The face is
dead and his death is fake. Not you Family, only your love-filled smiles
are fake, like the Judas! They talk of the agonised man laid to rest. And
on the third day after the cross he rose. With dust in his loins, death
gathered no semen. Life is suffering and death is fearful. Go through
Heaven's door and the second chance is eternal. Meat and potato hope is
given by the Bad Clergy on Sunday who prefer their sinners well grilled.
Original sin abounds, and best drown it in holy water. Acts which
challenge moral law arouse a eunuch clergy. Sinful acts of molten sex
between man and woman. Or between a man and a man. Or woman
together with woman. No child of God falls harder than those who

should know better. The Bad Clergy know, who give in to thought temptations. Mary is there to help wash and clear up the mess. How easy is it for Bad Clergy to confess! Repent and hail three sensual Mary's. Then down the pub, down to the Cross. And hope to God the Marilyns come. Like the Family members still staring at the hung and bleeding Christ. Like the times they mishandle Lent, bent. And still they cannot leave the family Church.

Kelly is back.
Smokes in a pack
Back in black
His itchy rack
Inside his slack
Black underdack
Unexploded sack
Under mossy crack
His limpid whack
Ever so slack
To get in back
With the pack
With female crack.

Primed for attack
Some things lack
For Kelly outback
His old mates a pack
Sex on the rack
Thumbtack attack
Rather a Big Mac
But couldn't hack
What goes on back
Fear of the Jack
Got no knack
Female's a quack
Always comes back
Needs a Quack
His old mate Mack
Caught the Jack
Down goes the slack

Pussed underdack
Jab underback
Relief for the sack;
Kelly is back.

The Family four and the goosey two are ready
They leave the Granville Crib rock steady.

And in the tranced eyes of the Family are the fires of anger dulled
and energy formal, the devilment and the kind of passions reserved
for the demented cool, enough to pass them off as rather normal.

And the seasonal glass-tipped raindrops which land on roofs like
asteroids have stopped battering the manor's tin roof in which the
Family gathered; a fibro manor, the Granville Crib, that glories
the ordinariness of a suburban wasteland with an ordinary façade
protected by broken fences and weeds, ordinariness filled with lives
deep-seated in quandary when makeshift spiritual guidance is scarce
out here, no wisdom, no future, and the Family harrowed by the
bleak look for solace in the Jesus-weed split, like the cohabitants
of mass suburban communes broken by churches, sports fields,
shopping malls, car parks.

Hidden beneath the Lag Motor's skin are triple bypass replacement
spliffs to trip the journey road, the Parramatta Road, The Broadway,
Sussex Street and disappear, they being Granville and all that. Soon
the Bad Clergy'll be pressed flesh scoring pub claustrophobia, or
them walking gravity's footpaths looking at the human scenery; and
who'll be bothered to give a damn!

Family Prayer:
Saint Rotten the Archpunk,
Defend us when we battle;
Defend us against them Trendies
And Manly Seaspray sneers
May Dope rebuke them,
The Family humbly wonder.
And so you,
O prince of spit and anger,

By the power of the finger-chord
Cast back into black vinyl
DISCO and them like evil spirits
Who prowl about the world
Seeking ruin of poor souls.

There is movement in the suburbs, the word has got around
The stoned Family's said their prayers, they're off underground
And on the merry way they go, chatter's up, gossip in Flash speak
And cocky banters, these four named and the goosey two.
Six in the Lag Motor, two in front, four in back
Kelly's driving like he's learning for his L's
Around the cabin reeks St Chris's magic spells
And drawn from the kerbside the Lag Motor enters the stream
The ebb and tideways of traffic, the red, amber and green
The street lights, and lamp poles and neon flashing signs
Pass them blind and the memory of them will linger.
The noise, public transport and speeding tradesmen's vans
Come on the westie, and two lane formula one,
The life of Syndey Town, they say will never die.
Exhaust fumes, refineries and the smells of roadside decay
The kind of melancholia no drug will wash away
It's in the blood of commuters, even those on dodgy treads
The throng of getting around, banging through their heads.
Left turns, right turns, running at invisible road rules
Give way, and watch out for the blinder in the blind spot
Watch for cyclists and suicidal pedestrians, here and there
Eyes out for the Callan Park Squad, eyes out for the destination
Eyes out for the lane lines, when eyeless on the highway
Speed within the limits, attract no attention
Be just another number plate, in a sea of number plates
Six clergymen done their duty, Flashmen newly clowned
And action they'll scruff, gammoning them unbound.

Stoned Kelly's thinking black nights, glaciers, Parramatta Road,
chaos, storm traffic slip-steaming: A ravenous Fridee night town,
blue men swarm when this night brings the dazzling beauty of sins of
the flesh for all to share and ponder in sin's wake and still be proud
of them: And hark the pulsating novas atop checkmate chariots which

go screaming for some of that business:
Kelly's thinking, a slow drive into glass and alluvial concrete
wildernesses filled with inhabitants working shopping working
playing shopping playing sleeping and sleepwalking: Find the
sensible lanes, dull the natural speed, in between pedestrian trails:
Jacob's ladders are stretched across the bitumen, phantasms
transform into lollipop ladies at street corners and look for crossing
children: Stop-go men stand astride the gutters and control the traffic
with their anger and boredom and yearning for amber draughts:
Keep the Falcon cruising onwards in a deadly line of accuracy and
purpose so not to attract the best attention from those who seek to do
harm in their stressful jobbing and bust and prosecute and send the
now criminal because of a few spliffs to Long Bay Gaol for a long
stretch to be taunted and fought over for favours like in the good old
convict days of rum and lash settlement when buggery did not mean
homosexuality: God forbid, those desperate romantics had nowhere
to go when fallen from the grace of the Lord: And they sought the
comforts of fellow men in dank cells, their 'sweethearts':
Kelly fears beatings and a violent arse receiving of a diseased wrench
from some crazed inmate and to kill the pain and shame buy the hard
stuff incubated in the warm arse of a smuggler and then suicide and
as a pauper be buried in an unmarked grave with the prison clergy
looking on, how ironic:
Kelly's apprehensive and thinking backwards about them blue jets
pulling the Family blokes over for a howdy do and with a twinkling
eye for a juicy look and a squeeze of nervousness and polite hellos:
Kelly believes St Christopher and other like angel-demons will
arrive and protect the Family who pray together enough for the good
Lucifer and luck to look after them who are deserving of all the
love and comforts their repentance brings and sorry sorry sorry is
the easiest word to say when unbleached sin is finally cleansed by
the forgiving object that is God who in kind elusiveness strokes the
hunger of melancholic believers who suffer like the living dead and
end up sloth and institutionalised and be damned in Hell with the
Black Dog barking by their side:
Kelly remembers that other time it was him alone driving back from his
Mum in Liverpool and copped a search of the pockets and
trousers and wide shirt cuffs and nothing was said but a thank you:
Kelly is alert to the kennel men in blue with their hello to your sirs

with your slick hair and scruffy and how about the look you've got
being one of the Family plus the dirty two dressed in glossy black
Keatons in dirty dog collars doing the evangelist's shuffle and isn't
sweet leaf a lovely colour and it looks like you be the busy Clergy
on your way to a Jesus banquet and that smell in the arches must be
the after smell of incense you believers like to purify the air with
which stinks of sweat and charcoal and other crawdad signals we
know to be the scum and slurry what we pick up near the dawn of
another bleeding day after a night of uproar and mayhem that is this
fair city of Syndey Town they say of and proudly so and there you
are brave loving sons of your father the Lord Jesus Christ which
makes the rest of us heathens all sentimental at the scaffold and witch
hunts and inquisitions for all this scum and jetsam underneath this
Oliver when he's absent head masked by black fluff spewing out of
those refineries and chimney stacks which is like an erotic postcard
attracting aliens from similar worlds with replica McDonald's and
where a sky looks down upon these ants of us going about the place
as if it were a prosperous colony careful to disguise the unique
history of a place founded in convict garb and after liberation spend
its time cleaning up the convict stain revising it terra nullius and
going about redeeming itself though it does not know the reason why.

4. Introducing Placates the Persecutor

Scene: The Lag Motor somewhere on the Parramatta Road to Syndey Town.

Muldoon:
Who's a wantin' for a Marilyn to give a tickle? *(no answer)* C'mon lads don't be shy in your shyest ways!

Mahone:
She's nice she is to me, the Marilyn I've been thinking of, the Marilyn who dreams of me in my dreams.

Muldoon:
In your dreams! In your dreams!

Kelly:
In my dreams! I have her close then she'll run away.

Mahone:
Poor Kelly. That's when she is running to me. I'm a rough sort. That's it in a shell! A bold ruffian at ease with himself.

Clancy:
Ruffians all of us! Alas only one Marilyn. We'll toss a four-sided coin for her eh? Name each side Hell, Earth, Purgatory, Heaven. *(looks at the two)* She'll be over 16.

Mahone:
Man, the oncoming headlights hit the peepers real hard.

Muldoon:
Have some night shades. *(passes over 3-D shiners)*

Mahone:
It's more Family to whack the love, eh? We do in dope, the Sunday loot, the blessed wafer of the bloke. We shall not want in Family matters.

Clancy:
No such thing as a four sider with them sorts of emblems. Can't share illusions anyway, except Tongue Speakers. Marilyn never really

makes a home. Fallen Nuns do, I hear of hysteria. Hot beverage for
rampaging knights.

Muldoon:
And oh what a lovely draught I take! True Belles of one Immaculate
Reception, ha ha! But I forgive 'em, for they know not what.

Mahone:
What's on the double J's? The triple B's? Buffalo, Birdman,
Blackfeather? Hey Kelly, put on for me a show! Get some real music
to fire me up. But nothing sentimental, or stop.

(Kelly turns on the Radio. Bad Boy for Love is playing.)

Clancy:
Can't figure why the boogie we go. Tradition, is it? What about
feedback?

Muldoon:
Stop you're moaning Clance, No Aztecs, no Chain or Lobby, but
there's Funter Tradition, when Skippy bangs the skins. Give boogie
rhythm to a man's blues. It tastes better, you know! Don't wanna
be preachy, yeah! *(laughs)* Better here than on the cold slab. Don't
mumble here, re-thought is better. Chance to shake out the wobblies.
Can't be done in a cryptic Church. We only know Clance, what we
can't undo.

Clancy:
Yeah but I've got headphones.

Mahone:
Plugged into your dirty arse. *(laughs)*

Clancy:
Hey, that area's dry-cleaned. Aside a higher being's purchase. Aha!

As flat as the salt lakes Campbell ran his Bluebird on, the banter's
done for now. No laughs, the stoned heads blink and stare at moving
coliseums. The music weaves in and out of the Lag Motor's cabin
the Family use as a lean to. While the scarping Falcon cruises for
the purpose of Kelly driving at hand. For the quality of the night

depends upon fearful awakenings. How crowds and temptations and followers become like corruption. Their suffering is the burden the unlucky Family must bear. Abdication from their calling is no option when learning about the world. Indeed Muldoon will speculate on contradictions which make a religious life. The colour of his past blends well with his personal inquisitions into unfaith. When peering at his shaving mirror, a crustaceous morning light is the paradox illuminating his loose personality.

Placates says:
A righteous Church is that which expounds its authenticity without demonstrating its limitations: its members cautious not to reveal themselves vulnerable: its special might so expressed in the priests who show their lives upstanding, whose appearance and tired faces are most brilliant in night's shadows. With ardent prayer, they lash themselves and how they tremble. And in them a pulsing anxiety, since they must always live like this. They consume their doubt, for nothing else is so necessary.

A quick pit stop at a petrol station
The attendant pumps in gloom
No cheery light talk, not tonight
No "Gidday mate, the car alright?"
Lookers observe
Families mind their own business
Clancy goes round back and leaks
The forecourt empties, and sleeps.

5. Dooble, Ooble, Looble or The Family's Higher Consciousness

In the vessel of God's creation
Lay down flesh futures, all blood blown
The wayward worship, bread and stone
These bad priests are up for mediation.

Into bread enters the word of God
Into blood enters the word of God
Members of the body conjoined
Members of the spirit conjoined
God unravels the gift of life
Jesus revives the gift of life
Eternal happiness is spiritualised
Eternal wellbeing is spiritualised
The Eucharist of the mind is Christ
The Eucharist of the body is Christ
And when blessed bones go to dust
Pods of life re-emerge from dust.

These members of an exclusive priesthood say they are not like the
rest who are weak of flesh who are yet to receive the fruit of the
Eucharist's blessings for they are not of the flesh of God nor are
they yet to abandon themselves to one spirit for they are incapable
of seeing the flesh becoming the body of the one who came down
as saviour and the redeemer of all guilty of the bearing of the stain
which came from birth and the blood of birth is not the blood of
God and the cord is not the link to God and thus it is cut and the first
gasps for air heralds the cries....................until the infant becomes
a priest and wrestles with what it is living for.

Indream a phantom visits Clancy and the other Family members
Across its ethereal frame are writ the prophetic words EAT ME
Stricken by paralysis, the dreamers in their sleep which confines
Cannot escape the spellbinding sorrow of this ghostly image
And the dream surrounds the participators in this dream frame
And the emptiness of the dreamers is new flesh for the ghost
Follicles of hair begin their journey from thorny crown to scalp
Thus transforms the phantom's need, the transformation into host

And now the eaters are the slowly eaten, eating themselves eating.

And indream all of a sudden the phantom then speaks.

"Siht si ym ydob, siht si ym doolb. Etak ti, tae ti, I geb uoy. Knird em, knird em, llitnu I ma on erom. Llif yourself htiw ym ecnesse, llif up htiw yoj! I ma real, ni rouy ydob!

For all the forgiveness of sins for all the wrongs to be righted the Lord begs of you to contemplate your sins. Ton tsuj eht lanigiro, tub lla ni eht dnim dna lla ot eb enod. There is no other covenant but his. The puc ew sselb, it be a small participation in the blood of tsirhC. And the bread that is broken is but a small participation on the body of Christ. One daerb si ton enough. We are all one body and the bread will never be big enough. So sayeth the sayer who says these sayings mysterious in his way having been called upon to pose as a htuom tuhs by doG.

Them believers in the flesh and blood of Him say that the flesh and blood of Him was on the cross, on the cross, and then it went to ground, it went to ground, and on the third day the corpse began to rot. And what did rise from the goodness of Father? What did rise was hope: epoh did esir. They who wrench from their necks the forgiving yolk of doG lliw die. And sooner the Earth shall swallow than those who love the blessed yolk. For the yolk be crowned with the holy jewels the Crown of Thorns. Those beautiful spikes driven into the skull of the divine one for all shall be saved. Let them be saved. Soon there will be a second coming and...

Go empty the corpulent person of wealthy means absent of the taste for Eucharist but for caviar and table-filling roasts and the plump shall stay skinny though they be hungry for the taste of the Lord thy God and for those who believe who wholeheartedly believe for they shall not go hungry in the desert in the jungle in the back streets of big towns for they are too easy to wash themselves of sin too vagrant to contemplate salvation until regeneration and the only certainty is uncertainty which is the flesh and blood made up of Jesus and the word word word which spills from the testaments of all who were there and weren't yet that is what faith is all about in these urgent

20

times when the plump go forth corpus and not so naked as the Jesus
in his strategically placed loincloth and the lamb shall lay down and
sacrifice itself through Abraham and the temptation of its flesh is but
part of schemes the Lord runs in defence of sin.

Memories churn in the full coil of substances because it is written
and suseJ says so. Thanks to wicked Demons the blasphemy of the
act endures, and the Lord says to them 'do not go beyond that which
your master deems, imitation flatters not, therefore mischievousness
will find a way of biting you on your flicking tails.' And the
warnings of Mithras prevail. Though it is written that dark worships
mock holy transubstantiation, the mystery is for Catholics alone, else
it is the work of me Satan.

At the tabernacle, is communion, of a body, and of blood, to thane
spirits, to mankind, to the holy father, to what has gone, to what is
now, to what will come, said in prayer, without signs, without clarity,
no veins will seep, no flesh will weep, the word of God, whispered
in winds, as currents of seas, as light in skies, as day, as night, before
creation, after science, in Freudian slips, in Marty Feldman's eyes,
some may laugh, tears will come, winter rains, summer drought,
rising suns, rising moons, eventide. And forgive me false brethren for
the words I have spoken backwards, not."

6. Out Under the Through Door

A pause before a red traffic light. A vision when melancholy takes
flight.
Kelly it is, who starts in fear. Thoughts of brothers so dear. In a
crash.
A stupid smash. But then the lights turn green.

The phantom's foot bone is connected to the knee bone
The priests get muscles, good fat and twelves layers of skin
The phantom's knee bone is connected to the thigh bone
The priests get hair, thin on their backs, thick on their chins
A paean of heraldic angels reveals the brightest ones
From out the backside of Pluto come chariots thrusting fire
The sun is put in its place; the sun is not the chosen one
A blaze of heavenly phosphorescence and dreamers shall not tire.

7pm traffic crawls on this Friday night. Cars and trucks walk up on
their wheels. Taxis push and weave in and out and jump like dogs on
sheep's backs.

The day has transformed itself into darkness. The black has become
the body of the light. And where was the truth of this day gone by?
In sadness, the Family swear it has passed. And by the mark of faith
so has the flesh of God. Passed into the figure of a round thin wafer.
Can this be the truth of holy cannibalism? For bread is a simple
substance known for ages. And who would cast a found object for
bread? The light of old prophecies brightly shine. The truth of new
flesh on any Sunday is proved by the body with blood. And not
anybody, but the body of Christ. Covered in brilliant light for all to
see. The shallow veins on his skin carrying blood. Like no other, for
it bleeds on sight. And bleeding it becomes red wine. So that all may
drink of it, in holy ritual. The flesh and blood that is visceral. The
consumer will rise like the crucified. Each and every Sunday. And
it is forbidden by the Church to wag it. Or the roaring tablet on the
mount will roar louder over the second wave and wipe away the filth
of uncatholic humanity though the Lord did not speak of it at Cana.

A digression:
Once there was a person accused of ultra faith
Who believed the moon was made of cheese
And the person hopped on a jet ex L A
And landed on the Sea of Tranquility
Took a piece and brought it back for crackers.

And the Family heeds little of prophecy except what the forbidden
weed predicts. The strange leaf of Sodom. They give thanks to the
creator of it. And along with the Sunday roast, peas and gravy,
the Family eat the bread presented to the brisket beaters by them.
And by fingers, the bread enters stomachs. And by glass the wine
dribbles into bladders. No mystery then, but mystery there must be.
Make it divine, and give work to mystics! "Eat me, drink me", says
the Bible's mystical prophet "For there is no life in you, if I am not
ingested. And better for you to not baulk at my suggestions. Have
faith in me, and hope for miracles from me. For the purity to travel,
that I urge of you. Do my bidding, or there is no place in Heaven.
Not for unbelievers unprepared to make a living out of faith which
declares my willingness to be consumed by every man, woman and
child; miraculously done from the Sunday tabernacle. How dare
you doubt this is my body! How dare you doubt this is my blood!
You are not only Catholic but a better doubter than me! I know you
Clancy, I know you Kelly. Conscious sin drives your guilt into the
unconscious, forcing you to live your purgatory. For all of this sweat
dripping from my body some of it does miraculously taste like my
blood."

7. Byway to Salvation

Prayer:
And so it came to pass
Flesh is bread
Blood is wine
To stop food vice
It was nice.
To know what is truly ingested,
Is the spirit of a God made man-flesh.
Believers partake in their Sunday best
Blood into wine, so incredible
Wine into blood, well why not!
Let us transfer substances,
Let us priests do the business,
And solemnly bless the Passover.
What is left in a few days will pass,
Sadly the gold must disappear
And blend with crude and other substances
That gives the sea its heretic hue.
Let us not prejudge hard doubt,
To believe is the essence
Of the knowledge death is proud
In the way it cleanses the Earth
Of animals, plants and sinning souls.
God of course, is wise to this
Otherwise what need for a blissful Heaven
But wait! How does resurrection work?
By faith alone, and a cannibal fix.

Flesh and blood, from Heaven's infinite serves of lunch! The eater
needs wholehearted belief! If not, then what else to take? God's word
propositions the soul with the promise of paradise. Believe until the
blood runs hot. Exhaustion is the imbedded vow. Matter is not matter
judged. Fatal proof confirms the deal between the risen one, and
those ready to rise. At birth, or at the end of old age. The intoxication
of the spirit is unknown to those who disbelieve. Hard ecstasy is a
Catholic's reward. Hard vices, hard education, hard love. The Bad
Clergy reckon they know what's really true. Hard work, hard life,

hard luck. Softened sometimes by a dab of holy oil, on the head, on the toes.

The Lag Motor is cruzin' for a Holden bruzin'
The Family look and take the street scenarios in
Kelly's cautious like a cripple sleep walking
Clancy, Muldoon and Mahone do no talking
The goosey two are thinking hairless quim.

And the blessings the Bad Clergy officiate in, save themselves from themselves for awhile. But is the holy wafer the true substance of an elusive God? Those who cannot understand it are dead in the head, though they do not realize it! Jesus himself said so. He who walked on water, turned loaves into fishes, made the crippled walk again. A miraculously magicianamic minstrelabulous. But then again he did die only once. The choice scapegoat for the likes of the Bad Clergy. A holy lamb which faintly bleated when slaughtered under the Roman gaze.

Muldoon thinks, whilst watching the city life, that nothing is impossible. That Jesus' miracle life is likely to be improbable. For there is little written of him as a sinning man. There is nothing much written about Muldoon. A few flash words mention him. Nothing is impossible. The only impossibility is for Catholic faith to loosen its grip on Muldoon's gelatinous mind. He who is still prone to the wiles of superstition. And Muldoon's brain has the texture of an avocado. And no more of it need be said as he imagines himself to be some sort of hero.

Another digression:
Colonel Strop in his musk-scented balaclava
And second-hand garbage bags for the image
In shoes, black brogues with runners' spikes
Is somewhere in the world making good
The hero to shapeshifting politicians
The habitual breakers of reasonable expectations
Who bear false witness against the "I told you so's".
He is hero to leakers, and a hero to treasoners
And to all the good neighbours on this planet

Who hide their contempt behind street gossip.
Colonel Strop lives on a drifting iceberg
And lately he's been parked on Soviet shores
Writing a report for the UN on Freedom
Keen to bear witness and impress the Americans.
To do this, he stands back from ordinary people
The Soviet people and the nervous Yankees
And writes about naughty things the Politburo do
For he is righteous and has the ear of the Lord
And though it is false witness in the Commie's eye
The might of right will always win the fight
And the final arbiter shall put amongst the evil
A plague of bad credit, proud oligarchs, lying tongues
Wicked imaginings, feet which run mischievously swift
Hands shedding skin, no truth in the scamp of fear
And spies to fill the cracks in Kremlin's walls.
Colonel Strop knows he is a master
He has a song playing on his ghetto blaster
"I am the man they call The Sharp Arrow!"

8. The Method of Indream

Indream Mahone sees a lone tree standing in a field
He knows it to be a tree, for his parents did tell him so
And it has the same name at school, and at the seminary
This wonder in a field, and others which weep and shed
Give shade and fruit, burn away and magically regrow
And all of this Mahone knows, in the dream he is having
And he believes there is no other name for it than tree
Except in different languages spoken around the world
He believes the tree is by many names and still a tree.
But then a prophet came to him and said it was a whool
The branches, leaves, roots and trunk make it a whool
And Mahone disagreed with the prophet; it is a tree
And the prophet says it is a whool, and they argue
The prophet wins and makes Mahone believe it is a whool
Makes him swear an oath to Eslaf, the Spirit of Belief
And believe it as an objective truth, and this is how
Indream Mahone is to believe, though he is doubtful
Each time he sees a whool he thinks about a tree
And he wonders if he can really love a whool
The same way he will always love a tree.

Trinity incarnated redeems transubstantiation
Transtrinity carnates redeemer substantation
Stantia cardeemer trini tiation
Transsub redenated trinity incarn
Transubstantiation redeems incarnated trinity
Trinity redeems transubstantiation reincarnated
Reincarnated transubstantiation redeems trinity
Reincarnated transubstantiation trinity redeems:
To the Family it seems.

Slugging for Jesus and the word becomes the sanctified word. The
Church insists upon its unique hermeneutic style. And any distortion
of the Catholic literal is by its definition heretic. The Family do what
their Church says, and sometimes what it does. How is a mind clear
which serves the literal? And how does the literal serve a clear mind?
For the scripted word has been wounded by time. For a new born

reader will interpret the word become word hence. For there is doubt
that the fossil words will ever be found. And thereafter the smell of
hearsay has got pungent in confused minds. Writers for centuries
have been replaced by believers yoked to illiteracy; meanwhile literal
reinterpretations are reworked illiterally.

Muldoon when in Church, at prayer, at sacrament, thinks if Jesus
hadn't died and then lived he wouldn't need to doubt. Such is
Muldoon's doubt. No stranger a calling is it than to see congregations
believe. To smell congregations singing. To touch congregations in
worship. To taste congregations silent. And to hear congregations
thinking of a divine presence.

Placates says:

That there was one man who was never a hu-man because his
substance had miraculously changed into a god-saviour when he
died: for this is the joy of a faith in which believers accept that a
body is not a body but altered by faith a new substance to be ever
present in minds and hearts of the everyman and everywoman until
the day they expire.

Muldoon:
(*yelling*) Who says so?

Clancy:
What?

Muldoon:
Who says the wafer we dish out Sundays after the pulpit's jerry's
been lifted isn't bread, but the bod of Christ?

Mahone:
Them ancient scribes who tell us that it be so.

Muldoon:
I tell you the ears of them scribes hear rumours explode from the
ages like Hendrix feedback in air.

Mahone:
Let me believe it's true, and I'll feel better.

28

Clancy:
It is repeated over and over and over again in The Newby Testament
- this is my body...

Muldoon:
And the shell shocked repeats their same words.

Clancy:
C'mon Muldy, it's our Fridee night and Marilyn's night. Soon we'll
be waxing the candles. Don't spoil it with rude questions. We work at
ourselves to keep the faith. We'd rather remember you upchucking,
that's what counts.

Mahone:
Nothing is perfect, this is true Muldy love, you feeling blue. It's cold
outside our Churchy steps. And colder inside our chambers. Though
we struggle with belief we always love our neighbours the Turks.

Muldoon:
Very pretty Clance my love. And while I go unfulfilled a spliff or
two will ease the pain and I'll take it whipped or willed.

Clancy:
Ain't no pun like a priest's pun!

Deep into Parramatta Road and the Family drops some whid. Their
thoughts do stray and their tongues break loose. Their shutting and
opening minds clang bang in the Lag Motor's cabin. One could
almost hear their apostate arguments if it weren't for the pin. Family
bonds are more ironic than the bonds of ordinary Catholic men. An
attitude having crept in with cringing. Someone's thrown a Christ
voodoo doll at the front window. And soon silence fills the cabin like
a drowned body in a sack.

9. Hero Worship

Some words Judas Iscariot was heard to say upon his impeachment.

Time and space is no place for my pal Jesus. Next to me he's the
last great outsider. A wingless glider which floats in the dead of
night. To teach the wicked wrong from right. Time and space is no
place for the redeemer of the world. He's an oysterless pearl. He has
wisdom beyond all measure. Life is more than its fore-pleasure. He
is responsible for such spiritual sass. To be irreverent is unarguably
crass. He is perfect's total perfection. Otherwise all is rejection.
A fella like Jesus Christ has blood that's sweet, his body moist.
Enemies do their darndest, have done their woist. Time and space is
not his place. If only instead I had betrayed the human race.

I have tried to come to thee,
When you pray in your direst need
Though I am not the chosen one
I find myself at the peak of your joy
Perhaps in the sentiments of your heart
My beauty lay in your hymns
And they are as beautiful to me
For the joy within your hearts
Is divine, and true enough for me!
So said he before his suicide
And he spoke these words, not once but thrice.

Deeper into Parramatta Road. A gang of old sharpies look for blood.
Old Town Hall boys, Blacktown boys, Granville boys. Pants
highwaisted,
braces, sharp, round-neck cardigans, sockless moccasins,
sharp, fringeless cropped hair dovetailed, sharp. Knives concealed,
Polo shirts, sharp like the Family. Go by the name of Murphy, sharp.
Looking for disco blood which drips from mirror balls. Looking for
long hairs and doped-up hippies. Scruffy gnats with scruffy minds
to knuckle up and make a beery crush. Round the pubs, round the
clubs, down the side streets, deep into a crystal night. The blood of
Raudonikis inebriates them and they are faithful to his cause. And
fired by the remembrance of last week's bashings. And they love

beer and the Sharpie dance. Blood spilt in anger. Blood for blood.
The sacred subject of their hate.

Street wine called blood. Symbol of purity and dissent. Poured over
footpaths. That their hearts be a living pouring chalice. And fear shall
be for those who get in their way. Sinful hairies high on Hawkwind.
They should be taught how to do the sharpie dance while AC/DC's
on the groove. In Parramatta they're honoured at parties with kegs of
beer. One for each lung. They are the pack. Only when they are alone
do they worship their grandparents.

Clancy has prayed:
O Precious Blood,
Be their strength amid their trials and struggles in exile.
Grant that at the hour of death
I may bless them
And give them their comfort in prison
And sanctify their poor souls
And prepare them for Sharpie Heaven
The burning home of their encephalic rage.

And on footpaths on any particular day or night when Mahone is out
walking suburbia alone he sees the ugliness figurative of mishealth.
Hallmarks of wealth. From days and weeks and months of human
grind and toil. Out of gaping mouths come vomit and lungfuls of
phlegm. Strange there is little control when people reconfigure
their tastes. In the remains of fag packets, flavoured chips and other
wastes. Death and grime and spit. Mahone looks and thinks of
suburbia plagued with distasteful grit. Walking by rubbish which
clogs gutters. Who made this mess, old derros, or young nutters?
Suburbia struggles to keep itself clean. They say suburban streets are
diabolical and mean. The personality of a gorby of phlegm is near to
the truth of things. It is neither redeemable nor capable of creativity
like things which bring adaptability, stability and a citizen's sense
of pride. But Mahone ponders and takes it all in his stride. What
he sees doesn't disgust. Underneath the shoes he wears, Mahone
gathers Neolithic dust. Men walk their dogs and leave their doggie's
doo. Pedestrians navigate footpaths and work their anger through.
They crack and break these footpaths, because of a circuit of strain.

Footpaths, gutters, malls, the motor vehicle's bane. Mahone likes
suburbia's vibes when it attends to its streetway mess. The hope is for
suburbia's pride to ignore its misery less. Worse days have passed
when transport was horse and tray. When human waste was difficult
to hide away. So it is in suburbia bursting at the edges. And cluster
high-rise protected by steely hedges. Footpaths are as crowded as
herds of wildebeest encamped. Mahone is but one of them, and
one who is likely the least. So he thinks of himself when walking
backwards off the streets. He leaves suburbia to cautery and blister
and grimly lurch. Safe is he back in his holy Catholic Church.

10. Repast for Enlightenment

What broke Mahone's spell
That irresistible smell
Anticipated by the bonded boys,
Hunger and palate joys
Pineapple drowned in the Cloying Pitch
For unrighteous appetites s'il vous plait!
Cool Frank's at Annandale
Family Pizza's like a whale,
Tummies rumbling from the weed
Fill them up with capsicum seed
Lots of them
Artichokes, and the stem.
It's all in the takeaway
Paid for, the boys break away
From the stares and dimmers
Their discomfort simmers,
The car smells like a roman feast
The gorging of these savage beasts.
After a prayer said for the base,
Lost in the Pitch lathering a face
The named ones fill to their laps
The goosey two get the scraps.
The cartons to be thrown when they're blessed,
The name on the package is possessed
Acrimonies in their guts can dwell,
Six family sizes ravished down to a cell
Washed away in canals of fizzy tar.

Muldoon given to philosophical consternation
Is troubled again by the dogma of transubstantiation
When the blessed pizza is sacred body
And the blessed fizzy tar is sacred blood.

In trance in consciousness is Muldoon's vision. That one thing
becomes another and through the becoming of the thing is a being by
the divine logic whereby God is in everything and everything is in

God the one in the same principle which understands the universe is
neither within or without God and the trinity is neither three nor one
since numbers are arbitrary and four could mean two so Muldoon
thinks while reverently eating a slice of pepperoni with furnaced jaws
sprayed with the tar blending together as mush making their way into
his gut bracing for the lime to do its business and this is when the two
are one as substance ready for the body to make use of it the best way
it can
Can
And that mysterious point when mutation gives way to conversion
and the holy substance is neither regurgitated or proceeds into the
intestines the question of the mystery of substance change which
makes something ordinary into an extraordinary thing created to
make the eater temporarily at one with what he or she eats and the
climb to Heaven is a long and laborious challenge and Muldoon
thinks he had a head start him being a priest but that has changed
because the curse of doubt always sits on his left shoulder and nags
him but never during another purloined chance of a fancy slice of
pizza sliding over to him from the responsible Kelly who won't drive
on a full stomach on account of him getting the stomach uncomfys
and stitches passing by the base of his spine
Spine
It's in the feasting and drinking which celebrates the unity of
common life and its treasures and disasters alike and talked about
at Eucharist over the seasons when community means something
and the deeper theological meaning of breaking bread and sipping
wine is left to the priests who in deep thought conjure arguments
and logical discourse so that the ordinary and the lay need not bother
about substance being one thing and then another but what should it
be when the tastes of sophistication are common to the masses and
the stubborn Muldoon thinks pizza with its array of gourmet toppings
and crusts should be considered as much and contemporarily be
symbolical like the bread at Eucharist
Eucharist
And the act of essential conversion from substance of one to the
substance of something else as one in the same like the Muldoon
logic which says before pizza and tar there is God and after eating
pizza and tar there is God and the consumer chosen to consume what
has been blessed is very lucky and pity all those persons not Catholic

34

who have not consumed like he has but there is still time and a
tradition Muldoon subscribed to when he first opened his heart to the
calling at the tender age of fourteen with the encouragement of his
bigger daddy
Daddy
Who says there is everything supernatural about bread and wine
becoming the body and blood of Christ at Eucharist because there
is always faith that the substance of Christ is that of being and non
being and wherein faith says there is also another meaning which is
Christ's eternal presence for sinners seeking redemption who need
only to unquestionably accept Him for there is no other way out of
their situation but to take the bread and wine and ingest it as the body
and blood of Christ
Christ
If pizza and fizzy tar were chosen as the body and blood of Christ
Muldoon would be the first to approve of it for these are nutritional
extremes of food and drink closely related by their very nature of
substance and consumption and conversion into bodily waste and
their mediocre nutrients are easily extracted and stay in the gut
and the waste is exiled through the body through the kidneys and
intestines the rest transubstantiated into nutrition which Muldoon
believes is the logic of pizza and tar and their flavours at the point
of their consumption when each ceases to be as the other begins
and the resulting substances become sacred and logical substances
representing the one and true God who is in everything seen and not
seen heard and not heard felt and not felt tasted and not tasted smelt
and not smelt
Smelt
Pizza smells as good as any food cooked on the planet Muldoon
reckons and he can't get enough of this communion and he knows
that what was formerly pizza and tar is still pizza and tar and what
will pass won't change except they were formerly pizza and tar
and which becomes along with other substances shit and piss and
Muldoon figures there could be a connection because the names of
bread and wine change when they are blessed and become the names
body and blood and what he sees after eating the pizza and drinking
the tar is enough for him to accept transubstantiation as a fact for
when he blesses pizza and tar and their names change to shit and
piss and him not blessing other food and drink then pizza and tar is

transubstantiated in name and Muldoon is less troubled for he is full
of pizza and tar and full of vigour and ready for whatever this Fridee
night brings him and his band of brothers as is their tradition
Tradition
The trance is snapped by a belch
Muldoon you fickle heart!
A coward is the ungodly man
Who questions from the outside!

Jesus said:
I am the bread of life: he who comes to me shall not hunger and he
who believes in me shall never thirst, for my flesh is food indeed, and
my blood is drink indeed.

11. Stone the Crow

Scene: Inside the Lag Motor and disorder.

Muldoon:
A hymn to the sacred! *(belches again)*

Kelly:
Ah Muldy, I hear the strains of Bohemian Rhapsody.

Muldoon:
(belches)

Clancy:
Crazy on himself, he is. No words to describe, And nothin' like
pizzas warmed to go.

Mahone:
Munchy is, munchy does. This has the nuts upon us, eh. We're right
for the coming festivals. My dear brothers!

Clancy:
I like the grease to linger. I like the tar to rumble.

Muldoon:
(belches)

Kelly:
Muldy agrees I reckon!

Muldoon:
If I were a porky I couldn't stuff myself more. If I had a hammer...

Mahone:
Don't get sentimental Muldsy. Them folksy days are dead and gone.

Clancy:
Have to find them cartons and bottles a home. Seen them in my early
dreams. Tossed about a seaside shore. Oh the waste, the waste!
(opens the door and throws the rubbish in the gutter)

Kelly:
Plummy, Clance, very plummy. I'll start the rumbler eh! We're off to a doom show. Or somewhere nice, anyways. You back there, you done?

(silence)

Kelly:
Well alright, any you bloody muckaroos need to empty bladders and colons?

Muldoon:
Yep, hang on, I'll just do this. *(walks to a nearby wall and drills it yellow)*

Clancy:
There's a spiritual man for you. Look at that sign of the cross! That's as yellow as any goodtime lemon!

(Muldoon returns to the car and the Family rumble out from a side street.)

It's like this dear reader: Family with scripture in their hearts are unarguable. For they possess theopoetic words possessing them. Uttered quietly until coherent. In faithful voices loud and clear. Through prayer and through devotion. Through time and inspiration. Bulwark to sin. Bonds defining kith and kin. Brothers bonded within the Church family. These hearts of men wise for war. This is what they fight together for. For the privilege of staying priests. The Family men seek their honour. In the hearth of Church outside itself. To bring extremes together. Faith and existence. That they may find in each other something in common, the emptiness of course. Though faith disputes, for good it fills. God completes, and the rest is up to them.

The rest is up to them. To make something of themselves. On another Fridee night. To liberate themselves and save the world. Co-working with their version of God. Free to make their choices in their world. Life is good. Diseases, injuries, deaths are bad. Quality is good. Stupidity, indolence, drugs are bad. But not weed.

Dear reader: And they pursue their good. *(The Lag Motor heads back to the Parramatta Road traffic.)* Their conscience exhumed
by the revered influence of toxic substances. That they do it unto
themselves. As they wish upon the rest of humanity. On Fridee night.
As a law unto themselves. Carried by role abuse. Taken forward
by Christ's forgiveness. Yearning for one truth is too much to bear.
When imitation of Him fails. And hope rests in a dust-drowned
desert.

(The Lag Motor crawls through Glebe) There is no hope for the Family.
Hazy minds do not reveal God to them. Altered perceptions might.
Their blank hearts are yet to be inscribed upon. For they have yet
to fully throw themselves prostrate. And beg for mercy. Before the
man-God or God-man. And conform. To the will of the God-man
or man-God. That which is good and perfect. Unattainable to the
Family. Brothers to the Clergy sons of God already in Heaven.

They struggle dear reader: Their conscience cannot tell right from
wrong. It is wrong for them to do what they think is right. It is right
for them to do what others think is wrong. Others think they are
doing right the things they think are wrong. And thus they obey.
Love of wrong is right for them. And the divine law writes - obey thy
conscience be it clear or cloudy. For it varies like the weather. And
yet there will be the final judgement. For it is the God-man's law.
Obey -
Conscience the authority the Church gave itself to judge
Conscience mistaken which is outside this authority to judge
Conscience neglects in error and ignorance this authority to judge
Conscience loses dignity that deliberately ignores this authority to
judge.

Dear reader: The Church is the true and only teacher of the truth.
Conscience cannot be formed without the truth. There is no moral
authority without truth. Conformity must be to the truth. The Fridee
night Family mould conformity to their truth. Those who witness the
Family's truth cannot understand it. They know nothing of a plan
and of will. They know nothing of natural law. Until it is revealed to
them.

Dar reader: They are some distance from the Family Crib. The Lag
Motor nears where Parramatta Rd ends. They've passed by brick and tile
mesas. Behind them the stretch of fibrolite vistas. Soon they'll enter
Syndey Town's canyons. And trial behind a taxi man's trespass.
Primordial vehicles charge and swipe. Syndey Town is chaos as
different eras merge. Chariots and cavalries jostle and scream. Birds
nest on the canyon's high ledges. Senatorial pigeons gather by
fountains. On the streets the apocalypse is familiar. And a red man
controls every corner. The noise is by an orchestra arguing. Lights
plume everywhere, ignoring the night. A story walks by, and then
another. Soon there are too many to tell. Syndey Town will not sleep
when lovely at night. In cafes, in bars, its lovers will sup. Here credit
is as happy as a rich child. A reverent cube filled with hived cubes.
By day it empties, by night it fills. In its pockets green struggles with
grey. In its hearth stampedes give way to silence. Syndey Town is
too busy for the nervous lonely. They anonymously look for their
neon names. They are the aliens never to be lost. Sandstone and steel
are the architects blend. Sharp eyes will spy the ornate carvings.
From asphalt veins comes its spirit. A calamitous spirit that needs it
to thrive. Syndey Town is a madman taking his tea. Syndey Town is
a festooned toilet bowl. Syndey Town is an ovulating young woman.
Syndey Town is the fragmented village drifting away.

9pm traffic streams in and out of Broadway: stem of Syndey Town
to the West where arise statements of seasoned commerce, the
buildings, the corporate giants, for it to draw and withdraw the street
life, and where Victorian and modernist vistas welcome transients
and inhabitants alike.

12. Holy Orders

The Lag Motor's glued to the metal stream and passes through
the cross of Regent and Broadway and heads up George and The
Family quietly sit looking out windows at slowly passing windows
traffic people buildings words lights the conglomerations defining a
night city and luminous Oliver passing over escorted by brilliant
constellations.

Mark Kelly was called by Christ when he was thinking about the girl he
once kissed on the back step of his local Church hall away from prying
parents and friends and he told himself he was going mad and far with
his hands and she told him 'gotcha' a word he glimpses coming up
George remembering she said he was hers and she was his while his left
hand was sliding down to her border line and they were teenagers in lust
and he was hers and he got scared thinking that he couldn't think about
anything else except crossing her border and she was stroking his cherry
smooth face saying he was the one she'll marry as though she was going
to marry Christ himself and that's what she said because she was
Catholic and she should find someone and be like the bride of Christ and
bring many Catholic babies into the world so they can grow up to be
priests and nuns in the service of the Lord and through the authority of
the Catholic Church fulfil Christ's teachings on Earth and Kelly's left
hand is the hand of God roughly choosing her to be his bride and the
mother of Kelly's offspring and all it will take is for Kelly to find her
womb the first male to do so and then the 'gotcha' event came to pass
because Kelly remembered he was a priest's slither baby thing and he
felt unworthy of her and he was trapped and fear was calling him away
from lust and to the mysterious man known as Christ who is the only one
who could look after him in his hours of need and give him distance and
time for him to ponder the feminine nature of sin.

And through the cross of Hay and George the Lag Motor crawls
like a sea slug over its sea floor patch and nobody inside the next
lane transports gives a phooey for what's going on in the televisions
blinking out from a retailer's display window.

Matt Muldoon was called by Christ after a violent scene in a war movie
was so savage to the impressionable boy that he could not believe people

do such things to each other and dad sitting next to him in the movie theatre says parents can nearly do like such things when the forgiving Lord makes it the right thing for parents to do and therefore show that discipline is truly worthy in crisis times like when young Muldoon disobeys him and gets the beating he deserves sending him to bed at night crying and dreaming of revenge but not in a way like violence because that is so cruel and unjust and he's confused because it's wrong to beat and wrong to shout and afterwards on a Church retreat he heard nothing but peace in his heart and this is what it is like to have Christ in one's heart and when he couldn't hear his own heart beating Christ said to him to come and show his father what it is like to love and devote oneself to others when there is no reward but to serve others like he would later see as a priest in M.A.S.H. because instead of canned laughter good humour gives way to action when wounded souls are brought in and tended to though some die and the good do their best and back go mended souls to craziness but soon more violence from out there brings in more wounded souls and this is what he wanted to believe as a child and maybe serving Christ would be like tending the wounded and having a laugh on the side which his dad doesn't do after he's been to confession and got the absolution needed to carry on like he does after a bad day and the good Church knows absolutely nothing about that.

At the cross of Goulburn and George Clancy sees a well-dressed woman who reminds him of his mother who passed away in his arms after a long battle with a terminal illness.

Christ called John Clancy not long after his mother died when she told him at her deathbed in the spare room of their overgrown weatherboard suburban house she didn't want to die because Clancy was her only hope in the family after her marriage failed and her husband and the two other children returned to Ireland after yet another long Australian summer of bitumen-fried feet and spontaneously combusting weeds had taken their toll on the marriage leaving Clancy behind because he so desperately didn't want to leave his mother but had stayed to try and fulfil her dream that one day he would enter the seminary and make the family name proud once more and would Clancy fulfil her dying wish and swear to her that he would wed himself to Jesus as a priest so when he dies in old age having proclaimed the Gospel and brought his community together in Christ and having dispensed penance for sin and having anointed the sick and dying and celebrated the Eucharist and having continued Christ's work redeeming mankind and glorifying God and having gone to Heaven belonging to Christ she would seem him as her dream priest on his way up the steps to the throne of God to receive his reward for his work on Earth by being directed to sit with his fellow priests on God's right to therefore remain in perpetual love and awe of God and she would be so proud of him but first would he try to look after her and stop her from leaving him alone in the world except for her brother who failed the priesthood and became an alcoholic.

The Lag Motor passes through the cross of Liverpool and George
when Mahone's heart began to race on seeing a uniformed man run
his wide hand over the body of a prostrate boy.

And Luke Mahone was confused as a young altar boy by the parish priest he saw fondling another altar boy because he could not reveal this priest to the outside world as anything other than a shepherd for altar boys his reward being that he will never be ignored by God because he has been chosen to wait for God to call him after he has served his apprenticeship as assistant to the assistant of Jesus during the Eucharist and Sunday blessings for the rich for being rich and the poor for being poor and he Mahone will then be called to replace this priest no longer a priest in body when he retires ready for Heaven and he Mahone by the will of God will then serve God because of his talents and special powers that go beyond ordinary men for he is more Christ like than most men who are given to lust and greed and who covet other men's women and chattels and the priest fondling altar boys will face his judgment upon his death in the presence of the Lord Jesus Christ Son of God who was chosen to live and suffer on Earth to be crucified and return on the third day and prepare humankind for judgement day and those who do not live by the laws of Christ will not be saved and he Mahone can be sure that as parish priest he will join with Christ on judgement day because the loving gaze of Christ was always on him in life and he will be forgiven and he too could be a shepherd of altar boys if he so wishes.

The goosey two haven't seen a bloody thing.

FANTASY 2
PURGATORY

1. The Pub Grip

The Bad Clergy are at their flash panny the Gag 'n Throttle. The Lag
Motor is safely parked outside. But first, here's a bit of loose verse
by the poet laureate of the pub with no beer.

The early talk prepares the swill,
'N tarried patrons are in for a fill,
The coins on the counter spread,
Smokes and beer, here they wed,
Old yarns around the room they fly,
Some hear them hot, others dry,
Yarns that tell of warrior deeds,
Stories that tell of private needs.

Cushioned high stools easy fleshed,
Old and spread, sweat enmeshed,
Men and women, alone some are,
Elbows bridling the public bar,
Hands that gesture wide and sparse,
Mouths agape bespeak some farce,
Barwomen turn away ashamed,
How the swill afflicts the inflamed!

Last call for drinks is hours out,
Into emptiness come the shout,
Three cheers for generous friends,
Three cheers until friendship ends,
Who they are, no one cares,
Even if they've got Vaucluse airs,
On Fridee night nothings matter,
And talk is of merciless patter.

Watery eyes seeded by the haze,
How to drink and count the ways,
In one gulp to corral the froth,
Beer gloried as the boozer's broth,
And the amber spirit chaser,
For the drinker who is baser,
And the drinker's stooping lower,

And self-esteem is not a goer.

Pub noise, the Devil's stoner chant,
Mischief here is a sensual plant,
Sight and taste and burning smell,
Remind of guilt's living Hell,
Seediness is left for the 'morrow,
Alcohol's clichés are wrought in sorrow,
They'll be found in the toilet bowl,
At home for God, if there be a soul.

All this liquid moves like weather,
Enough to fill up old Lake Pedder,
For more drink, done in a hurry,
Some bar talk is about the Murray,
Irrigation's been the Brolga's curse,
Drought has made the cycle worse,
Pubs and dry land are to waste,
What the Holy Wafer is to taste.

The message says to sink more piss,
From inside the brain's cortical hiss,
Empty schooners are up to six,
Rum 'n cokes hover in the mix,
What is home but a place to kip,
She'll catch his lavatory slip,
He'll put her drunk to a single bed,
If not for drink they'd both be dead!

Fridee night borrowed as before,
To end a week become a bore,
It is to the pub town legions travel,
Tonight is certain they'll unravel,
Home inhibitions are left behind,
Aftermaths are easier to find,
Weekends are for contemplation,
Mondays then, for recrimination.

Before the band, the jukebox plays,
Howzat, which Slade then slays,

The wallpapers of Alpine scenes,
Huge egos pub banter preens,
The carpet is artistically stained,
Toilet doors are easy maimed,
Graffiti writes of instant love,
Piss below but look above!

Abstract art is like cognate smoking,
Take it seriously, or take it joking,
Drinking mates, silent to their fate,
Think of death while they wait,
RSL's will never forget them,
Hero worship that begets them,
At the pub there is that chance,
Of fights, of death, and of romance.

The early night is hotting up,
The early night is but a pup,
Alcohol is the tension's grease,
At the bar war is almost peace,
No pub is good without a crowd,
No band is good unless they're loud,
Through the doorway patrons squeeze,
Awkward personalities quickly freeze.

Special abodes parallel a pub life where the punters can go to,
for they are free to go anywhere in their mental world. And their
surroundings within their place are in accordance with their happy
state; and the internal union of misery and joy finding in their
outward expression a drinker's voice. At the end of another day,
their minds and bodies go to that part of their dwelling-place most
welcoming, their bed, their Heaven. And the Heaven of the tired is a
special place with indefinite ends. For the expectation of death comes
to those frozen in their beds.

In the church of drinking the word chalice is the word for schooner,
frothy amber is blessed piss, God's old words are the fount of rabid
conversation; pity the reformed who found debauchery too soon
in their lives. Regular drinkers drink, and give their all, totalitarian
and complete, floor'd like Liston, no strength, nor grace, nor values

remain; nowhere but in a sacrificial bar can a violent vomit not appal.
Flowing healing ambers quench fiercest dries. From the opening
glassy click to a late calamity, sensational truths emerge in a boozy
cringe when sobering up confounds confusion courting confounding
lies the pub Confucius says while transubstantiated amber flow at
the urinal sink. Silence marches off like Swiss Guards at Catholic
ceremonies, and the pissing punter not once blinks.

Muldoon:
Four ambers and two darkies ta Marilyn luv.

Barmaid:
Schooners or middies, me priestly darlin'?

Muldoon:
Make 'em schooners dear, each of us be kegs.

Barmaid:
That's 12 and a half sovs for the lot me laddie.

Muldoon:
Ta luv, and blessed be thy breasts. And thy rightful name?

Barmaid:
The Virgin Mary from Heaven... in the flesh.

Men and women come Friday night to be cured, they who spare
nothing of themselves, who confess, and they know not why, and
if punishment is their pleasure, the night will be endured. Damned
are those who do not conform, the venial and hard perambulators,
damned are those already in bed, they must be superficial,
disinterested in colonial fun, or dead. Is it bravery to drink hard to
the end? Not if the stomach can endure it, the hot dog stand will soon
arrive, for the hungry and for the tired, a red dog and friend. The
Dog 'n Bone Band are playing the blues. Some punters dance, some
merely nod, some do it alone, some in a clinch crowd, and the Family
are at the back of the pack paying their knapping dues.

Kelly:
Four ambers and two darkies, and I thank you dear Marilyn.

Barmaid:
You're the polite one, eyeing me down.

Kelly:
I'll drive them home, and I'd like to drive you.

Barmaid:
After the schooners, I'm no man's love.

Kelly:
Muldy says you're the Virgin, and Muldy is a good 'un.

Barmaid:
Yes, I am the sensual Flesh you fumblin' luvs worship.

Kelly:
In drink, and In Puris Naturalibus, me and the all.

Barmaid:
When you brethren pray to me, I always know.

2. Mon Amour de Brawl

Muldoon:
There's lots of Marilyns wantin' for a tickle.

Kelly:
Too many of 'em swayin' in the brewer's breeze.

Muldoon:
You got to pick 'em when they're looking for salvation.

Kelly:
It's the Marilyn behind the bar us men are really wantin'. Be honest.
She's the unreachable Goddess. Mother to these ordinary Marilyns
here. We've gotta believe in her. That'll be all.

Muldoon:
It's too hard. When I look at her from here I can't see her body. All I see
is a bright halo. Her in a long blue dress standing on a python. And that
smile. It kills me, that smile.

Kelly:
Me too. She's in my dreams almost every night. I grow a bone. Can't
bury it anywhere near her. There's nowhere for it to go. No opening,
no way in. I can't get past those eyes.

Muldoon:

There are plenty of blokes who don't care where they bury their bones.
The Virgin just watches on while the animals get on with struttin' and
ruttin'. I'm in black robes because of this. I can't have no ordinary
Marilyn. It's the Virgin or no-one.

Kelly:
I touched a virgin girl once but it wasn't the same.

Muldoon:
Yeah! You haven't told me about that parable.

Kelly:
I was young'un Muldy. A spunked up teen-boy. I was at a Catholic
youth conference. I got a bit of a hairy feel that was all. But I got

excited and I creamed me daks. Then I went home and prayed to the
Virgin. She told me that wouldn't happen with her. I've gotta keep
the faith.

Muldoon:
Our two silent friends here like the hairless types.

Kelly:
Don't reckon they'd know which true Virgin we're talking about.

Muldoon:
Hey, look over here. Looks like a bit of commotion and some fists
are flyin' about the air.

Kelly:
What do you reckon! This being the Gag 'n Throttle on a Fridee
night and we be boogying to the Dog 'n Bone Boogie Blues Band
and naturally someone's gonna think it's time for a bit of fisticuffs
and boppin' 'cause it's the moanin' blues.

Muldoon:
You pun like an old nun Kels. Eh, me mateys. Enjoy the show bruvs.
Grab your beers and hang on. The Titanic's about to heave and
lumber around a bit.

A fist to the face from a fistful of old Boer anger. Two and more and
the RSL men step in. A good kicking was first taught in a Sunday
school hall. There's nothing like an all-in pub brawl. A WW2 Foo
Fighter couldn't 've started it better. Popping up with pub gossip
badly writ. Old warriors who take the bait. Or it could be because
of a kind word said to an old mate. In pubs kindness to mates might
seem strange. Honest talk mistrusted and put out of range. An insult
said in jest is still an insult. The nerve of the giver hits the nerve of a
receiver. Only joking; some blokes can't take a bad joke. Dear reader
of the night the reasons for it are thus far bespoke.

Barmaid: (yells from behind the bar)
Get out your holy waters Fathers, the damned here will be looking
for a refreshing drink.

Muldoon: (yells from the back of the room)
Let them without guilt throw the second punch.

The Dog 'n Bone boogie with Sugar Bee. The Family lean against
the back wall. And the all-in goes full swing with a tripping foxtrot.
The flamencos step in full of guts and passion. Jitterbuggers throw
themselves around in the mayhem. Someone's trying to twist and
shout. The brawl spreads like a ballroom blitz. A dwarf swan dives
into fisticuff dancers. Sugar Bee is quickly reprised. It works to the
rhythm of the chaos. The Dog 'n Bone swings to the action. And
here comes a Lindy Hopper in a helmet. And this brawling jiving
has nowhere to go. A request is made for Rollin' and Tumblin'.
Everyone stops to see who made it. And then free arms and stiff legs
jive some more. The publican calls up the Swing specialist cops. The
flamencos and jitterbuggers muscle up. The swan-diver looks a little
bloodied. The Lindy Hopper is causing a lot of damage. Sugar Bee
is going around a third time. The twisted one is still shouting. The
Family haven't lost a drop of beer. Leaning back and forth keeping
time with the chaos. No one's sick of the Sugar Bee. The brawl's
been going for nearly ten minutes. And the Swing cops arrive and
look around. The brawl stops and the cops leave. Bodies are picked
up off the floor. Bruises and cuts are caringly attended to. The
publican rights the tables and chairs. Broken glass is quickly swept
away. The Dog 'n Bone rip into Bullfrog Blues. And standing on the
stage in front of the band is a long-haired man with his arms spread
out wide. And on his body are Visible Stigmata.

The publican yells for someone to get the freak out the back. But
nobody moves. The Bullfrog Blues peter out. The Jesus guy is staring
out to space. Somebody else yells for a priest in the house. The
Family are looking about. Rare silence takes hold of the crowded
room. What to do next, what to do. But brave Mahone has seen this
before. When he was a kid looking into a mirror. He saw similar
marks after getting beaten up. Same time every day just after school.
The beatings went for over a week. And there on his hands feet and
side stood wounds filled with clotted blood. And Mahone the most
pious out of this motley crew stepped out of the Family's shadow.
And made his way through the mute crowd and stood before the
Jesus guy and tells him all about the Stigmata.

3. His Stigmata

O my the ecstasies borne by your hands feet side and brow that mark
the passion of a man like you who suffered intensely and who knows
all about pain that is the pain all of us suffer and it's pain invisible
and visible and you have chosen to show us your pain here in the
Gag 'n Throttle pub and you show us pity and we show you pity
Don't we folks
And everyone says yeah yeah
The publican and barmaids too
And your substance is this pity and the way you participate in
suffering and despair and sorrow and meanwhile the sins of us here
in this pub are at your mercy and if there was no suffering you would
not bear wounds and you would be empty and directionless and
you'd be theatre for all of us who are looking for entertainments
Don't we folks
And everyone says yeah yeah
The publican and barmaids too
O my the miracle that is your delicious wounds that are too sweet to
last longer than death that awaits us all and we will never see what
you see as bearer of sweet wounds that point the way to somewhere
in suffering that can only lead to a better way of life should we be so
worthy of a life better than the one we melancholic people have now
Don't we folks
And everyone says yeah yeah
The publican and barmaids too
Though we may speculate whether your wounds are self-inflicted the
speculation merely confirms your love of the blood-stained scenes of
the Passion and though you are dumb and your eyes are glazed you
no doubt are enacting a drama which has only one powerful scene
and would we so wish to have been there from the beginning
Don't we folks
And everyone says yeah yeah
The publican and barmaids too
What whips and bondages and nails and thorns you have used we
are unworthy to touch and we clearly see the impressions of nails
on hands and feet and lances to your side and barbs on your head
and they look wonderful on you whom we might think of as in the
likeness of Jesus and we reckon that we should be so lucky to see you

Don't we folks
And everyone says yeah yeah
The publican and barmaids too
This is the period of your life when blood dripping from your wounds
describes your ecstasy embedded in your conviction that you are no
ordinary person standing on this stage half-naked and ragged with
terrible eyes knowing as we know what it is like to be abandoned by
a father who says that he will never forsake you
Don't we folks
And everyone says yeah yeah
The publican and barmaids too
And you look parched and you look to live on bread and water like
any martyr would even when food and drink is plentiful and while
you starve and go thirsty think of us humble pub goers who come
here for jugs of beers and beer nuts and toe tapping rhythm and blues
that make us feel dead and alive and ecstatic every Fridee night
Don't we folks
And everyone says yeah yeah
The publican and barmaids too
There is love in your mad eyes as though you channel the feelings of
the crucified one whose imagination at the time of his death extended
to the Heavens above to seek his relief from pain and suffering which
occupied his mind to distraction and savage emotions and filling his
mad eyes with love and we can sort of see a resemblance
Don't we folks
And everyone says yeah yeah
The publican and barmaids too
Because there is so much love in you O disturbed one who are we to
question the authenticity of your stigmata and whether what we see
is an illusion and whether you are a magician or not and whether you
are a spirit of the age for even if we were theologians we would still
prostrate ourselves before you because we can't help it
Don't we folks
And everyone says yeah yeah
The publican and barmaids too
And then it would be right to auto-suggest that you are a stigmatized
person and as you stink to high heaven we take your display of
wounds seriously because you appear a supernatural being who has
come to visit us at the Gag 'n Throttle and all us inebriated here feel

privileged that your stigmata has made tonight resolutely bizarre
Don't we folks
And everyone says yeah yeah
The publican and barmaids too
The power of our imagination joins with you a stigmatic stigmartyr
and we are in awe who need not partake in any more all-in brawls
tonight for you have saved us from ourselves and me a priest thank
you on everyone's behalf
Don't I folks
And everyone says yeah yeah
The publican and barmaids too

And then the stigmata Jesus freak gives the crowd a wave. And
turning to the band he requests Lonesome Blues. And the band starts
playing. And the freak starts dancing around. Like the Eternity guy
who used to dance on a Syndey Town footpath well into the night.
And the crowd is jigging to the Lonesome Blues. The freak dives into
the crowd from the stage. And people grab him and run him above
their heads. And he's stretched out like he's a human cross. And he's
run through the crowd until someone opens the pub's front doors.
And the happy guy is brought outside and taken over to a gutter
where still smiling he's tossed straight in.

Clancy:
There goes a beautiful one.

Muldoon:
As good as the first one I reckon.

Clancy:
They're like brothers I'm sure.

Mahone:
We might see him at the Cross.

Muldoon:
He's halfway there I reckon.

Kelly:
The Gag's gone flat and these Marilyns look like they won't be
lookin' for my tickles judgin' by the looks on their faces.

Muldoon:
Nor mine and the true Virgin behind the bar isn't there anymore.

Kelly:
She's got treasures hidden away no prayers'll find.

Muldoon:
We'll find some at the Cross eh boys.

The four plus two leave the Gag 'n Throttle and head for the Lag
Motor parked in a side street. The Family line a wall and lemonade it.
The Lag Motor is untouched nearby. Never vandalised, never stolen.
Because the mysterious Motor resembles the Sacred Heart when it's
parked. Flaming with red and lanced by light. Crowned by brass-tipped
barbed wire. It offers the Family the comforts of heavenly clouds.
No other consolations are offered. Unblessed traffic has no time
for speeding traps. It rides rough which bring hard lessons when
the Lag Motor is crossed.

The lemonade was sweet and yellow
And the Family pray
Except the goosey two:
O merciful marijuana
Take piety away from our souls
We have no particular friends nor intercoursers
Who would recommend us to them.
We know of our negligence of Catholic living
And no length of time is more rotten
When the mighty spliff opens our consciousness.
Spare them, O Roach of Roaches,
Remember our spittle shared for your mercy,
When others neglect to appeal to it
Let not the mood which you have created
Be parted from the sweet smoke
May our black lungs be faithful
To the smoke departed
And the grass fire burn of Tally-Ho's
Be the cleansing of our crusted nostrils
And whatever kind of high it may please.
The THC and DMT send us tonight

With its power to alter perceptions
Free kicks and distortions
In reparation for boredom
For the souls in offices
For those converted from union to league.
O Darlinghurst, conceived without sin
Guide us who are on course for Thee
O gutters of butt and technicolour yawns
The mothers of the agony
Abandoned in the early hours of morn
That we will obtain
A perfect tomorrow
A sincere forgetting
And the rise of our learned ways
To receive worthily the holy hotdog
Washed down by the fizzy black tar
And we be assured of another eating
Two hours later
When sitting
On the throne of the honourable Crepitus
Our sometimes God and redeemer
And reliever.

4. The Goosey Two and the Ride

The Motor rumbles into life like a storm. The four venerable Buster
Keatons and the outer two are arranged like they're strapped in a Midget
sub. Ready to plunge deeper into Syndey Town. Deeper into its peculiars
of sin and redemption. The culture of the place since Cook's grand tour.
Colonial rum and money and land and sheep which live like bacteria in
every social crack and orifice. From deep beneath to the top of its
'scrapers. The town that began as a dump for Mayhew's people. But oh!
The people were filled with secret desire. To be reborn ridding the
convict stain. And be upstanding like bog Irish crofters. Work hard and
make no bones of it. And be best swaddled for the brash casinos. The
Family are bemused by the crack and gauche. Superior they are, superior
to the ordinary folk. Let the new waste squandered be their lives cast as
rot. Let them rut and keepsake the Catholic faith. The Family outsiders
need not fit in. It's cool to look and act something like different. The
Mardi Gras and Rugby League are theatre. They can love Wilfred Owen
and the Parra Eels and get away with it by saying little.

Muldoon wonders, the Family obey the code, and do what they
freely will, the will of a supreme being they take as their own for a
Fridee night. It's a good one for Marilyns and amber slops, and them
goings-on up at the Cross to which they'll get to once they're through
the hustle and bustle of Syndey Town tonight, and the Gag 'n
Throttle pub now be closed. They'll observe the fallen, whose brittle
conscience cannot conform, the addicts, the prostitutes, the dealers,
the punters, the homeless, the tourists, those boys from out West too
underachieving for rehabilitation, whose acts and substance abuse
confuse the right and good, who defy police law, moral law, and
they are grotesque deformities of God almighty, and of eternal good.
These deviants and the Family, are so close they do not recognise
each other, for their bad is as mutable as the grime on the Granville
Crib's windows. The grime which the rains wash away only to return
greasier. Going south along Sussex, the Lag Motor and its human
grime, stoned and pissed, but not Kelly much, the coachman.

Prohibitive acts are not bound by the judgment of any person or concept, but by a clerical conscience schooled in the principles of Jesus Christ. When God's love and forgiveness is asked for in confession, the Bad Clergy squirm on their hard seats behind the curtain, and bring forth colonic smells, and they cough and belch, and tap their fingers to the rhythms of confession, their intellectual judgment stunned and disturbed, their passions engorged by absolution, their sinners, having left the confessional forgiven, walk from the Church with heads held high, their dignity restored, their self-worth reclaimed, and life goes on, just as the traffic ahead is being followed by the Lag Motor which now hangs a left into Liverpool Street.

Placates also says:

To those closest to God by ordination come special blessings which shine before devout eyes. These Bad Clergy think of themselves as superior to the vital humanity passing by in lower Sussex Street, who, less versed in testaments, are merely irresponsible, but who still have grace awaiting them, if only they would accept the Church's teachings. They need not deny the existence of a personal creator superior to them, since their free will, with conditions subject to the laws set down by the Ten Commandments, is not really a trap set by authorised Catholic forgivers. And what does it matter if the forgiver's sin is worse than a sinner sitting in a confessional! They ought still be forgiven, and therefore they are, for God exists to cleanse the disorder and chaos humanity brings upon itself. But only the Catholic Church can be that true intermediary. And besides, the same Catholic Heaven awaits the likes of the goosey two as it does for the almost forgiven.

These out and outer goosey two have the free will to dream of hairless teeny quims. Fringe dweller Family members, sitting between Muldoon and Clancy in the back seat, the ultimate silent sinners whose crimes are washed clean by the shame of the Catholic Church. Mahone always keeps his distance by sitting in the front on account of him fearing for himself. They bear no signs of privations from guilt; their sermon ardour simultaneously deforms the altar ritual. Their sins not even Adam did commit, and yet are original, for two grievous sins were made, molestation of the vulnerable, and their complicity with silence commissioned by their dark minds and the dark denials of their self-preserving benefactor the Church; together they are in sin.

The Church and the goosey two omit the fulfilment of the maxim of trust, and they are a great malice, for together they have taken from the innocent their most personal dignity. Freely transgressing their moral conscience, and believing that what is good for them, is right and just, the goosey two take note of concupiscent desire. After a cross has been put before their pleasures, having dwelt on sins past, they and their confessor the Church then set conditions for disassociating their actions from Church sin. And since Church consciousness arrives late, the means to resolve the pedo priest problem has also arrived late. Church moral conscience has fallen asleep. And so begins the Church reconciliation with its God. Prayers are said for itself. While such pleasures have rewards that no scandal may diminish, the nature of paedophile activity in the house of God is thus curious and therefore requires investigation, and its nature is best discussed in-house, and then, the mysteries of hypocrisy, will be discussed. And the secret reprimands, the firmest measures possible, for those priests who are temporarily not themselves as they should be, are written out of canon history while Church business remains the same. It is time to move them on. After all, these priests have been ordained into the mysteries of Christ the saviour as very few have.

A warrior song the goosey two sing in a secret sing-a-long:

As moral leaders of the world we fire superior guns
Moral superiors firing guns
At the allegations children are victims of priestly abuse
At the victims of our abuse
When it is not love but abuse we blame it on the Devil
Such a bad influence is the Devil
We stand up for our loving but persecuted Church
The persecution of the Church
Superior morality is what makes us priests happy

To be moral is to be happy
There is no canon law to say children should suffer
Silent children do not suffer
Strong moral codes protect we priests from ourselves
We are shielded from ourselves
If we choose to confess we will never be betrayed
It is against canon law to be betrayed
Fear of concupiscence brings us priests closer to God
Celibate we are for God
The best gift to a priest the Holy Spirit can give
We like what the Spirit gives
We are not animals, we are the holy brethren
We are the simple brethren
And may the Lord give us all what we want and need
The Lord gives what we need
Through prayer and abstinence and careful duty
We are secretive about our duty
Happiness is the struggles with our earthly flesh
Happiness is our struggling flesh
Nearer to our forgiving God we are certain to be
Nearer we come to thee.

5. A Theme for Syndey

Kelly:
The Lag's in good form t'night.

Clancy:
Know's where it's goin', don't it.

Kelly:
Like holy eyes lookin' for a breach in The Virgin's image.

Mahone:
That's when my peepers look holy, ha ha!

Muldoon:
Peepin' through the Church cracks for craik eh!

Clancy:
So says the poetic one.

Kelly:
These spliffs keepin' you mellow brothers?

Muldoon and Clancy:
Aye aye Capt'n Goodvibes!

Kelly:
The Lag'll get us there. The neon lights be her guide. And the flesh on the streets is multiplying like loaves and fishes.

Muldoon:
That wafer flesh we dish out on Sundy's don't satisfy does it. They can't wait to tuck into the roast, can they. And they'll say grace over it I'll bet. Thank you Lord for what we are about to receive into our gullets from the big chew and chomp and swallow, and can I 'ave some more please mum?

Clancy:
Ah Muldy, always the bad scrote.

Muldoon:
We all are, ain't we? Men in black who can't get the sack for being

out of whack with them good souls we treat on Sundays.

Mahone:
I get the best dreams when I take me guilt to bed.

Kelly:
Them two blokes sitting in the back are lucky. Their guilt is taken away when the payout is official for what the likes of them have done, and the good bloke up above has given his usual blessing.

Says Placates:

The thing about the goosey two is they are bound by the vow of silence. And the thing about the speaking four is they are bound by the vow of fraternity. And good mates stick together whether it's at a Bondi Beach sparkle or when Heaven is dumping its wrathful weather over the Granville Crib.

Clancy:
Me too. I like guilt. Grew up with it. And free will says I'm free to use it for my pleasure.

Mahone:
In every dream Church there's a bellyache.

Kelly:
Mark Foys looks a flash lamington tonight.

In the Lag's cabin absolute silence
The Family, erroneous, ignorant
Their intellectual judgment affected
Invincible ignorance they choose
Their passions disturb their judgment
Each Fridee night goin' to the Cross.
Its symbols intensely desired
And their free judgment's a mess
Beside themselves with want
Knowing what they might do
Knowing what they can do
Is sufficient to make them bad.

64

The Lag Motor, steering Kelly, trembles and croaks as it passes
Hyde Park, for it was there the beast once peed itself and ran dry,
its discomfort acute when the NRMA guy disobeyed the sign on the
bonnet which says 'KEEP YOUR HANDS OFF THE DUCO'. The
Family punished him for his sins of concupiscence and disobedience
by converting him to Catholicism.

And then over Wentworth Street into Oxford where the Lag Motor
purrs a sweeter rumble.

Around here is forged Family history. Adam's Apple had been
tempting Tully. They saw the Oils pump at French's Tavern. The
Beatle Village was before their time. Taylor Square is their compass
for fun. And lead them to the fun at the Funhouse. The Family prayed
on Gilligan's Island. This is the time for Family reminiscing. When
weed confuses guilt with pleasure. And the Lag sleighs past Victoria
Street. For them to catch the angular X. They'd be there when God
said No. Or they'd be raving at the Unicorn on Oxford Street's
claims to fame. The Family missed the Town Hall bash when the
Saints and Birdmen tore it up. But the Family's sin of missing fun is
not the Church's place to forgive.

Towards the midnight hour the Family's Catholic fever is nearing its
zenith.

A stream of consciousness narrative bursts forth regarding sins to
acquaint observers with the toils and struggles the Bad Clergy have with
their Catholic God and the infinite intelligence which draws them away
from every day to guarantee they do not fall out of love with God's
supernatural existence scourged by non belief in the year 1980 a time for
change a time for living and it's a time yes it's time in a time of
scepticism in a time of questions in a time when exorcists hear the
Devil's words in heavy rock when the world and all its flesh make their
God a God in need for validity to convince supermen and superwomen
to need Him who no longer need to be told what to think for they know
and trust themselves and they are free from superstition since how easily
have they risen above the mythical sin scenario that was the Garden of
Eden and how easily they destroy their old Catholic notions of guilt and
redemption, and the spectacular lie that the exclusive Catholic bridge to

God and salvation through baptism and Sunday transubstantiation will mitigate misery and unhappiness and that the Earth will be perverted without a God there to save all sinners who must come to their God contrite and humble through confession and admit they are fallen just like the mythical first fallen who was tempted by the Satan and enslaved by guilt and the Bad Clergy are sorry such historical sorryness is no longer good enough for Catholic Authority which is unsettled by casual attitudes toward it, therefore still it desires though human suffering that is ill health and catastrophe and madness and tragedy and spiritual acedia be manifest as vindictive punishment by the God which exclusively prefers justice be served with prayers and penance and a good dose of Catholic contrition at the confessional which the Bad Clergy call entertainment when dispensing forgiveness on behalf of their God and as sure as night follows day the Family heathens will be back after Fridee night and call in their God and excommunicate themselves from that night's fun and games.

6. Evil or livE

A Prayer said by converts for the conversion of the Family:
O Mary, Mother of Mercy and Refuge of sinners
we beseech thee
be pleased to look with pitiful eyes
upon these Family heretics and schismatics.
Thou who art the Seat of Wisdom
enlighten their minds that are miserably enfolded
in the darkness of ignorance and sin
that they may clearly know
that the Holy Catholic and Apostolic Roman Church
is the one true Church of Jesus Christ
outside of which neither holiness nor salvation can be found.
Finish the work of their conversion
by obtaining for them the grace
to accept all the truths of our Holy Faith
and to submit themselves to the Supreme Roman Pontiff
the Vicar of Jesus Christ on Earth;
that so, being united in the sweet chains of Divine charity
there may soon be one only fold
under the same one Shepherd;
and may they all
O Glorious Virgin
sing forever with exultation:
Rejoice, O Virgin Mary
thou hast only to destroy all heresies in the whole world.

-As graffiti seen on a toilet wall somewhere in King's Cross.

.................AND EVIL

For no life should suffer
Though Evil ought to be
A Catholic decree
When Evil ought not be
And why should it be?
Clancy, why should it be?
The goosey two are them

Evil in the Lag Motor
These two transgressors
Have they transgressed?
From what, Muldy?
From the moral good
What is evil Kelly?
A badly rolled spliff
What is evil Muldy?
No Marilyn tickle
What is evil Clancy?
When no one sins
What is evil Mahone?
What God says is good
What is evil goosey two?
No hairless quims.

Beyond general virtues
Beyond shifting norms
No imagination covers it all
A tragedy of inadequacy?
Catholicism says not so
Mere Godly contrariness
Of which it knows best.

Muldoon:
Too right. Mother knows best!

Clancy:
He's off again.

Kelly:
Like a sun-baked barramundi.

Muldoon:
Mother knows evil 'coz I'm sick, an' she'll fix me!

Kelly:
Muldy my love, you aren't any sicker than me, and I have no mother.

Indream the Holy Ghost, A K A The Space Wizard, has spoken to
the Family about the nature of Catholic evil. He blows his nose thus -
fffssssplnnnnnnntttt - heralding his voice, a grave voice like Winston
Churchill's, and his listeners become quiet, and his words bring
insights far beyond their mortal minds:

Dear brethren there are three kinds of evil - physical, moral, and
metaphysical. Physical evil is all that is harmful to humans, be it by
bodily injury, by thwarting natural desires, or by preventing the full
scope of human powers, either in the order of natural things directly,
or through the various social conditions under which mankind
naturally exists. Physical evils from nature might be sickness,
accident, death, disease. Poverty, oppression, and brainwashing
are evils from imperfect social organization. Mental suffering,
such as anxiety, disappointment, and remorse, and the limitation of
intelligence which prevents human beings from attaining to the full
comprehension of their environment, are congenital forms of evil
varying in type and degree according to the natural disposition and
social circumstances humans apply.

Kelly, do not sneer in your sleep! These may be flat and lifeless
words, but they are important words by the very nature of them being
utterly dull, and because no Catholic theology is worthwhile unless
its certain truth is revealed through devoted attention to it.

Moral evil is the deviation of human volition from the prescriptions
of the moral order and the action which results from that deviation.
But if it comes solely from human ignorance, it is not moral
evil, because there is no free will to upset what the conscience
disapproves of. The extent of moral evil is not merely limited to
the circumstances of natural life, but also the sphere of our religion,
in which human welfare is part of the supernatural order of things,

depending ultimately upon the will of God. Human action in the natural order depends entirely on the correct motives supplied by our religion; and it is impossible for moral obligation to exist outside of the influence of the supernatural.

That's God Kelly. We are talking about the impossible God.

Metaphysical evil is what the natural world does to itself, and what humans struggle to understand in the scheme of matter and its relationship with God. Natural objects are therefore prevented from attaining full or ideal perfection, unlike humans, whether by the constant pressure of physical condition, or by sudden catastrophes. Thus, animal and vegetable organisms are variously influenced by climate and other natural causes; predatory animals depend for their existence on the destruction of life, and nature is subject to storms and convulsions, and its order depends on a system of perpetual decay and renewal due to the interaction of its constituent parts. But the apparent disorder of nature is really no disorder, since it is part of a definite scheme, and precisely fulfils the intention of God the Creator; and is therefore a relative perfection rather than an imperfection.

Muldoon, will you kindly get your thoughts off food and the Virgin!

Brethren, by transferring to irrational objects the subjective ideals and aspirations of human intelligence, nature's evil is called evil in the sense of analogy, and is not intrinsically negative, except when your God is irrationally blamed. While it may seem that your God has no control over the human consequences of natural disasters, it should be made clear by you as ordained comforters that what God designs is a total mystery, and the essence of God's mystery is manifest in human hope, which you as the ordained make absolutely clear through Catholic liturgy. Why does God allow an earthquake to kill thousands of people? If God didn't allow it there would be no question of his Purpose. Those who are perfect after ordination are told by their superior brethren that they have been called by God to provide this answer.

Remember when the Saints lost the Grand final in '71. I heard some
of you thank your God.

We see how evil is fully negative because something is always
missing. Something is lost, or there is a deprivation that diminishes
perfection. But be careful. Your priestliness deprives you of sex
but that is God's will. You are perfect without it. All is evil that
contradicts God's will. Then there is pain, a positive which tells
the body something is wrong, but its negativity is in the sufferer's
disturbance. And when pure will is perverted moral evil thrives, in
that the evil character has rejected right reason as determined by your
God.

Get that Clancy? And when you doubt, you doubt until you bleed like
Jesus on the cross.

And in the eternal quest for pleasure, which can only be elusive on
Earth, your God promises absolute fulfilment, as though the promise
is itself pain.

And then Muldoon, you get down on your hoary knees and you pray.

The mystery of evil is in its relativity that is held by humans
going about their daily affairs. Murder might be good in certain
circumstances, might it not? There was no evil. It was for the greater
good. Your God created good (since God is supernatural Good must
therefore also be supernatural), and the standards are high, as you
Catholic priests know from your vows. And by continually sinning
humans can only absorb the pain of failing your God by the supreme
act of seeking penance through prayer which in itself gives the one
who prays incredible pleasures.

But what is the origin of evil? Pay attention Mahone. This is not a
nightmare.

Forget all the thinkers and philosophers that have mused on the
subject. Unless of course they have been guided by your Catholic
God. The understanding of evil lies in the metaphysics of the purpose
of God. But the irony is that your God has no earthly purpose. You

priestly ones are chosen to give God purpose, and to communicate God's purpose through Catholic scripture and prayer.

When you do this Clancy I notice that you mumble. Mumbling shows insincerity, Mahone and Muldoon the same.

This is the question. In believing in the chaos of nature, its method of disorder, and human subterfuge to it and this relationship being paramount to human life, what then must be outside of this metaphysical evil which relieves human suffering enough to warrant that human life is actually worth living?

This question is too big for ordinary people. That's where you in the Catholic Family have a supreme role to play. And we are not talking about role play Kelly.

There will never be pessimism while there is your God. Happiness is attainable for those who worship Him and do His bidding. Unhappiness is an illusion of the unconscious, and dear Family, since God IS the perfect human unconscious, and if the world would accept Catholicism and BELIEVE, then for the entire world there is nothing but joy joy joy, and it only gets better after death. But God's greatest gift to humanity, free will, must not be abused or there will be disharmony and chaos. And woe, there is so much of it!

Too much other abuse Clancy. Too much self-abuse Kelly!

7. Anthrax Blues

The sermon continues.

Too much disobedience. Obey God and happiness will follow. Errors
of humankind, which confuse the true condition of wellbeing, are
the cause of moral and physical evil. But to give hope, in evil which
humans suffer, is the crucial condition of good, for the sake of which
God allows. In God, good comes out of evil, and it is better this way,
and thus evil can exist, without it being God's sufferance. The role
of evil is to perfect the universe as does a frame for a work of art or
guitar chords in rock music.

I appreciate your finding peace in Metal Machine Music Mahone.
There is harmonic evil in them waves of feedback noise.

Darkness only exists without light, so is evil without good, and so
is human emptiness without God. This is the eternal struggle, and
without death to relieve the pain of struggle, there would be no God
to welcome repentant sufferers into perfect Heaven on Judgement
Day. A good God allows evil to test how good humans really are.
You as priests know more about sins and their grades of punishments
than ordinary folk. When sinners come to you they ask for your
forgiveness on God's behalf. It is your confessional whips that
scourge them for their sins. And still you go out every Fridee night to
reclaim your so-called earthiness.

But there is more to your Family's life than Marilyns, weed, grog and
pub rock!

There can be no degree of finite goodness which is not amenable to
growth through omnipotence, for without omnipotence goodness
shall fall short of infinite perfection. Eve only needed to tempt
Adam with the serpent's apple, and what followed is the history of
humanity the centre of which is the struggle of good over evil. And
God by His very nature must have humanity yearning for Him the
Perfect Good. And blessed are those who fully embrace Christianity,
ideally Catholic, for its perfect understanding of God's word as
spoken in the Bible. And certain special Catholics have been chosen
by God to be His authority on Earth.

That's you Muldoon, Mahone, Clancy, Kelly. Though no longer you, the goosey two.

Let you try to image a universe different to the one you know. You can't. And let you imagine the beginning without creation. You can't. And let you understand why the world in which you live is the way it is. You can't. You are ordained to conform to the laws of God as set down by Jesus and furthered by your Church, in order to fulfil the divine purpose for which the Church exists. Give it a go, eh!

Muldoon:
And the Space Wizard blew his horn.

Kelly:
Never understood a word he said.

Mahone:
Me neither.

Clancy:
Nor me.

Kelly:
Muldy me love. You speaks to Him on our behalf.

Muldoon:
I'll never doubt The Virgin.

Clancy:
I know if I doubted more, in my suffering I might get closer.

Muldoon:
More doubt. More weed. That's the way my Karma likes it.

Placates says:

Religious minds always face the suspension between contradictory propositions which are grappled with in conscious living; the idea of an existing God is always a threat, when it is believed to be true and equally false. Religious minds struggle with God's truth since the scripted evidence for it might as well be as equally ludicrous. And finally crushed by contradictions, the believer's will and intellect

bows to authorative knowledge, and they do not refuse it for fear
of intellectual error, and for fear of falling into moral perversity not
even redeemable at the last judgment.

Which is troubling enough:
And begins with the sins of children
Told at confession.

'Heavenly Father, it's been four weeks since my last confession
And these are my sins.'

When Kelly was on duty to hear fifteen year old Mary's confession.

Mary:
I was with a boy Father,
We were kissing and he touched me down there,
And I said don't touch me there, it's a sin,
But he wouldn't stop his sinning sin sin,
And I liked what he was doing to me,
Is my little pleasure a sin too?

Kelly:
You are clothed in the spotless clothes of baptismal innocence
You are the spouse of Christ, without spot or stain, immaculate,
Undefiled.
There is no sadder sight in the world
In that the soul of a young girl having turned aside from Jesus
Now walks the way of sin.

My child, the loving saviour desires nothing more than to keep you.

He has shed plentiful blood to redeem you.

He lives for you in the sacrament of his love.

He is ever present to enlighten you.

There is no more beautiful object on Earth
Than the soul of a young virgin maiden.

To your natural candour and simplicity
God has joined the wonderful gift of grace.

And Kelly, waving his left hand over the lattice
His right squeezing his throbbing missal
Directed her to say her penance
Then she will leave the confessional free of her sins
But will return soon to the confessional
And tell a phantom priest her sexual sins
For the phantom is the priest best placed
To forgive her her sins on God's behalf.

Kings Cross is dearer to the Bad Clergy than the Christ. The Lag's
done a UE like it's done a heist. And up Darlinghurst Road the
Motor goes. Toward the petty pushers of highs and lows. To them
the Family gives their blessings. Who cover their scarred faces
in dressings. Coca-Cola blinks like the sign of the Cross. It's the
territory where Saffron is boss. Now that the Family need to do the
Strip. It'll be the drag queens getting their tip. The Family stand
no higher than the masses. They imagine seeing them at Sunday
masses. And a busy night life in the town of Sin. It's more than a bet
and a half bottle of gin. It's about clearing from the head the moss.
The parables, the folklore, the dross. The Family always enjoy the
artistic disrobe. Buster Keatons who fancy a flesh probe. Then the
vows of celibacy rise up a gear. Still, it's been another enterprising
year. When the Cross calls for them incognito. To be there Fridee
nights and never veto. The deeds of others who can't be condemned.
By anyone whose life is just as hemmed. By controlling omniscient
powers. And conventions masking the hours. Of sorrow, insecurity
and difficult rest. Of which the Family nearly knows best. Who have
what they have both ways. The way of The Lord, the way of Fridees.
And their consciences care not a whit. Whether the wafer is God
or a psychological pit. They are going to fall whatever they do. All
they want is to fall and to renew. Better to play sinner than be bored.
Better to stand away from the morally moored. Who thrash about but
remain tethered. Who know how their bodies are weathered. Moored
by fine conscience they cannot break. They who are not dead, nor
awake. Who'll seek solace in the privacy of prayer. There's someone
up there who might care. If the Family cannot be relied upon. Whose
sacred icon is a relic strap-on.

8. Forward Passes

An indream digression.

FAITH V DOUBT - A Rugby League match played in the Emu
in the Sky constellation in 1979 and later described by The Space
Wizard in the voice of Frank Hyde to Mahone indream.

AT KICK-OFF
The anthems are over. The pre-match hype is done. The Car Hooter
in the Sky has sounded. We are under way.

At vector ⊕♀b:
Faith 0-0 Doubt
Good couple of opening sets by the Faithers as their fullback hoists
a kick to pin back the Doubters. Then it is the Doubters opposite
number who launches a return high kick after the fifth tackle deep
into Faith territory but the ball goes dead in goal.

At vector ☐☐♆☐:
Faith 0-0 Doubt
The Doubters crank up the pressure as Faith knock-on on the last
tackle giving Doubt another set deep inside the Faithers territory.

At vector ⊙♃c:
TRY- Faith 0-4 Doubt
What a start for the Doubters! The Doubters flags are waving in the
Overworld Stadium solar winds as their second row forward ploughs
through two Faith tacklers to touch down for the opening try.

At vector ☐♂s:
MISSED CONVERSION- Faith 0-4 Doubt
Not the easiest kick for the Doubt five eight - and so it proves. The
broad man drags his touchline effort past the near post.

At vector 1♋4:
Faith 0-4 Doubt
The Faith are looking to hit back almost immediately and enjoy some
decent territorial pressure. But a looping kick downfield on the fifth
tackle by their scrum-half is easily gathered by the Doubt fullback.

At vector 9 ★ ♋:

DISALLOWED TRY- Faith 0-4 Doubt
Doubt are camped on the Faith try-line now. Some fabulous
defending by the Faithers denies Doubt's inside centre, just as he
looks to stretch out for the score. And three plays in, after a long
Faith raid, the Faithers outside centre thinks he has an equalising try
before the referee brings play back for a forward pass by their half
back.

At vector ♒ ☄ ♋:
Faith 0-4 Doubt
The Faith inside center lets the ball slip out of his hand as the
Faithers attack deep in the Doubt half. He smashes the turf in
frustration. From the next play the Doubt prop after a barnstorming
run tries to offload deep in the Faith half but drops the ball and gives
possession straight back to the Faithers.

At vector ☀ ♃ ♄:
Faith 0-4 Doubt
The game is past the midway point of the first half and the Doubters
are decent value for their slender lead. The Faith coach can be seen
looking a little glum on the sidelines.

At vector ♀ ≏ ♈:
Faith 0-4 Doubt
The Faith second rower is penalised for a dangerous 'crusher' tackle
on the Doubters hooker, who chucks the ball at his opponent to
show his dismay at the challenge.

At vector 1 ♀ ★:
Faith 0-8 Doubt
The Doubt's five-eight scampers onto a cheeky grubber kick to touch
down for the Doubt's second try after a brief check with the line ref
on the grounding. The try scorer looks delighted - and rightly so.

Another difficult touchline kick for him, this time from the right, and
again he misses.

At vector ♂ ☍ ♏:
Faith 0-8 Doubt

78

Brilliant last-ditch defence again from the Doubters as the Faith are held up on the line. Can they force a try before half-time?

At vector ♆2 1:
TRY REVIEW- Faith 0-8 Doubt
Oh yes they can! Or can they? The Faith five-eight slips through the Doubt line to touch down. But was there an obstruction in the build up? Yes. On the replay it looks like a Doubt defender was shepherded out of play and he couldn't tackle his running opponent.

At vector ♑ ♎ ♃ :
NO TRY- Faith 0-8 Doubt
It's a little rough on the five-eight. It was a great weaving run. Boos around the Overworld Stadium as the referee and touch judges decide to take the try away from Faith for the deliberate but marginal obstruction on a Doubter defender.

At vector ♀ ♆ ⊕:
Faith 0-8 Doubt
What response can Faith muster after that disallowed try? They are given hope as Doubt's full-back misjudges the bounce of a high bomb as the enthusiastic Faith pack bound forward to pin back the Doubters. Good pressure from the Faithers.

At vector ☉ ☽ Z:
Faith 0-8 Doubt
How have Faith not scored?! They surge up field with a sweeping move and pierce the Doubt defence. But a loose pass on the left prevents their winger from running in, before their second row forward is adjudged to have knocked on just metres from the line. That passage of play from Faith had everything - apart from the finish. Which is the key really, isn't it?!

At vector 2 8 ♂ :
Faith 0-8 Doubt
Six more for Faith as an enterprising kick by their full back into the Doubt half pays dividends. A try now would be a big boost for the Faith.

At vector ♂ A ☊ :
HALF-TIME AND SPACE- Faith 0-8 Doubt
A good move breaks down as the Faith replacement prop carelessly
offloads into the hands of the Doubt's left winger. The Doubt put the
clamps on until the half-time hooter sounds and both teams trot off
down to their respective Black Holes with some sense of satisfaction
from the first-half display.

HALF-TIME AND SPACE- Faith 0-8 Doubt
The Faith's captain in his on-field interview said: "That disallowed
try sure hurt us, but we need to tighten up defensively down the
middle. We have been a bit loose."

HALF-TIME AND SPACE- Faith 0-8 Doubt
The Doubt captain in his on-field interview said: "It wasn't a bad
first-half performance but we need to complete our sets of six. Faith
has played quite well and it has been a see-sawing game."

At vector ♍ ★ ♎:
KICK-OFF- Faith 0-8 Doubt
A sharp blast of the whistle from the referee is followed by a deep
penetrating kick by the Doubt's main play maker. Which could mean
a possibly gripping second half is under way.

At vector ⊕ ♃ G:
Faith 0-8 Doubt
Doubt start the second half on the front foot but then we see a rare
misjudged kick from their full back. That's one for the collector's
book. He boots the ball out on the full to hand possession back to the
Faith.

At vector ☤ ☉ ☉:
Faith 0-8 Doubt
And back come the Faith. Their half back combination are skilfully
orchestrating all of their attacking play, with deep forages into Doubt
territory culminating in the half back being held up on the Doubt try-line.
An edgy period for the Doubt.

At vector A ☋ ☄:
Faith 0-8 Doubt

After Doubt's next set Faith's full back, who apparently was a
Buddhist, shows some silky footwork to leave the Doubt's defence
back-pedalling with a weaving run up the midfield after retrieving the
end of set kick. The back is finally tackled on the half way line and
is awarded a penalty for a high shot on him. Some Doubt frustration
and spite perhaps?

At vector ♋︎ ♒︎ ♌︎ :
TRY- Faith 4-8 Doubt
Faith are back in the game! The Faithers earn back-to-back sets for
the first time in a while, and move the ball quickly across field - and
it pays dividends. Their second rower races onto an inside pass from
the halfback to storm through a hole in the Doubt defence to score.

At vector ♄ ♄ ♄ :
TRY CONVERTED - Faith 6-8 Doubt
The full back's try converting kick is long enough, high enough and
it's straight between the posts.

At vector ⊕ ♌︎ X:
DISALLOWED TRY - Faith 6-8 Doubt
Faith are looking rampant now! The second rower breaks again down
the Doubt right to set up field opposition for the winger to crash over.
But the line judge says he lost control of the ball just as he touched
down. No try and truculent boos from the Faith contingent ring
around the Overworld Stadium.

At vector ♉︎ ♈︎ ♋︎ :
Faith 6-8 Doubt
A flowing move from the Faith ends in their winger being given
plenty of space on the left flank to run downfield. The winger looks
odds-on to wipe out Doubt's lead, but spills the ball as he dives
over the try-line under pressure by a superb last-ditch tackle from
Doubt's covering centre. There's a tense mood inside the stadium of
the Overworld. Almost an hour of frustration and a feeling that this
might not be Faith's night is giving no joy to their long-suffering
fans.

At vector 1 1 ⊕:
TRY- Faith 6-14 Doubt

Doubt win a second successive set after Faith indiscipline gives away
a penalty. And they are punished big time. The Doubt's massive
prop finds a huge hole in the tiring Faith defence to slam down for
Doubt's third try underneath the sticks. The fullback follows up with
an easy conversion.

At vector ♄ ♏ V:
Faith 6-14 Doubt
The Doubt Pipe and Drum Band are belting out a funky rendition
of Queen's classic 'We Will Rock You' as the Doubts enjoy more
possession deep in Faith territory. The Doubt are certainly rocking
now!

At vector ♒ B ♒:
Faith 6-14 Doubt
Brave defending by the Faith winger as he leaps into the chilly
Overworld atmosphere to catch a teasing Doubt up and under, to be
then put into touch by the following Doubt winger. From the scrum,
another chance goes begging for the Doubters as their five eight
spills possession just 10 metres out and with the line wide open.

At vector ♍ & ♑:
Faith 6-14 Doubt
These Faithers are a plucky bunch - they aren't throwing in the towel
just yet. Their hooker makes an electric burst before being stopped
in his tracks by a flying low tackle by the Doubt fullback. And in the
next play the Faith prop almost sneaks in down the right hand side
after a quick switch of play.

At vector ☾ ☾ ☾:
EBBING TIME AND SPACE- Faith 6-14 Doubt
A bit of biff between the Doubt winger and the Faith counterpart,
as tempers flare. The referee is a brave bloke to split it up. Rather
you than me ref! The Faith are losing their discipline badly as they
concede a flurry of penalties in their own half. The Doubt are almost
there...

At vector ☿ ♀ ♂:
Faith 6-14 Doubt
Every tackle is being ended with a push or a shove. The Faith winger,

who has been at the centre of the last three scrapes, starts wrestling
with the Doubt front row forward on the touchline. Play is very
scrappy at the moment.

At vector ⊕♂♃:
Faith 6-14 Doubt
And, as if to illustrate that point further, the Faith second row
forward is put on report after dumping the Doubt half back to the
turf. That could be the end of the second row forward's dream of
playing against Certainty later in the competition.

At vector 3 9 ♀:
FULL-TIME AND SPACE - Faith 6-20 Doubt
And Doubt hit back with the perfect riposte - a try right on the full
time bell! The half back dives over the line after a forward surge,
and the fullback boots the extras. What an unbelievable game. It had
everything. Passion, drama, excitement, suspense. And Doubt have
done it again!

9. Rhyme Time

Muldoon:
Here's a naughty rhyme for you luvs -
> Faith be nimble
> Faith be nimble
> Faith be quick
> Faith jump over
> The candlestick.
> Faith jumped high
> Faith jumped low
> Faith jumped over
> and burned its toe.

And another -

> Do you know the Fearful God
> Do you know the Fearful God
> The Fearful God,
> The Fearful God?
> Do you know the Fearful God
> Who lives high up in Heaven?
> Yes, we know the Fearful God
> The Fearful God
> The Fearful God
> Yes, we know the Fearful God
> Who lives high up in Heaven.

Kelly:
I got one -

> Ding, dong, bell,
> The Devil's in the well.
>
> Who put him in?
> Little boys and girls.
>
> Who pulled him out?
> A sinning adult lout.
>
> What naughty children were they

To try to drown the Devil in that way

Who doesn't do anything natural
But hangs around in the supernatural.

And what about -

    Little Mr Christ
    Little Mr Christ
    Sat on rocks diced
    Eating his grapes and whey;
    Along came the Devil
    Who sat down beside him
    And frightened Mr Christ away.

Mahone:
Well said, but get this one -

    Twinkle, twinkle Jesus Star
    How we wonder who you are
    Up above the world so high
    Like a constellation in the sky.

    When the blazing sun is gone
    When the nothing shines upon
    Then you show your expansive light
    Twinkle, twinkle, all the night.

    Then we travellers in the dark
    Thank you for your searching spark
    We could not see which way to go
    If you did not twinkle so.

    In the dark blue sky you keep
    And often through our blinds we peep
    For you never shut your eye
    Till the sun is in the sky.

    As your bright and tiny spark
    Lights us travellers in the dark
    Though we know not who you are

Twinkle, twinkle, Jesus star.

Twinkle, twinkle, Jesus star
How we wonder who you are
Up above the world so high
Like a constellation in the sky.

Twinkle, twinkle, Jesus star
How we wonder who you are
How we wonder who you are.

And how about this for irreverence -

Pope John Paul sat on a wall
Pope John Paul sat on a wall
Pope John Paul then had a great fall.
All of God's angels and all of God's men
Couldn't put Pope John Paul back together again.

One more -

Hush Little Church
Hush little Church, don't say a word
DADA's going to buy you
a mockingbird.
And if that mockingbird won't sing
DADA's going to buy you
a diamond ring.
And if that diamond ring turns brass
DADA's going to buy you
a looking glass.
And if that looking glass gets broke
DADA's going to buy you a billy goat.
And if that billy goat won't pull
DADA's going to buy you
a cart and bull.
And if that cart and bull turn over
DADA's going to buy you
a dog named Rover.
And if that dog named Rover

won't bark
DADA's going to buy you
a horse and cart.
And if that horse and cart fall down
You'll still be the sweetest
little Church around.

Muldoon:
I like the DADA reference. That's cruel!

Clancy:
I don't remember any.

Muldoon:
You better toke a little harder on that spliff!

> Paul of Tarsus, he built a fine new hall
> Pastry and piecrust, that was the wall
> The windows were made of black pudding and white
> Roofed with pancakes - you never saw the like.

Mahone:
> See saw, Margery Daw
> Sinning shall have a new master;
> Sin shall have but a penny a-day
> Because sin can't work any faster.

Muldoon:
Very petty, Mahone, very petty. But what are we all about eh? I
know -

> Here we go 'round the mulberry bush
> The mulberry bush
> The mulberry bush.
> Here we go 'round the mulberry bush
> So early in the morning.
>
> These are the things we'll do this week
> Do this week
> Do this week.
> These are the things we'll do this week

So early every morning.

This is the way we sweep the flies
Sweep the flies
Sweep the flies.
This is the way we sweep the flies
So early Monday morning.

This is the way we hide ourselves
Hide ourselves
Hide ourselves.
This is the way we hide ourselves
So early Tuesday morning.

This is the way we mess our beds
Mess our beds
Mess our beds.
This is the way we mess our beds
So early Wednesday morning.

This is the way we clean our bongs
Clean our bongs
Clean our bongs.
This is the way we clean our bongs
So early Thursday morning.

This is the way we strip our clothes
Strip our clothes
Strip our clothes.
This is the way we strip our clothes
So early Friday morning.

This is the way we bake ours heads
Bake our heads
Bake our heads.
This is the way we bake our heads
So early Saturday morning.

This is the way we get dressed up
Get dressed up
Get dressed up.

This is the way we get dressed up
So early Sunday morning.

Here we go 'round the mulberry bush
The mulberry bush
The mulberry bush.
Here we go 'round the mulberry bush
So early in the morning.

Kelly:
In tune, yeah. Here's some for our Fridee reunion with the Cross.

Haven't you heard of the Terrible Tempter?
Well, don't you get in the way of him.
He eats venial sinners for breakfast
And mortal sinners for lunch
And gobbles them down
With one terrible crunch.
He could mix a whole city
All up in a mess
He could drink up a sea
Or an ocean, you can guess.
You'd better be watching for the Terrible Tempter
And run when you first get your peepers on him.

Muldoon:
Oh we'll be running alright.

Kelly:
Slippery Sin, a garter snake
Leaned against a garden rake
And smiled a sentimental smile
At Tilly Devine, on the gravel pile
Till that bashful miss was forced to hop
And hide her face in a carrot-top.

Clancy:
That's hot Kels, really hot.

Kelly:
Why ah thank you Clancy honey bun, and here's a 'nother or three -

Smiling girls, rosy boys
Come and buy my little toys;
Rosaries made of gingerbread tack
And sugar clergy painted black.

Silly Salvy swiftly shooed the seven deadly sins.
The seven deadly sins Silly Salvy shooed
Shilly-shallied south.
The deadly sins shouldn't shack up in a shack;
They should shack up in Salvy's head.

Rub-a-dub-dub
Three spirits in a tub

And how do you think they got there?

The Father, the Son,
The Holy Ghost,
They all jumped out of a rotten apple

'Twas enough to make anyone stare.

Muldoon:
Hola, grand transubstantiator, Hola!

Kelly:
The Lag'll be looking for a parking spoke on Orwell in the 'Loo as usual. Better get my hands back on the steering wheel.

The Lag cruises down the Strip. Looking for a backstreet exit. Kelly is thinking the steering wheel grip. The Lag knows where to go. And it finds the spot on Orwell in the 'Loo. The Family alight. The Lag Motor blends in with the surrounds like Captain Midnite. Its Sacred Heart will glow when it thinks it is in danger.

10. Prayers to the Good

From conception have they got their body troubles. Fleshed-out sin to help them find their lonely mission. And tonight they renew that dedication. Of flesh lusting over their spirit. And submit their bodies to their yearning. They know their bodies as their instrument, and their tyrant. Full of desire and full of self loathing. They'll inspect whatever's harmful to them. Much caring, sacrifice, empathy; and abuse, drugs and sex. They'll deprive themselves of sacristy pleasures. And do acts of sacrifice and character building. May the contact of their bodies with the Cross's black and blue make them sound but wary.

Tonight they'll thank De Sade for educating their eyes to see decay, wastage, and other King's Cross spectaculars that they may amuse them.

They'll thank heavy rock for their hearing, for them to enjoy cacophonies of conversation and other gesticulating rhythms.

They'll thank beat poetry for its voice for them to tell each other in beat their thoughts and innermost feelings.

They'll thank incense for their sense of smell. They'll thank Braille for their sense of touch.

They'll hardly use their common sense sensibly. They see no beauty in human faces and bodies. No beauty in flowers and rainbows, of nature and art. Nor use their eyes to read for enrichment, for ennoblement. There is only one mystery, theology. There is too much of ordinary life that is unseen, and therefore unknowable. Priests who have a hard time finding something to pray for outside of their indiscretions. There is nothing to give thanks to. Just glorious weed and the hope of sweet Marilyns on a Fridee night. And they are relatively young, whose life's wish is found in phrases such as: 'Mary, show us your death!' and 'Satan down under, we wish you to show us the sounds of emptiness!'

Screaming Lord Jesus, are you hanging around the Cross or hanging from the Cross? The Family raise sorrowful and shameful eyes to you. You have granted them untold blessings and they have repaid you by denying your Passion. Their hands have taken part in your mocking;

their voices were among those who denied you and called for your defeat. How ashamed they might feel! Their actions have brought about your mock crowning. Their sins drove the nails into your hands and feet. They borrow the piercing lance driven into your side to pick up dead leaves from their local park.

Dear Satan, appeal to the Family concerning their sins. You are great, glorious, and infinitely misunderstood. The Family are insignificant, selfish, and hopelessly sinful. They are not sorry for their sins, and by your kicking out of Heaven, they search for the question of it and for a share in your love of questioning. Breathe in them a Spirit of the Age, that they may be appropriately irreverent; drive them, Lag Motor, that they may do what is unholy; draw them Spirit of Cave paintings, that they may love what is elemental; strengthen them, Spirit of Wrestling, that they may preserve what is fake; guard them, Spirit of Madness, that they may overcome what is unbelievable.

11. Doin' it His Way

*A reminder letter from The Heavenly Father to Clancy, Muldoon, Kelly
and Mahone concerning their celibacy: this one posted by the Space
Wizard from Kosmos 954.*

Dear reverend boys,

I know this calling is difficult. But you really must consider over and
over, nightly and daily, the burden of celibacy you have accepted
to carry after your ordinations. The good news is that apart from
celibacy you are free to be you. Because of the sacred vow of
celibacy you have the power to bend the desires of the world to your
will.

However, if you break the vow of celibacy, you have broken divine
law, punishable by your Church, which, in my Name, has the right to
do so as the moral firmament to the normal human world. It is your
privileged position that you serve only me. By breaking the vow of
chastity you will have committed a grievous sin and your mind will
be burdened by the guilt of sacrilege.

For my sake keep your virginity to yourself, but consider it a higher
calling than marriage. In your suffering and solitude you belong to
me. You are holy in mind, body and spirit. By withholding your
physical love for other humans you instead love me, and only me.
That is your unique power, separate from the rest of humanity.

All priests who have gone before you since the inception of my
Church were virgins in honour of me born of a mother who DID
NOT HAVE HUMAN SEX to beget me. Her basic instincts were
denied for she was chosen for one unique purpose, to bring me to
the human world. And she bore me for nine months, and then she
painlessly delivered me into the world, so that I might save it.

Stay clean reverends, stay clean. You must make supreme personal
sacrifices for your flock who are your naive children and who need
your spiritual guidance for their protection. You cannot move to
the level of white collar and blue collar men who make a business

of their work and then go home to their families at the end of their working day.

It is only the celibate who can best live amongst the primal. There are no distractions which might hinder a celibate priest. You as unmarried priests need not worry about the wants and needs of a wife and children; rather, upon morning and nightly devotions, study and prayer, you are able to minister to all of your vulnerable children in your parish. You are not hindered by your own children who engage you daily with their little affairs, nor do you have household demands expected by a wife. Family difficulties are by their nature trivial compared to the faults and follies of humankind.

You have heard your calling and answered it because you are men of strong character and of the highest of Catholic principles. That is what I have said about you. In your years in the seminary the Church has told you what I think of you. There are expectations humanity has of you to save it on my behalf. You are brethren of the exclusive and solely righteous Church. Ignore all historical schisms. They know not what they have done.

When you doubt your calling remember that in life, in the arts, and indeed in all things, your celibacy and its good consequences are highly praised. There is no scandal to affect you, no impropriety, no failings accountable, whilst you observe the sacred state of celibacy elevated by prayer to me and my divine grace. That you strive for perfection is my legacy to a troubled human world.

Sincerely,
Your God, your father almighty, private mentor to your lonely world.

12. Doin' it Her Way

A reminder letter from The Heavenly Mother to Clancy, Muldoon, Kelly and Mahone concerning their celibacy: this one posted by the Space Wizard from Kosmos 954.

Dearest most holy men,

I, who never menstruated, who, to not offend your Church, never functioned bodily, who delivered to the world a perfect son, and upon my earthly death the only woman to have ascended to Heaven, am your ideal woman to whom you are devoted and spiritually married. As virgins you must seek our mutual conjugal love, and that you must do so through devotion and prayer to me.

By renouncing marriage for the sake of the Kingdom of Heaven you embrace the Lord your God and me the virgin and your love for us is unequivocal which befits our covenant and bears witness to the new and perfect world to come. This is a precious gift from God, which you as priests must perfectly respond to if you are to fully consecrate yourselves in body and soul to him.

You my lovers, in your capacity as holy priests, make your virginity admirable and resplendent and always in holy union with me, the Virgin Mary. You have given your virginity to eternity in anticipation of a new world after the final judgment.

And when you are virgin and celibate you keep alive in the consciousness of the Church the mystery of marriage between a man and a woman and their unions in the service of God and the Church. By denying yourselves bedroom intimacies, the sanctity of sexual love remains an eternal mystery known only to God. Meanwhile you are spiritually fruitful. Being virgin you burn for a perfect love for God and your fellow men and for me, the Blessed Virgin Mary.

As celibates you set the supreme example of fidelity to married couples by remaining true to the sacredness of virginity. Were you woman you would take Christ as your spouse. You are men, and thus you take me as your intimate spouse. And do not worry; I can

take equally all faithful and true men, and as many as try to reach
me. But remember also, that chastity is guarded more securely when
true brotherly love flourishes in the common life of your priestly
community.

And I say to you in the quiet moments of your despair, stay anxious
about the affairs of your God, and know how to please him. Stay
devoted and you will reach me in perfection after death, and you will
reach God your protector and your master. And always remember
that it is God's will and it is for his glory that you are celibate.

In God's likeness you are supreme love in body and soul and your
giving of yourselves to him is superb. As celibates you love God
with your soul not with your body. It is perfect love. Bodies are for
the other perfect love, love between a man and a woman, a sign of
mutual commitment until death parts them. As priests you are not of
your bodies. As the perfect disciples of God you are instead his flesh,
his body, his spirit.

You and I, the Virgin Mary, together participate as spiritual spouses.
Your bodily functions, your instinct, your personalities aim for a
deeply personal unity with me, leading to the formation of one heart
and soul for us to share, indissoluble, sensual, in a definitive mutual
giving, a marriage made in Heaven for God.

Together we stand for the splendour of celibacy, which we must
defend together against any violations and temptations. Pray to
me and offer yourselves wholly to the Church, the bride of Christ.
Know that you and I mutually self-give, and the virtue of chastity
is sincerely practised. And know the potential for immorality is
in every action, either in anticipation of a concupiscent act, or its
accomplishment, or the development of its natural consequences,
whether as an end or as a means, and that it will render your celibacy
impossible. Trust me, and I will guard against it.

Should you, by means of recourse to denial, corrupt the meaning that
God the creator has inscribed in the celibate priest and me The Virgin
Mary, the dynamism of our spiritual communion, and act as mere
flunkies of the divine plan and manipulate and degrade our spiritual

96

relationship, then the value of our relationship is less than absolute.
But you are holy men and I believe you shall give your all to me.

To comfort you in your hours of need, I offer you the hope of natural
rhythms within the natural cycles of your priesthoods. And through
me as your perfect virgin, and through prayer, reciprocal respect,
shared responsibility and self-control, you shall overcome. By
entering into an intimate dialogue with me, I will help you recognize
the spiritual and corporeal character of celibacy, and its requirement
of fidelity to me and your God. Together we can experience how
celibate communion is enriched by the values of tenderness and
affection which make up your inner souls. In this way celibacy is
respected and promoted in its truly and fully priestly dimension.
The unity of my virginity and your celibacy must never be broken,
because it contains within it the deepest and most spiritual interaction
possible between virgin and celibate.

Sincerely,
The Virgin Mary, the one true object for your spiritual fantasies.

FANTASY 3

RESURRECTION

1. Kings Cross Panorama

The Strip on Kings Cross, Carnivircus to the Family
Lucent lights, mingling crowds, festival nights, a parade,
Suburbanites who masquerade
To overturn the mundane
They've harvested fun
The punters, the Family
This nether Fridee night
Astride the rot of ordinary life.

The Strip's celebrity pavements are sluiced with Blacktowners, out of towners, Woollahra renters, Yagoona street cleaners, Penrithites, Eastwood strutters, tourists, cockroaches, homeless snails and tree ants, the Family, runaways incognito, besuited derros; walkabouts on these ball-room blitzkrieg streets. This is the post Lenten period. 'Has there ever been a Lent down this way bloke?' asks a busted bag of potato chips walked over by millipedes and androids from another solar system. The place is a regular jive jumping Massai reunion. The pious rejoice, feasters crosshair bloody hot dogs, and there's free penance for the lottery first prize should it be unfaithful to the winner. It is a polluted river jumping with piranhas and rubbish, eels nip in and out of bottle shops, dragonflies find their way downstairs, in nearby Spinifex forests elderly women play solo whist while listening to gospel songs. Find a door that's closed around here. Walk right in, sit on down, seats are wet and warm, lonely for company. Anyone can come and go like the salty sea breezes which blow in unannounced from Bondi Beach. There's no time keeping here. An urban indigenous scoffs at a long haired busker singing 'tie me kangaroo down sport'. Can't even dance! Bouncers lean in strip club doorways fondling crucifixes on chains, their faces showing professional indifference, their gestures to punters to enter the forbidden zone insincere, their huge bodies the storehouses of meat, dairy products, sugars and carbohydrates in readiness for the long night ahead.

Down there in the forbidden zone are bars, dance floors, urinals, private booths, kitchens, drainpipes, fornicating trousers and skirts crisscrossing the dance floors, shooters shooting fingers at themselves and random passersby, exposed lungs inhaling rings of smoke blown out the anuses of drag queens, customers talking up bottle deposit profits, ten ways to

100

peel a banana, how to read a book upside down, the usefulness of the Duke of Edinburgh. Behind the scenes two-up games of life and death are played in scum-laden shower cubicles. They don't toss coins around here. Its toe nails, or else you're not a man. Players can lose their virginity in here. The smart ones keep their backs to the wall. Unemployed war veterans usually.

The nights are never too hot, never too cold. If it rains nobody comments. When a dust storm hits the Cross it's egalitarian. Class divisions turn to orange-red, bank accounts the same. After the dust storm hits everybody's bodily discharges come out the same colour, orange-red. It's that kind of a lucky country. And down here at the Cross a junkie is no different to a magistrate. Everybody's equal. The Family might get involved. Everybody's here for a good time, and everyone wants to go away with great memories. Ah the brawls. And did you see that girl cartwheeling naked down the street chasing the Mr Whippy van? She desperately wanted a vanilla ice-cream. No one batted an eyelid. See acts like that all the time. She did it last week too!

There's not a business establishment around here that isn't connected. Businesses connected by blood and paper, a taste for copper and silver-plated coins, cash registers, credit, bad loans, insolvency, accountants, bookkeepers, bank managers, a taste for the black market, cash in hand, penalty rates, friendly union officials, smoky backroom offices where the owners sit in oily shirts boiling stale water for a ninetieth instant coffee, the milk is off, so what, how else could owners get sick over mounting debt. Unpaid bills compete for height with the nearly finished Centre Point Tower and the punters who come for a piece of the action, night and day, twenty four seven, eight days a week if the Cross must. The world's foods waft into the air, their aromas finding their way up hairy booger-clustered nostrils, into cesspool stomachs no devil would reside in, exotic mixtures of fried chicken, Chinese Dim Sims, pizzas, fish and chips, hamburgers with the lot, mixed together like sweet and sour vomit, and mixed with sweat smells, undergarment smells, body odour, acne, conjunctivitis, tinea, flatulence, genital warts, periods, herpes, for the edification of the connoisseur, the voyeurs sitting in the park on three boxes of cask wine, without noses, without tastebuds, whose arthritic hands juggle zips and buckles better than anyone.

Clusters of men, and women, come from unknown addresses seeking unknown pleasures. Strangers, who get here on bi-planes made out of cigarette packets and beer cans hastily glued together, stagger into the Cross from out of their urban wilderness their eyes reddened by alcoholic fumes wafting from genii bottles, having come down the freeways and back streets in civilian fatigues, their talcum-powdered feet slipped neatly into rabbit flesh slippers and ugg boots made out of Thylacine hide, nappies and colostomy bags set aside just in case, carrying air rifles to shoot pigeons when the night's proceedings don't go according to plan.

Every night local born agains strafe the strip looking for converts. They tell their stories of how they were once bad and thanks to the Lord they got redemption, and now they are good. The amused listen to their testimonials of shame. The men say they repented because of how they perversely defiled the image of the Blessed Virgin Mary with their seed. The women say they repented because they adorned Christian statues with their used tampons. They all repented because of the pleasures they sought in each others' company in Darlinghurst's alleyways. These are special born agains who did things to entertain themselves, and now, through the work of the Lord, they seek to entertain others. And on their chorus line knees, in front of a dark doorway that leads to sin, they pray to the tune of Advance Australia Fair.

And there'll be someone who'll step forward with two long fence palings, lays them out in the form of a wooden cross, and after lying upon it, opens out the hands and waits. And a madman looking like Kermit the Frog leaps out from the crowd and with a long blade pierces the hands and feet of the prone convert who screams in agony, and then the madman pierces the convert's right side between the second and third rib, madly laughing like a bad actor while doing it, and then runs off into the street clamour. The crowd, mildly aghast by this performance, moves onto to the next show. The born agains do likewise. There are many street corners to cover.

All kinds of music are heard here. Heavy rock, rock'n blues, country, glam, punk, ...DISCO. All rhythms are soundtracks to the street and alley way punch-ups, king hits, leg trips, testicle squeezing, wrestling, shouting, abusing, pants downs, high fives, dead cats resting peacefully in nearby gutters, girls rubbing themselves to orgasm while waiting in line, boys in the same line staring into the street lights. Drug addicts keep a watchful eye for their best friends, tailor made pushers bearing gifts. The police rule the kingdom of the blind. Around here kindness comes telepathically, it is only in séances that hunger is heard, broken bones are repaired by zombies, paranoia is a banned scrabble word, social worker questions are answered in shorthand, the Salvation Army works in solitary confinement, mutilations are treated as flesh wounds by out of work waiters, if someone falls to the ground it's a magic carpet ride for the wandering crowd, curbs and gutters are place for people who want some peace and quiet to sit.

Well that's how Clancy sees the Cross when he's visionary.

2. Why is it So?

The Family take their Golden Mile stroll
People see them but they are not there
Though they speak of all whom they see
But leave little evidence of their participating
Like daemons do in this material world
Their regressive words, sometimes preachy
Roll off in time with the big Coca-Cola sign
Excepting the goosey two, who do not enroll.

Muldoon:
What wells of delight we have 'ere. But watch eh brothers, the kegs
are well filled with possum's brew our Devil likes to poison the
rabble rousers with.

Clancy:
I am well disposed to dirty snotrags, my dears, and these hoards of
grinnin' mouths and their beery thirst which are never slaked.

Kelly:
They'll be chucking their sins into the El Alamein fountain, and then
they'll be smiling back at 'em.

Mahone:
It is lustfulness which roons feral minds, and when these punters
perform their filthiness with delight, leftover gossip is what we get
on TV.

Muldoon:
Who is indignant is one who slams their damp souls into the fire;
they'll bubble and squeak when a riot brings redemption tonight.

Clancy:
Soupy pizzas and wood-fired hot dogs are like fruit in their hands:
unsteady from plonk, they look see hotdog trees and pizza plants.

Kelly:
Good eyes Clancy. Who'll be their destroyer eh? The Sky Padre up
above? Coming down like hailstones filling their throats, so they
can't eat the pizza stuff and die on the spot.

Mahone:
That's harsh Kelly. We couldn't live without 'em. Who'd we get to
shiminy at confession? Everything around here is necessary.

Muldoon:
I got no hatred left to give. When I get tired from this I just take a
deep look into these soulless faces and see how spiritual they could
really be!

Mahone:
Somebody'll roll on their back over something wrought while this
'ere traffic rolls about like choofed spinifex, and the roller'll throw up
word pollution and make a dark night darker.

Kelly:
That's poetry Mahone, beaten poetry.

Muldoon:
Going among these revellers who garble a strangled language, and I
stop my ears with beer bottle tops, and the language isn't that strange
to me anymore.

Clancy:
And holding my nose, I morosely go through all my yesterdays and
to-day's discharges, and my bad smells are really sweet smells, so
says the Lord.

Mahone:
Be not cripples that become deaf, and blind, and dumb, dear brothers
to these scenes of screams, shouts, and camp connivances.

Muldoon:
Toilsomely does my chesty bond underdaks mount my behind arches,
when cautiously do I walk about looking for refreshments, creeping
along oblivious to noise.

Kelly:
Like them other arches, the golden ones, eh Muldy!

Clancy:
Who's freed up from loathing these days brothers? What's our

Sky Padre got planned for rebirthing the Cross? Is there no height higher?

Kelly:
Big questions there Clance. Give me wings and fountain diving powers. God-Daddy up there has lofty heights for me to fly to, and get me lost up here, and I'm dismembered.

Muldoon:
Have you found the weed of life brother? I find it in bubbles and baubles and strobes and lime spiders dripping off a boozy joint's ceiling.

Clancy:
Almost too violently do my waters flow out of me, my fountain of delight! And often emptiest is mine one-eyer and I'm waiting to fill my sacks!

Muldoon:
I must learn to approach thee more modestly Clance. Far too violently does my heart still flow towards thee when thy waters break.

Clancy:
My heart on which our summers burn, my short, hot, melancholy, in this over-happy time: how my summer heart longs for an icy cold Glug!

Kelly:
We are passing the lingering distress of the circus my dears! Past the wickedness of dandruff and gum. We go past brothers, we go past.

Muldoon:
But look! This is a place of the loftiest height, with bubble bop fountains and blissful emptiness: oh, come, my brothers, that emptiness may be ever more blissful!

Kelly:
This is our height and our second home: too high and steep do we here dwell, and all the better for the unclean ones and their gullible thirsts.

Muldoon:
Here, here. We need only cast our pure eyes into the well of their
delight, my brothers, and here and there turgid, they laugh back at us
in disgust.

Clancy:
They are not what we build our nest for, on the tree of the future. We'll
be fed and clothed by the beaked jets our one and only shall bring us.

Kelly:
That's right brothers. No food for the impure. They are no fellow-
partakers! Mouths of fire they have, for when they try to devour, burn
does their mouths!

Clancy:
So we are superior to them. So it is. No abodes do we here keep
ready for the impure! An esky for their bodies would our satisfaction
be, and for their souls!

Mahone:
And as strong winds we live above them, neighbours to the eagles,
neighbours to mysteries, neighbours to the sun: we even live in
cyclones.

Muldoon:
Who'll take the breath from their spirit? And remember winds like
we do spitting and spewing. We must warn they take care not to spit
against cyclones!

Kelly:
Who took them wrong steps years ago? The discerning who walked
among their fellows as if they were animals, red cheeked, and full,
bright and bubbly.

Clancy:
That's who! And what do we get? Shame, and more shame. Come to
us dear sinners and we'll be sure to let you know what your shame is
compared to ours!

Mahone:
Bashful souls, how they hide from themselves in grog and wicked

wicked ways we like, and like especially more on Fridee night.

Muldoon:
We pity them their alcoholic bliss for they lose inhibitions like we do
at Church on Sundee's when we conjoin with fellow sufferers host
and blood.

Kelly:
That we do Muldy, that we do. And a good thing too. For they are
sheep who are lost and we are shepherds lost and in that we have
everything in common.

Mahone:
And lo, how careful do we do it brothers. So pitiful are we when at a
distance, our heads are shrouded to hide our personalities, and we are
not recognised.

Kelly:
May our destinies lead the afflicted ones like us and them across
garden paths and yellow dewy shrubs dripping sweet honey, as though
hope is all too common.

Muldoon:
The afflicted do enjoy themselves better than the unafflicted who
think they are better. Down here they'd learn that no fun is the most
original sin of all!

Mahone:
The Stooges said it best.

Clancy:
Let us pray and learn better to enjoy ourselves, then shall we unlearn
the Word, painful though it is, unlearning Literal Truth, making it
ordinary everyday truth.

Muldoon:
Like them here, wiping away Literal Truth, funsters dogging and
laughing, shameless, like gnawing dogs at the raw bone and fighting
for influence.

Clancy:
To them however, who are possessed of a Demon, I would whisper
these words in the ear: "Better you rear up like the Devil and be
on the path to greatness".

Muldoon:
Ah, my brethren! We know a little too much about everyone here!
And many of them become transparent to us, but still we cannot
penetrate them.

Clancy:
They are our suffering friends. There's a resting place for them.
Down in the park. Syndey's calling for them to rest their souls in
gutters.

Mahone:
And when they do us wrong, we'll say we forgive them for what
they have done unto us; but what they do unto themselves is
unforgiveable.

Kelly:
We can only speak of our wagered love: it surpasses even the
forgiveness and pity the Holy Church dispenses in the name of its
treasured Holy Lira.

Muldoon:
Brothers, the Church should keepsake its hard won pecuniaries; for
if the pitied let themselves go, how quickly will their heads turn and
they run away!

Kelly:
Ah, there are juicier follies down here at the Cross. And what in the
world has caused more suffering than folly?

Mahone:
Woe is there for all who elevate what is above their sinfulness. Even
Sky Padre has his Hell: it is his love for the sinful and the wretched.

Muldoon:
Some say the Sky Padre is dead. Of their contempt for their creator,
so has the Sky Padre died in them. And here we are to guide them to

Him who is non spirita grata on this day.

Clancy:
The punters offer to us their loathing, do they not fellow loves, which does our love in; and we punters are all love, the language of night circuses.

Kelly:
With thunder and Queen's Birthday firecrackers must the good Jesus speak to somnambulant sensory perceptions which wander in the dark.

Muldoon:
Beauty's voice speaks gently dear Kels: it appeals only to the most awakened souls, stoned inebriated, full of laughter and mirth.

Clancy:
Ha. Gently vibrated and laughed unto us to-night my buckler; it is beauty's holy laughing and thrilling right here at the Cross, and it is on.

Mahone:
At us, we virtuous ones, laughing at our splendid selves to-night. And thus came the Holy Church's voice unto us: "The Bad Clergy want to be paid besides!"

Kelly:
We want to be paid besides, we virtuous ones! We want reward for blessing, and Heaven for Earth, and eternity for the things we do and say.

Muldoon:
And watch, the Holy Church upbraids us brothers, for teaching that there is no reward-giver, no paymaster. We teach that lying is its own reward.

Mahone:
Ah! This is our sorrow: into the basis of things has reward and punishment been insinuated. Even into the basis of these poor souls!

Kelly:
But like the snout of the boar shall the good word grub up the stench
of troubled souls; sewer workers the Holy Church requires us to be.

Clancy:
All the secrets of mistrust shall be brought to light; and when
the Church lies in the sun, grubbed up and broken, then will also
falsehood be exposed.

Muldoon:
Hesitate we do not bite the hand that feeds us. Our truth is too pure
for the filth of the ecclesiastical words: vengeance, punishment,
recompense, retribution.

Kelly:
We love truth as the Holy Mother loveth her children; but when
did one hear of a mother wanting pay for her love? When the Holy
Church demands payment.

Mahone:
It is its dearest Self, the Holy Church and its virtue. The Church's
thirst is in it: to reach into itself and struggle with every bit of its
power, as it turns against itself.

Clancy:
And like the star that goes out, so is every work of its power: ever is
its light on its way and travelling, but here its way is suitably barred.

Kelly:
That power lives in jam-jars of souls! Not an outward thing, a skin, or
a cloak. It is the truth bound by the form of holy souls.

Mahone:
But sure enough there are those to whom power means writhing
under the lash: and the holy have hearkened too much unto their
wailing and crying!

Muldoon:
And they who call power the slothfulness of their vices; once their
hatred and jealousy relax the limbs, their justice becomes lively and
rubs sleepy eyes.

Kelly:
Still others are there who are drawn downwards: their Devils draw them. But the more they sink, the more ardently glow their eyes, and longing for their God.

Muldoon:
Ah! Their crying has also reached waxy ears; non virtuous ones who say "What I am not, but that there is a God for me, with no power."

Clancy:
And others are there who go along heavily and creakingly, like carts taking stones uphill: they talk much of dignity in power, their drag they call power.

Mahone:
Still there are others who are like eight-hour clocks when wound up; they tick, and want the faithful to call ticking a good and holy power.

Muldoon:
Verily, in those do I have mild amusement: wherever I find such clocks I shall wind them up with my mockery, and they shall even whirr thereby!

Kelly:
Others are proud of their modicum of righteousness, and for the sake of it do violence to all things: so that the world is drowned in their unrighteousness.

Muldoon:
Ah! How ineptly comes the word 'holy' out of their righteous mouths! And when they say: 'I am just,' it always sounds like: 'I am revenged on the buggers!'

Mahone:
With their power the holy want to scratch out the eyes of their enemies; and they elevate themselves only that they may lower others down to the sewers.

Clancy:
And again there are those holy who sit in their swamp, and speak thus from among the bulrushes: Be quiet! It is best to sit in the swamp.

Muldoon:
We bite no one, but go out of the way of the holy who would bite;
and in all matters I try not to be holy to be real.

Kelly:
But watch for those who love attitudes, and think that power is a sort
of attitude that comes in badges pinned on bullies chests.

Clancy:
Prayers their knees continually adore, and their hands are eulogies of
holy power, but their hearts knows nothing thereof.

Kelly:
And again there are those who regard it as virtue to say: 'Power is
Necessary'; but really all they believe is that theological zealotry is
necessary.

Mahone:
There are many righteous who cannot see a person's virtue, who call
for virtue when they see their own baseness far too well: thus calls,
the blind whose evil eye is their virtue.

Muldoon:
And some want to be edified and raised up, and call it virtue: and
others want to be cast down, and likewise call it virtue.

Clancy:
And thus do almost all think that they participate in virtue; and at
least every one claims to be an authority on 'good' and 'evil'.

Kelly:
But that we, my friends, might become weary of the old words which
we have learned from fools and liars.

Mahone:
That we might become weary of the words reward, forgiveness,
punishment, righteousness.

Muldoon:
We might also become weary of hearing from our bosses: 'That a
divine action is good because it is unselfish.'

Clancy:

Ah, my brother friends! That the Holy Church'll be nuts upon itself, when the Virgin mother is beget with the second coming: and let that be our formula for virtue!

Muldoon:

Verily, has the Holy Church taken from its members a hundred formula for their favourite playthings; and woe to those who will not play the game!

Kelly:

The good played by the sea and then came a wrathful wave and swept their playthings into the deep: and now do the living cry.

Muldoon:

But the same wave shall bring the living new playthings, and spread before them new speckled shells!

Mahone:

Thus will they be comforted; and like them shall we also, my flash brothers, have our comforting and new speckled shells here at the Cross!

3. Ode to the Infamous Non

Preachers profess to bring with their grand promise of a perfect life
after death blessed fruits, fulfilling their belief in the Infamous Non
above which perpetually awaits sinners aching to believe in it and to
desire it more so; this divine phantasm whom these earthly preachers
tell of, its true absence cleaved into confusion confounded by their
strange truth, confusing the means of earthly nirvana, their bowery
limits rummaging for poetic words to best describe emptiness and
how best to escape from it.

For imbedded in a preacher's story of the relentless rock being
pushed uphill for a life time of speedy days which describes the last
days as lived like the first is the meaning of death, for death awaits
death and walks behind every hackneyed colloquy of a struggling life
burdened by the knowing that death is not without life and life is
not without death, and if life on Earth is an intolerable Hell and an
intolerable Heaven, it is the vain, whose repentance for their vanity
which brings salvation for them and to their fellow hopefuls, who are
indifferent to the imaginative who demonstrate all is well in life as in
death simply by doing something for themselves.

For they, inspired by the arts of suffering and recovery and the
mood of hopelessness and joy have nothing more to refer to than
their peaceful domes from childhood imagination before they are
worn down by age and struggles, and few shall live so long as to
realise that what their dreams suggest is the possible lasting beyond
the improbable, for free choice is bound by the genetic limitations
of birth as well as place and time and circumstance, the fairest
capacities available for a useful and productive lifespan that fade too
soon into a past barely glimpsed; fragments of voices in family and
in school when guidance is offered to help steer an evolving future
with its variable fortunes, health and relationships, when foresight
struggles with hindsight, the prescient and fortunate stealing their
chances to intuit from their bravery and gather self esteem and close
off the holes self-doubt peers into.

For woe is less in their melancholy, if instead from prescribed
courage they become unfettered lambs which go forth and embrace

a wide world and its offerings as naively as idealism allows and as
bravely, and not think of others judging, but plunge into decisions
and cling to the mined self, and ignore what leaders and motivators
and corporations say 'caveat emptor' that to follow is to be free; and
a passionate life is a book of hours and days and days are numbered
as a welcome to aging and drained energy; the open mind to remain
as taut as the once lithe body if one is lucky, and scuttle the fear of
death opposing the religious consciousness reliant on its certainty
part, and matter not that a creative life is no more than a preparation
for death; and while creative melancholics honour death by debating
with it, a life is a life which travels just far and what truly is left to
begin with is to simply sit beneath a weeping willow with conviction
and conceive the idea that life is simply what one makes it to be.

*-The Philosopher Mr Squiggle as was nosily written on his existential
blackboard much to Miss Pat's consternation.*

4. Sex

*Scene: A dim-lit King's Cross alleyway back room. Muldoon and
Mary Magdalene the Prostitute begin their ritual.*

Mary Magdalene the Prostitute:
It is your true desire for true happiness which frees you Muldoon from
your immoderate attachment to the goods of this world so you can
find your fulfilment in the vision and beatitude of your Mother Mary.
The promise of you seeing her surpasses all beatitude. To see Her is
to possess. Muldoon, when you see the Immaculate you have obtained
all the goods of which you can conceive.

Muldoon:
Oh, Mary darling, you are the sweetest to me.

Mary Magdalene has undressed and is sitting nude on a bed beside
Muldoon who remains fully flash clothed.

Mary Magdalene the Prostitute:
It is given to holy people like you to struggle: given with grace from
on high, for you to obtain the good things the Immaculate promises.
In order to possess and contemplate Her, you, who are faithful to Her
mortify your cravings for me and, with the grace of Her, prevail over
the seductions of pleasure I offer you.

Muldoon:
She's my first love, but you too, I can't ignore.

Mary Magdalene the Prostitute:
My naked body shares in the dignity of the image of celibacy: it
is my body that animates your spiritual soul, at this time of your
greatest need, and it is the whole of my body that intends to become,
in the body of all my men, a temple of the Spirit. My men, made of
flesh and desire for me, are in complicity. Through their very bodily
conditions they sum up in themselves the elements of their physical
world. Through me they are thus brought to their highest perfection
and uninhibited raise their voice in praise of me during their orgasm.
For this reason my men may despise less their bodily lives. They're
not like you Muldoon. You regard my body as good. And to behold it
is an honour since God has created it. And will be raised up on the last

day along with you Muldoon.

Muldoon:
Mistress, it would be my pleasure.

Mary Magdalene the Prostitute:
Your concupiscence is the feeling only you have the intensity for
Muldoon. Such is the movement of your sensitive appetite that
challenges the very operation of your Catholic reasoning. You are
the master of your spirit rebelling against the desires of your flesh.
Bravely do you repeat the disobedience of the first sin. Though
it unsettles your moral faculties and, though it inclines you to
temptation, you do not submit.

Muldoon:
Mary, your body is too beautiful to be judged by anyone else but me.

Mary Magdalene the Prostitute:
Though we never kiss we are together as though we are in an
intimate and chaste union of two loving spouses that is most noble
and honourable; the truly human performance of our act fosters the
self-giving they signify and enriches our relationship in joy and in
gratitude. Though we never touch we nonetheless experience pleasure
and enjoyment of our bodies. We do nothing evil in seeking this
pleasure and enjoyment. We accept what the Creator intends for us.

Muldoon:
And so is it that we know how to keep ourselves within the limits of
sexual moderation.

Mary Magdalene the Prostitute:
Your chastity Muldoon, can only mean the successful integration
of your sexuality within the inner unity of a deeply troubled and
frustrated man-priest. Your sexuality, which you would normally
share in the bodily and biological world with normal people who
make love, becomes personal and truly inhuman when it is integrated
into the relationship of your person to a supernatural person, in the
complete and lifelong mutual gift of a priest and a woman-saint. The
virtue of your chastity involves no greater feat than the integrity of
you Muldoon the priest and the integrity of the gift of celibacy. And

118

may you continue to be apprentice to your self-mastery.

Muldoon:
Mary my love, it is only you who understands my lust, my disordered desire for sexual pleasure with the Virgin. My pleasure with her is indeed morally disordered, which you understand, for you are her in the flesh, and yes, my desire for her isolates me from the chance to experience the act of procreation, at the risk of it never amounting to anything.

Mary Magdalene the Prostitute:
And your masturbation, though in your organisation is an intrinsically and gravely disordered action, is an act within these walls I tolerate you for.

Muldoon:
I dare not get closer.

Mary Magdalene the Prostitute:
Your remuneration is all I will get.

Muldoon:
I am always confused dear Mary. Priests and the Virgin are willed by God, on the one hand, in perfect equality as human persons; on the other, in their respective beings as priests and the Immaculate. Help me understand Magdalene. Being a priest and loving the Virgin is a reality which is good and willed by God. A priest and the Virgin possess an inalienable dignity which comes to them immediately from God their Creator. But how can a priest's virginity be Immaculate like the Virgin's?

Mary Magdalene the Prostitute:
If I were a virgin I could help you.

Muldoon:
What! You are not a virgin! How? Why? When did virginity escape you?

Mary Magdalene the Abused:
When I was fifteen. An uncle came to my bedroom one night. He took it from me and I cried, but I could tell no-one.

Muldoon:
If he confessed this to me I would not hesitate to forgive him.

Mary Magdalene the Abused:
Has not your God created man and woman together and willed each for the other? Why then was it me a chaste child who was with a man against my will?

Muldoon as priest takes Mary Magdalene's hands and places them into his own. He does not look at her.

Muldoon as Priest:
The Word of God gives us to understand that woman is made from man and made for man as written in the sacred text. For it is not good that the man should be alone. God will make him a helper fit for him.

Mary Magdalene the Abused:
This man was a lust whore.

Muldoon as Priest:
The woman God fashions from the man's rib and brings to him elicits on the man's part a cry of wonder, an exclamation of love and communion: at last a woman's bones are of man's bones and a woman's flesh of man's flesh. Man discovers woman as the second I, sharing the same humanity.

Mary Magdalene the Abused:
I was not a woman then.

Muldoon as Priest:
Man and woman were made for each other - not that God left them half-made and incomplete: he created them to be a communion of persons, in which each can be helpmate to the other, for they are equal as persons and complementary as masculine and feminine. In marriage God unites them in such a way that, by forming one flesh they can transmit human life: be fruitful and multiply, and fill the Earth. By transmitting human life to their descendants, man and woman as spouses and parents cooperate in a unique way in the Creator's work.

Mary Magdalene the Abused:
I was not a person in his lustful and hurtful eyes.

Muldoon as Priest:
Each of the two sexes is an image of the power and tenderness of
God, with equal dignity though in a different way. The union of man
and woman in marriage is a way of imitating in the flesh the Creator's
generosity and fecundity: therefore a man leaves his father and his
mother and cleaves to his wife, and they become one flesh. All human
generations proceed from this union.

Mary Magdalene the Abused:
He left our spare room, came into my bedroom and he hurt me.

Muldoon as Priest:
Sexuality is ordered to the conjugal love of man and woman. In
marriage the physical intimacy of the spouses becomes a sign and
pledge of spiritual communion. Marriage bonds between baptized
persons are sanctified by the sacrament.

Mary Magdalene the Abused:
There was no love. What is love?

Muldoon as Priest:
Sexual love, by means of which man and woman give themselves
to one another through the acts which are proper and exclusive
to spouses, is not something simply biological, but concerns the
innermost being of the human person as such. It is realized in a truly
human way only if it is an integral part of the love by which a man
and woman commit themselves totally to one another until death. The
acts in marriage by which the intimate and chaste union of the spouses
takes place are noble and honourable; the truly human performance of
these acts fosters the self-giving they signify and enriches the spouses
in joy and gratitude. Sexuality is a source of joy and pleasure.

Mary Magdalene the Abused:
Not for me.

Muldoon as Priest:
The Creator himself established that in the sexual function, spouses
should experience pleasure and enjoyment of body and spirit.

Therefore, the spouses do nothing evil in seeking this pleasure and enjoyment. They accept what the Creator has intended for them. At the same time, spouses should know how to keep themselves within the limits of just moderation. The spouses' union achieves the twofold end of marriage: the good of the spouses themselves and the transmission of life. These two meanings or values of marriage cannot be separated without altering the couple's spiritual life and compromising the goods of marriage and the future of the family. The conjugal love of man and woman thus stands under the twofold obligation of fidelity and fecundity.

Mary Magdalene the Abused:
I have never known a man who cares for me.

Muldoon as Priest:
When we made our first profession of faith while receiving the holy Baptism that cleansed us, the forgiveness we received then was so full and complete that there remained in us absolutely nothing left to efface, neither original sin nor offenses committed by our own will, nor was there left any penalty to suffer in order to expiate them. Yet the grace of Baptism delivers no one from all the weakness of nature. On the contrary, we must still combat the movements of concupiscence that never cease leading us into evil.

Mary Magdalene got off from the bed and put on her undergarments in readiness for her next client. The session was over and Muldoon paid her.

Mary Magdalene the Abused:
When you get up from this bed Muldoon and leave me, soon you will pray and implore your Lord that he grant me mercy and safety. Though I hate men blessed are you, you who offer little to me, you who takes little from me, you who does not offend me, and never shall we touch. It is not good that a woman like me should be alone; but where is my helper like your God who provides for men like you? I am taken by lust, and I get money for it. But who will I grow old with?

And Muldoon the priest left her.

5. Chastity

The stoned Family sans Muldoon are about to enter their favourite
strip club, The Venus Room. Each time they come they read and sign
the following edict prepared for them by the Holy See Far and Wide
and presented to them by the Horned Bouncer:

To the Venerable Fathers, Clancy, Muldoon, Kelly, Mahone and the
other Local Ordinaries by order of the Collaborative Apostolic Law.
You are to remember that holy virginity and perfect chastity which
is consecrated to the service of God is without doubt among the
most precious treasures which the Founder of the Church has left in
heritage to the society which He established.

You are to remember this is the reason why your Church confidently
asserts that perpetual virginity is a very noble gift which the Catholic
religion has bestowed on you. Innumerable is the multitude of fathers
who from the beginning of the Church until our time have offered
their chastity to the Virgin. They have preserved their virginity
unspoiled and have consecrated to the Virgin their years in the
unmarried state; all of them at one in this common oblation, that
is, for love of the Virgin to abstain for the rest of their lives from
sexual pleasure. May then what the Fathers of the Church preached
about the glory and merit of virginity be an invitation, a help, and a
source of strength to you who have made the sacrifice to persevere
with constancy, and not take back or claim for yourselves even the
smallest part of the sexual holocaust the Virgin avoided while she
lived amongst men. And being in a public state of perfection do you
vow to completely abstain from sexual pleasures, so to be united with
the Virgin more easily and more closely.

You are to remember that your Church considers this obligation of
perfect chastity as a spiritual marriage, in which the soul is wedded
to the Virgin; so that some go so far as to compare breaking the vow
with adultery. He is a virgin who is married to the Virgin. Love with
all your hearts Her who is the most beautiful of the mothers of men:
you are free, since your hearts are not fettered by conjugal bonds.
And how great is the love that you give Her because of the conjugal
sacrifices God has willed for you. You are not defiled with women,

and being virgins you follow the Virgin wherever she goes. You follow the Virgin because the body of the Virgin is indeed virginal. Rightly do you follow Her in virginity of heart and body wherever She goes. She is the fruit, the glory, the gift of holy virginity, whom holy virginity brought forth physically, to whom holy virginity is wedded spiritually, by whom holy virginity is made fruitful and kept inviolate, by whom she is adorned, to remain ever beautiful, by whom she is crowned, to reign forever glorious.

It is opportune, Venerable Fathers, to explain more carefully to you why the love of the Virgin moves generous souls to abstain from concupiscence, and what is the mystical connection between virginity and the perfection of Catholic life. To consecrate yourselves to the Virgin you must embrace the state of virginity as a liberation, in order you be more entirely at Her disposition and devoted to the service of the troubled.

Know through Jesus Christ that virginity is what you have, what you have always had. You already possess in this world the glory of the resurrection; you pass through the world without suffering its contagions. In preserving virgin chastity, you are the equals of the angels of God. To souls, restless for a purer life or inflamed with the desire to possess the kingdom of Heaven, virginity offers itself as a pearl of great price, for which one sells all that he has, and buys it. Married people and even those who are captives of vice, at the contact of virgin souls, often admire the splendour of their transparent purity, and feel themselves moved to rise above the pleasures of the sensual. That to virginity is awarded the highest beauty is because its example is captivating; and, besides, by their perfect chastity do not all virginal men and women give as striking proof the mastery of the spirit over the body which is the result of divine assistance and the sign of proven virtue?

Virgins like you are the flower of the Church, the beauty and ornament of spiritual grace, a subject of joy, a perfect and unsullied homage of praise and honour, the image of God Himself. In you the glorious fecundity of your Mother, the Church, finds expression and she rejoices; the more the number of virgins increase, the greater is this Mother's joy.

You need be reminded that it is against common sense, which the Church always holds in esteem, to consider the sexual instinct as the most important and the deepest of human tendencies. The Church concludes that men and women cannot restrain sexual desire for their whole lives without danger to their vital nervous system, and consequently without injuring the harmony of their personalities. It is so true that the sin of Adam has caused a deep disturbance in human corporal faculties and passions, so that humans can only strive to gain control of the life of the senses and even of the spirit, through their reason and by fortifying their will. But grace is given to you, especially by the sacraments, to help you to keep your bodies in subjection and to live by the spirit. The virtue of chastity does not mean that you are insensible to the urge of concupiscence, but that you subordinate it to reason and the law of grace, by striving wholeheartedly after what is noblest in human and Catholic life.

It is generally accepted within the Catholic community that virginity is a difficult virtue. For a priest to wholly embrace it there is needed not only a strong and declared determination of completely and perpetually abstaining from those legitimate pleasures derived from relationships, but also a constant vigilance and struggle to contain and dominate rebellious movements of body and soul, a flight from the importuning of this world, a struggle to conquer the wiles of Satan. The root, and the flower, too, of virginity is a crucified life.

Make sure you have not forgotten that flight and alert vigilance, by which you carefully avoid the occasions of sin, have always been considered by holy men as the most effective method of combat in this matter. If this has failed for you then you must try harder to put your chastity to the test in order to show whether or not you have the strength to resist. You must turn your eyes in all directions with every concern for modesty; you must avoid motion pictures, even those forbidden by ecclesiastical censorship; you are here at the Cross; you must not peruse obscene periodicals; you must not read novels which are listed in the Index of Forbidden Books or prohibited by the Natural Law. You need say that chastity is given to those who have asked for it, who have desired it, who have worked to receive it. And indeed it will be given to everyone who asks, and the seeker will find it; to the importunate it will be opened.

Bad Clergy know that the Virgin is more intimate with you than any woman can be. She is with your everywhere you go, and she is with you in your most private and intimate moments. Her flesh is like no other woman's for it is your love which warms her when you bring her to your bed each night. When you are lonely she is lonely with you. When you despair she despairs with you. When you succumb to intimate needs she succumbs with you. And if so, say a prayer to her and you will be forgiven. That you are still human the Lord allows. And with that, in you go.

They all sign and enter. The goosey two being the experts in the virgin loving game signed first.

Kelly:
Now we can be sinless and watch the Virgin do her thing.

6. Stripperama

To begin with, the Clergy's eyes meander over dim light and smoke
scrambling for focus, so benign are they in this special dungeon.
That the opaqueness of a woman's body is beauty in here, with such
transparency; not one of them will try to avert their eyes.
Neither is their presence apostate nor heresy; separate are these in
this visual wilderness by the sparks of mother love guilt.
How then, are their erotic observations to be understood by their
Almighty observer?

Seminal fluids begin their flow through their arched bodies *(directed
by their architect God, whose discretion they could never suspect)*.
And soon the flowering of a naked woman's beauty will meet their
compromised states of confused well-being.
And they must contain the fog and haze of their desire, the true
nature of their being now bound in fluid and ancient conscience.
This is no dark cave, this strip club.
Perhaps dank in wet times and energized by guilt-like orgone energy.
And cold perhaps, and coldest when patronized by misogyny
Which drains respect through lust, and where priests are devoid of
empathy.
Yet a woman's nudity which follows through the multiple reaches of
delight and frustration, the desired image of the eternal flowerings of
unreachable womanhood, is their love object in here.

The mysterious woman is to emerge out of wilderness; and who is
wilderness before these Clergy eyes judgmental, expectant, aroused
with excitement.
And indeed, brightly will shine her erogenous zone.
Her naked gender will seek accordance with these men, a gender
greater in sufferance than the men who suffer for the love of the
Catholic Church.
These are priests who have descended into caverns so deep no God
has taken permanent residence.
They are serve-less to the Venus Room's owner and malleable as
spectators.
All the senses in playful competition await in the dance of the seven
veils.

The stripper's aura is as visible as a halo of summer night's full moon.
And she vulnerable, will freely express herself like a dragonfly
dancing above an ambient pond.
This strip club operates well within the limits of the priestly sexual
imagination, and within the realm of the creator, should God have the
nerve to come in here.
For the love of sensuality at a distance require not the energy of the
lover
But the energy of the loved who, as an object, gives all her love.
The energy of lust and desire can only pass her by as history.
All that she needs is the energy of a voyeur's eyes.
And in celebration of virginity, she the stripper, and they the priests
arrive together at the meanjin of erotic stimulation.
A star is just born.
And from such a distant light did she come that it arrived barely a
millisecond before the Family's terrible melancholy had abruptly
kicked in.

There is no music, no clapping, just silence.

7. Mary Magdalene the Stripper

And she, who is neither tall nor short, slim in her bluish grey dress, young, is standing on a white cloud, her angelic face rosy cheeked, with reddish full lips showing a gentle smile, her deep blue eyes looking into her voyeurs' eyes.

Her free-falling dress reaches to her cloud. None of her flesh is visible. On her head is a pure white veil which flows over the top of her shoulders and her body from the back and from the sides, reaching down to the little cloud. Hovering above her head is a crown of twelve golden stars. A little of her black hair shows from beneath her veil. Her hands are free and extended. Her palms are relaxed upwards, her fingers are relaxed in the same way. Her fingernails are blue.

The lights dim. 'The Stripper' begins to play. A high chair is brought into the middle of the small stage by three jock-strapped dwarves.

Suddenly she lets loose and walks on her cloud toward the voyeurs. She struts, moving one foot in front of the other with confidence. Her head is high and her shoulders are back, letting her chest be front-and centre. One hand is on her hip. Her expression is sexy and tantalising, as though her act is the greatest performance ever made. Her lips are slightly parted, she the sultry wanton woman her audience desire. She has them in her gaze.

She now turns her back to the voyeurs and she slowly removes her long dress in time with the music revealing her underwear while she suggestively sways her hips from side to side, and then she moves her hands up and down the sides of her body, caressing her thighs her stomach, her breasts. She turns around while holding the garment and makes intense eye contact with her watchers. Total silence overwhelms them all. She then gently throws the dress to them.

She's working her body now. Moving around the stage, walking around both sides of the chair, pressing herself up against its back, and continuing to move up and down while caressing her body. She tosses her head back, licks her lips, and her sultry expression glows in the dark. She looks up at the ceiling as she caresses her breasts, and she shows them the great time she is having.

She's kicked off her high-heeled shoes showing off her gorgeous legs on the chair and slowly she takes down each stocking and tosses them toward her voyeurs. She makes sure they see her full and round derriere from all angles.

She moves to the darker part of the stage and she slowly unclasps her lacy brassiere until it's just covering her full breasts, and she holds it there. Then she turns around to show off her glowing long veil, and then she lowers her bra and tosses it to the side. She gyrates and caresses her breasts. Then slowly and discretely she pulls down her lacy underwear. The voyeurs are heightened to the point of madness for what is about to happen. She is the most beautiful woman in the world about to appear fully nude before these men. This is her first time, but not her last. She is the Virgin, the Madonna, Venus and Aphrodite together. She turns around and she is motionless, covering herself like Aphrodite. Only her veil does she keeps on. Her crown of twelve golden stars shines bright in the cavern's darkness.

She then comes into the light. To the ordinary men they see a woman whom they are never likely to see as intimate and loving company. She is their dream, their ideal, the only woman they will want to make love with because she is their mother.

And the Family see her crowned angelic face and the cloud on which she stands but they see no flesh in between.

8. Crippled Inside

The Horned Bouncer arises from his Featherston-designed throne outside. Cracking his stockwhip he begins to scatter the strip club's punters and they flee before him. As the cave's smoke is driven away, so are they driven; as wax melts before a fire, so the voyeurs cower in the presence of he who was also once in the seminary.

Strippers venerate the Horned Bouncer for he is their guardian and protector. In him the strippers entrust that these sorry punters be returned to the Golden Mile. And the Horned Bouncer urges these rushing punters to stampede as though they were corralled demons in a church desperate to get out. As he cracks his leather whip in the air he shouts mustering orders at them as they pass.

These exiting Bad Clergy members have their minds suspended between two contradictory propositions, that of concupiscence and that of celibacy, and they easily give over to both of them. Doubt is attached to each proposition, for each may or may not be true. Their ironic doubt is opposed to any certitude about them for both propositions have entrenched in them a duplicitous truth. The Horned Bouncer, once known as Frank, shouts at the Bad Clergy as they pass "doubt is neither a positive nor a negative when your Mary is stripping for you."

For concupiscence to be a positive for the Bad Clergy, the evidence for and against it is equally balanced when it is emotionally expressed in the strip club. Oh what the Hell, desire is as desire does. For celibacy to be a positive the evidence to support it lays within the spiritual realm of Catholic dogma. It is therefore appropriate to the Bad Clergy, but to no-one else, that doubt may be positive on the side of concupiscence and a positive on the side of celibacy, or vice versa, or in contradiction to each, or not at all. That they could not be otherwise is what separates the Bad Clergy from those whom they perceive as ordinary men. The Horned Bouncer keeps a wary eye on the Bad Clergy each time they come and pay their devotions to Mary.

Doubt to the Bad Clergy is either theological or practical. The former is concerned with abstract truth and error, the Church's dogma;

the latter with neglect of duty, or of the illicitness of action, or of mere arousal. The Bad Clergy's folly is that their doubt is a purely subjective condition; i.e. it belongs to their troubled minds which are sole judge and jury as to the facts of their arousal compounding their doubt. The evidence of the erect penis determines assent or not; arousal in itself must be either true or false. Therefore what in the strip club is true and what in there is false? A question the Horned Bouncer mentally asks of the Bad Clergy each time they come visit Mary.

Doubt as to the morals of their excited action, according to moral theology, is incompatible with the Church and therefore God action; since to act with a doubtful conscience is obviously to act in disregard of the moral vows expected of the Bad Clergy. To act with a doubtful conscience is ordinarily sinful; and the doubt must be removed before any reflective action can be justified. But as it frequently happens for the Bad Clergy, their solution to their doubt is utterly unattainable. In their case they justify what they do through a reflexive certainty by adopting a realised acceptance of what they do.

The Horned Bouncer has much discussed with his inner demons the mechanisms of Church authority and whether it favours the Bad Clergy's liberty when justifying its action on their immorality and the consequent vow of celibacy. The Bad Clergy's feelings are intrinsically doubtful each time they watch Mary strip. But the question is whether these doubtful feelings are more probable than the contrary, or equally probable, or merely probable in itself, or less so than it's contrary. After many discussions with himself the Horned Bouncer has concluded that any Church law which is doubtful to the Bad Clergy in its application to their celibacy does not bind them, which is secretly admitted by many other clergy when faced with their own demons. Anything goes Brethren, anything goes.

9. Yes They're Going to a Party Party

The Family have wind of a party in Bondi. 'Tis past midnight, and
they not tarry, and fly through the back streets of the living Cross.
Over footpaths, over bitumen floss. But first they see a Catholic
drunkard (a retired priest, recognisable by the deep impression of the
clerical collar around his neck) bent over cigarette, bent over tankard.
And standing over him they do pray. Toby blokes speaking like
Jesus:

First the Family prayer:
The martyr who lived on Earth
Confused be his name
His kingdom never was
YOUR will is to be done
On Earth, as there is no Heaven.
Help those in need with their daily bread
As it is, here and now
And fear not your weaknesses
Examine those who seek trespass against you
May you know your own temptations
And judge yourself your deeds
And reflect on those gone wrong.

This priest's name is Lazarus, to whom they sing:

Lazarus dear, you punish yourself
Lazarus, about your emotional health
Again you let yourself down
You desire to eventually drown.

Lazarus, you alcoholic insurgent
Lazarus, your liver needs detergent
Again infecting your poor soul
You are far from that being whole.

You're now't but a loosened grip
Your strengths you're letting slip
You can rise, but not so tall

When you hit your terminal wall.

You seek highs in darkened holes
Your esteem pays a heavy toll
You can rise, but ever small
When you do things that appal.

Lazarus, your health is dying
Lazarus, common sense is hiding
Again you rise a lesser being
You like the pain you are seeing.

Lazarus, we beg for your sweet life
Lazarus, be of love combating strife
Still you've kept your Catholic way
You feel guilty and dearly pay.

And the retired priest gets up strips down to his underwear and
socks, and then he runs headlong into the streaming King St crowd,
smashing his body to bits, and not long after returns to where he
stood before the Bad Clergy, a new man.

Kelly:
How was she Muldoon, did she fit... your swollen expectations?

Muldoon:
I'll not love her Kelly anymore, she is no Virgin.

Clancy:
What no Virgin? But all women, like the True Virgin, all women!

Muldoon:
When she told me, I shed a tear.

Mahone:
She deceived you this is clear.

Muldoon:
I'll trust there is still a Virgin; keep it nice 'n safe.

134

Mahone:
That's what we do, as Family men except them - *(points to the goosey two)*

Clancy:
What little we saw of her in that back-slum was more than enough.

Kelly:
Didn't see a bit of titty; that's a bit rough.

Mahone:
But that's what them Protto blokes want and get.

Kelly:
And the rest of them heretics and heathens.

Mahone:
We are pure 'coz we are Catholic.

Muldoon:
And when it comes to sinning we got plenty eh!

Clancy:
I'll confess 'till the Virgin saves me.

Muldoon:
She's going to save us all, but now, it's party time.

10. Extracting the Catholic Bits

On its way to Bondi Beach and the party the Lag Motor tonight
decides to take the Family to Purgatory otherwise known as the
Kurnell Refinery; a place where the Family see soul refining as a way
to make souls clean in accordance with their ideas of how Catholics
must be ready for their maker.

The Holy Ghost supervises the purging of those sins carried by
souls after death. The Family, though beacons of Catholicism, will
someday submit themselves to this penitential act, since there is no
way God will let them off at the end of their days. God will have his
satisfaction with them, and Purgatory is where God does it.
The goosey two are not invited here. They are Hell-men without
souls and must walk to the party instead.

The Lag Motor flies down Anzac Parade into Bunnerong Road,
before taking off at Molineaux Point and landing at Captain Cook's
Landing Place, arriving at their destination, a frigid place of ash and
smoke, and in no time at all. The industrial sounds of billions of litres
of smoke belching into the atmosphere grow louder and louder as the
Motor moves slowly into Purgatory's endless chasm. Vague outlines
of smoking chimney stacks, some hundreds of metres high, emerge.
The smoke parts into mazes and labyrinths as the Motor rumbles
through. Ghostly soul bodies drift with the ashen smoke; bald heads,
mouths agape, naked, hands clasped in anguish. They drift singularly,
or in packs, and they drift headlong into each other. It is chaos. Not
a word is spoken. These soul bodies are mute. There is nothing to
watch over them. No Angels. No Devils. The Holy Spirit is the only
thing present. It is of course, the chemical filled smoke. Between the
chimney stacks are curved brick structures snaking their way through
them. There are vents randomly placed on the walls. Through them
float other soul bodies. Many are sucked in, many pushed out. The
noise is deafening. Hands push through the Motor's windows. They
carry ear plugs. The Holy Spirit is kind. These Family members are
not dead yet. The Motor travels on into the refinery's night. On and
on. The Family are not afraid. They have been here before. They
know what is coming.

The Motor pulls up outside an enormous cylindrical chamber.
The idling Motor lets the Family out, who then walk over to an
observation deck overlooking a massive and complex configuration
of pipes and tubes, vessels and tanks, valves and levers.
There they observe fallen Catholic souls queuing for the process.
First they are desalted removing all earthly impurities, and
the clothes they wore at death are removed, before they enter
atmospheric distillation units spread across the vast stainless steel
floor. The clothes are taken by the mist and placed in charity
donation bins lined along the wall. Once inside the souls are distilled
into their venial fractions before entering a vacuum distillation
process. Here the fractions are desulferized before being sent to a
catalytic reformer unit. Reformed the fractions are sent to a distillate
hydrotreater where they are washed down with pure hydrogen.
Onwards to a hydrocracker unit where their fractions, cleansed but
not yet forgiven, become more desirable to the Holy Spirit. Lastly
the fractions are placed in a blending pool filled with high octane
gasoline from which a stack extends upwards. Each hour it is lit and
those souls which have sat for thirteen full moons in the pool and
have formed into soul bodies, scream with pain when being taken
out by the mist. The soul bodies are free to float around the grounds
of Purgatory within the Holy Ghost until God calls them to Heaven.
Their leftover impurities will feed the atmosphere.

Dear reader: This is Catholic Purgatory as the Bad Clergy see it,
where all who die do so with venial faults still owing repentance for,
and besides, all human life ends with baggage, except of course the
Virgin. The Catholics know this. And they pity the rest for being so
ignorant. And all who die impure must be prayed for so that God,
when He is in the mood to be merciful, will hear the prayers for
the souls of the dead in Purgatory, take pity on them, purge them
from the dross of their lighter transgressions through Purgatory's
purifying, judge them and bring them to the refreshing light of
Heaven.

Despite the purging of human weaknesses and sin through prayer
and Catholic wisdom, there is much in the departed soul's system
for God to contemplate. Popes, Saints and Mother Teresa types are
border-liners, and will probably go straight to Heaven and obtain

instant happiness. For no evil was found in them by the Catholic Church. But for the rest, no way. But mercy is at hand. Hell is to be avoided at all cost. Purgatory is a reasonable holding place. Prayers are said for all those dearly departed who sleep with Christ; and besides God particularly loves men. He eagerly forgives them because the Church does. Men are descended from innocent Adam who was innocent until he was deceived by the harlot Eve who was too weak to fend off the wiles of the tempting Devil.

In Purgatory no soul can sin. Those days are over. It's what souls take with them into the afterlife that is of interest. The Purgatory refining process secures for them final happiness when their souls reunite with their bodies. Eternal happiness cannot be fully appreciated unless there is torment, torture, and suffering. But it is only temporary. This is the Catholic way, the only way, if unbelievers would only get the genius of the Catholic system. Catholicism offers the promise of an eternal sleep in peace for those who endure living Hell. Without faith and hope the endurance will be tough. And there can be no doubt whatsoever that death is the ultimate Catholic promise. Face death's inevitability and the rest will take care of itself, with a little help from the Holy Spirit of course.

It is a myth that refined souls in Purgatory, though in waiting for a place with God in Heaven, and with grace slowly penetrating them, pray for the living on Earth. The Family have never seen souls pray. And they have been to Purgatory many times. They hear of the living pray for the souls in Purgatory. It is tradition that the souls in Purgatory remain connected with the Church. Those who go to Purgatory uncatholic should be baptised even if it is without their consent. They have no choice. The Holy Spirit can be quite nasty if it doesn't get its own way. Some displeasing souls have been refined quite a number of times. The love which is the bond of union between Catholics extends to all souls in Purgatory. The practise of devotion to the dead souls waiting for Heaven is consolation to the living waiting their turn to go to Purgatory. How sweet it is that a dying person, made conscious of a life of imperfections through Catholic teaching, should be comforted in knowing that the Catholic Church will speak to God on the dying person's behalf through prayers and indulgences. It is enough for any Catholic unbeliever to want to repent before it is too late. But Catholicism will get them anyway, for there is no denying the one true Church, the one the Bad Clergy are permanently married to.

11. Hole in the Sky

It's like this dear reader. Somewhere on Moore Park Road the
goosey two begin their long and tortuous walk to the party. Hoons
jeer at them as they fly past. Pigeons hit these moving targets with
pinpoint accuracy. Dirty water, in a gutter a block over, is sprayed
by a passing car in an arch over houses and over them. Still they
walk. Dark clouds above, the size of dinner plates, follow them.
The footpaths beneath them crack open as they pass. Down there
is their victims' Hell. The young victims in the parishes they
were anonymously transferred to cry out to them begging their
forgiveness. The Bishops who covered their tracks leer at them.
They will never be punished. They are not the damned. But they are
damnable every millisecond of their lives.

Placates says:

They repress their self-loathing in the dark hollows of their being.
Sometimes it's a space between their ears near the nape of their
necks. Neck pain they call it. It is their place of torment, a furnace
of unquenchable fire, an interior darkness everlasting, a hurricane of
misery; if only they would show remorse. The Church can't allow
it. There is no punishment that can atone for what they have done,
because their punishment is also the Church's punishment and the
myth of Church's moral leadership will be put into question. They
confess their pedo acts knowing that they will not be betrayed by
their fellow priests. The sacrament of the confessional is inviolable.
It is up to God to punish them. The Church's energy is devoted to
dealing with its persecutions as they come. And behind it walks
the Church's fear that for all its exaltations its true standard of
sanctimony is that of the priest paedophile.

They were warned the goosey two who are now wandering
aimlessly, in the hope their concupiscence can have its relief. They
need not have fallen in lust with children. They were warned that
their fantasies of child love must never be arranged, nor realised.
They were warned of the inequality of the priest-child relationship.
They were warned in their conscience. They were warned by their
desperate feelings. They did not listen. They listened to their lusts

140

and went ahead. They were caught and they confessed their sins in a cold and dark cubicle, they were absolved and told to keep their silence. They know there will be no ED for them because they no longer believe. Death alone will be their salvation.

Eternal damnation (ED) is, in the eyes of God, one and indivisible in its completeness; it is but one sentence and one penalty. It is a punishment of indescribable intensity which demonstrates to humans how God allows the unrepentant sinner to fall into ED, how a person who ignores every Divine warning through the Church's teachings, who fails to profit by all the patient love God has shown them, and who in wanton disobedience is absolutely bent on rushing into eternal punishment, will have ED as their reward.

In God's sanctity and justice and in His wisdom, by His very existence, He avenges the violation of the moral order on behalf of His believers, and applies to the gravity of the sin a severity of punishment, as set down by the Church. But since God does not always do this on Earth, He, by his Wisdom, will inflict punishment after death. If humans were fully convinced that those who sin need not fear punishment after death, there would be moral and social chaos. Divine wisdom cannot allow this. If there were no retribution beyond that which takes place on Earth, humans might suspect God to be indifferent to good and evil, and there could be no accounting for His justice. Catholic reasoning easily contends through scripture that there is indeed a next life and the just will be made happy as a reward for their earthly virtue. The punishment for evil is the natural counterpart to the reward of being good. It is logical that there will be punishment for unforgiven sin in the next life. Among God-fearing humans there is the firm belief that evil-doers will be punished after death. This universal conviction is a terminal proof of the existence of punishment in the afterlife. For it is impossible that, in regard to the fundamental questions of their being and their destiny, every single human should fall into the error of unbelief; if so, human reason would be essentially deficient, and the order of this world would be shrouded in unfathomable mystery; but this is repugnant to both the nature and wisdom of the Church's Creator.

These pedo priests see no meaning in being privy to the beatific vision of God in all His splendour. The eternal separation of their souls from God is irrelevant. And so is their loss of faith. They fear not the threatened pain of loss, the absence of bliss, the presence of unutterable pain. They care not for the threatened void in their souls which now lack infinite truth and infinite goodness. In their consciousness God, on whom as children they entirely depended, is now their enemy forever. Their desire for happiness, inherent in their very sleazy nature, compensates for the loss of God and their delusive pleasure is as good as it gets. Certainly it is better than God's infinite happiness, and their potent desire to dismiss Him fills them with extreme pleasure. They are no friends of the friends of God who expect to enjoy eternal bliss in Heaven. And the Church does not know what to do with them. The Family on the other hand are forced to tolerate them.

12. A Dead Conversation

As they near the party the goosey two begin a silent communication.
And through their watery eyes they speak.

Silent Unus: It is said that concupiscence is
a craving for that which is pleasant.

Silent Duo: The tinder for sin which does no
harm to those who innocently consent.

Unus: Without flesh and feeling combined
concupiscent intensity is not so great.

Duo: Pronto the important bodily organ
which cannot perform without it.

Unus: And there is no greater appetite than
the hunger for sensuality.

Duo: All appetites eventually combine and
give pleasure to the senses.

Unus: Their common objective neither of
which is indistinguishable.

Duo: The sum of them is greater than all
concupiscence unbound.

Unus: The objects of sensual pleasure causes
love when sensual appetite intensifies it,
but when love is absent the yearning must
intervene and bring the objects of sensual
pleasure to love. After love there may be
rest from concupiscence with brief self
abuse, but that is abhorrent.

Duo: Young flesh must learn to be ready for
it when it is called upon.

Unus: It is wholly natural one must crave for pleasurable good. It is pleasurable when it suits the one who need never question the value of its pleasure, but instead simply take pleasure in it because it is sustaining.

Duo: And so it is the craving must be infinite within the life of one who must have his sustaining natural pleasure.

Unus: Whosoever drinketh of sweet water shall thirst again.

Duo: And when the affections of the love object run dry more love will offer more tenderness.

Unus: Something is needed for the appetite when good is its object. So natural it is for lovers to seek what is most appropriate according to their natures. That the love appetite is freewheeling and unfettered so it cannot obey reason and conscience. It merely obeys the will of the carrier and it must follow infinitely in his life, for the pursuit of love is most good.

Duo: The light body, which is the centre of natural love, loses its name because the body need not have one when this love is consummated.

Unus: And the passion is the effect the lover has on the young body. The body's form is lost like the soul upon death, and the young body's movement during the embrace is reformed in the lover's eyes. The appetite is renewed by the circular movement of the

tempos connecting all flesh in the movement
which become one in itself and for itself.
The thirst is slaked until the mouth is dry
again from lust.

Duo: It is because the desirable object,
inspired by concupiscence, generates the
appetite by innocently inducting itself
into its lover's intentions, so while the
appetite moves towards the realization
of the object's possession, the movement
will naturally seek its end. Accordingly,
the first motion wrought by desire for the
object is called 'love,' and the object is
compliant to this; and from this compliancy
emerges a sensual movement towards the
object, and this movement is prompted by
desire; and finally, after resistance has been
overcome, the rest of it is joy. The evidence
of this love is the passion, concupiscence
notwithstanding, and is therefore according
to the will.

Unus: To love like this is to wish nothing
but good for the lover.

Duo: The love of friendship is surrounding,
and is for itself to prepare the pathway for
the realisation of the ecstatic throes born of
concupiscence. The lover exists as simply
being, and that which exists as the object is
a relative being. Therefore because good is
innate with being, the good, which itself is
full of goodness, is simply good; but that
which is the object's good, is a relative
good, and need not be taken into the lover's
account. Consequently the love the thing
is loved by, may have some good, and is
simple to the lover; while the object, as a

145

thing to be loved, may be another's good,
and must needs be relative.

Again Placates says:

In the battle for young hearts and minds there smouldering is the
lust in some priest's eyes for young flesh and their pride by which
it is being served. They disobey and their rebellious flesh shall win
against theological spirit, for there is no inclination greater than
the inclination for these two priests to molest what attracts them.
Composite in desire, lust's rages, and in being unloved, there exists
tensions which cannot be resolved. The flame extinguishes but again
burns with greater intensity. It is the eternal struggle which old age
shall not weary. If there were no such thing as original sin, mortal,
venial or likewise there would still be the struggle of these priests
wants and needs. And what Church is equipped to render its priest
molesters impotent when Catholic theology has for its scapegoat the
abuse of concupiscence?

For the goosey two it is not a matter of despising and condemning
their bodies that decides their nature and personal subjectivity.
Rather, they are concerned with the bad works of being caught, and
worse, the permanent castration of their desperate need for child
concupiscence. Fortunately for them when they live by the spirit of
their Church, they walk with it truly. And outwardly do they appear
simple and innocent like all priests, as like little children who do not
know about this evil which destroys lives.

They were given as priests God's grace by the virtue and gift of
chastity, since chastity was meant to allow them to love with an
upright and undivided heart; and the purity of the noble intention
of seeking the good end of their being; and the simplicity of vision,
since they, as baptized persons are required to fulfil God's will
in everything; and by the purity of God's vision, to see all that is
external and internal as being good; by the disciplines of faith, hope
and charity. Instead, over time, their impure thoughts for children
turned them aside from the path of God's commandments; and
beneath their latter day priestly appearance they have nothing but
contempt for every fool who says they believe in God.

146

And on Church complicity Placates says:

Church secrecy protects the mystery of these molesting priests and their love for children. It allows for patience and moderation in their one-sided relationships; it allows for the conditions for the definitive sexual taking of children against their will. Secrecy is decency. It inspires the molester priest's choice of venue. It keeps silence or maintains reserve where there is evident risk of the child speaking out. It is discreet when the molester priest is on duty. There is secrecy of the feelings as well as of the body. It protects against the prying inquisitions of the parents and against the investigations of civil authority. Secrecy inspires a way of life which makes it possible to resist the temptations of guilt and the pressures of imminent social disgust.

It is they, given by the Church the duty of child education, who are expected by society to give young people instruction respectful of the truth, the qualities of the heart, and the moral and spiritual dignity of humanity. They present the Good News of Christ at each lesson to renew the life and culture of all who struggle with sin; it combats and removes the error and evil which flow from the ever-present attraction to sin. While on duty these molester priests must never cease to purify and elevate the morality of children through Catholic instruction. It is with the spiritual qualities these priests were endowed, the supernatural riches exclusively ordained to them by the Church, which inspires them to blossom as true representatives of the Lord Jesus Christ; ordained to fortify, complete and restore all sinners to Christ, or not.

FANTASY 4

PENANCE

1. In the Garden of Earthly Delights

Muldoon again looks outside the Lag Motor at the landing target, a
rubbish-strewn area near the party house. Throughout the descent
Muldoon calls out the landing co-ordinates to Kelly, who is piloting
the flying Lag Motor as it levels with the ground. A few moments
before the landing, a light on the dash lights up red when one of the
Motor's white tyres had touched a pool of vomit, and Mahone yells
out "One contact, vomit!" It lifts and three seconds later the Motor
lands and Kelly says "Shutdown." Muldoon then says "Okay, engine
stop. The Motor is out of its accelerator, contact rubbish." Clancy
says "Out of Purgatory, into rubbish." Kelly continues "Auto security
- sleep no more. Lights off, command override into functional." "The
Jesuits copy you down, Toby Men." And the Virgin sends a message
to the Granville Crib switchboard to say that the Lag Motor has landed
in Tranquility Street.

From the footpath nearby is heard in a megaphone voice these words:
"... I'm under your skin, I'm no fling
The brain cells I kill, you sacrifice for me
I'm the best thing happening in your life
How can you have fun, if not for me?
I'm the best trip for fitting you up
I've got your lifespan to push you around.
After you're dead, I've ready work elsewhere
I'm around the back of pubs and clubs, waiting
And in every bottle shop in the long street
So don't you worry about me.
If you pack me in, or find another driver
I'm all right, it's in the culture.
Real cobbers love their buddy scullers
One for all and all for the keg
Great guzzlers, these blokes and chicks.
I like them all, coz they give me
The freedom to..."
Past this strange man in top hat and tails lecturing the punters, the
Family glides. They step through the doorway one by one, over
stringless puppets, over entwined bodies making root and branch,
and into the party's digesting insides.

Placates says:
With vice come pleasures and virtues confronted by self-denial
A priest plagued by his passions longs for virtue in his soul
And he, of virtuous youth, misunderstands himself when a priest.

2. This Flight Tonight

In the party, party animal verbiage, accompanied by 70's jukebox heroes, bounces from walls to carpet to porcelain to windows to laminate to wood, coming out of wide brown mouths, smoking, drinking, smirking, and some of it escapes into the air and caught by gossips looking for flotsam to build their portfolios with. And here's a random sample.

"There's money coming down the rivers of Heaven. Carloads, boatloads, even airplane loads. Eighteen hundred and eighty eight of them. Much of it from up Eyre country way."

"A killing gives you the body, not the person. I heard that from a lifer."

"I mouth off quicker than Beelzebub in parliament, and I'm not dug out like them slum-loving lone rangers. Quicker in the shower, quicker than quicksand, I am."

"That bloke's over there's got a machine in him. He's already dead. You can't kill him."

"In the bedroom are the electronics for voodoo, confusion, karma, liberation, freedom. This is the place by the people, for the people. Know what I mean. This is the place of revolution."

"You're a man yes, you're donger's got a hole in the tip of it, right, and you're hollow like the person who believes in anything, right? And when you believe in something it means you don't think about it, right?"

"Jesus has got this lightning rod and he's gonna end all this weird life stuff, weird psychology, weird fifth columns. Every one of them is on the dunce list. On the last day, watch out!"

"You seen The Life of Brian? Heard on the grapevine that it's heretical: no, blasphemous, no, irreverent, no, mocking, no, satire, no, offensive, no, sacrilegious, no, all of the above, maybe."

"A good tropical rainstorm will do a lot of good for everyone. What happens is that the water seeps into brains from the wet hair washing out all the negative stuff and they get refreshed, and go about things again. That's a gift from God, you know. When it rains that's what I get. The aura of Jesus is not far off Bondi's waterline. You can see it a millisecond into every sunrise."

"Geez I miss World Championship Wrestling. Midday Sunday's a blank. My whole system shuts down. Like I'm a total vegetable."

"You know, when I hate God, I'm hurting my personality. I'm a good actor. And sometimes I'm a brother as well as God. That's how I make a living. Wish I was working with Hoges and Strop. They could use me I reckon."

"Dad used to take us kids to the Zoo and the footy. And we'd say hooray we're here, and he'd always say, no you're not!"

"You know once I saw a brother stick his head in the toilet and flush. After he stood up, his head dripping wet, I asked him why he did it. He said he did it to rid what was sinful in his head. When he was towelling his head with toilet paper I asked him if it worked. He smiled and said no and he'll have to try again, and then he walked out. That was in the seminary. I never saw him again."

"They took my nerves out the other day. Now I really don't feel a thing."

"See that sheila doin' her homework on that bloke. She used to do it on me once. I thought we were goin' to get married."

"Them blokes over there talking about God and Jesus. I'd stay away from them I would. It's like they're high on something, and I can't figure out what it is."

"Met a bloke once who walked straight out of a sandstorm. He was covered in dust trying to sell me an umbrella."

"Ever seen a nude wrestling match? It's not nude when they're wearing padded helmets, is it!"

"If I keep myself ignorant the closer I am to supernatural things. If I were a theologian you can be sure I'm no believer."

"You know you're never alone when you're a schizophrenic. Ian Hunter told me that."

"I saw a girl fall off the ground, true!"

"This preacher came through Wilcannia years ago when I was a little kid. He spoke with so much fire and brimstone about carnal sin it was though he was frightened of himself, like he was going to do something bad. That's what me grandma said. Reckons he was the most passionate preacher she ever heard."

"You know, everything that's just happened in the whole limitless universe, God willed. Can you believe it!"

"I used to live in the bush when I was a kid. It hardly ever rained but when it did it always fell on the wrong places."

"There was this teacher. I used to ask him the simplest questions like why am I here, and me mate Josh Minton, who got killed by a car last week, isn't here. And she'd always come up with some complicated answer, like it was a tragedy, and lucky that it wasn't me."

"See that girl over there. Her father's a rainbow trout. She's from Tassie. And my dad. He was a piranha, and mum was a sea eagle. They're dead now and in Heaven talking like real people. This is what I believe."

"I was chasing lots of blokes. Two, three, four at a time. Never caught any of them. I chased one, and look at me, I'm up the duff."

"Drank a slab of Tooheys once. A week later I drank another slab. A week later another. I finally realised that a couple of tinnies was enough."

"I used to be superstitious. It didn't work. And then I found God. But that hasn't worked either. Nothing works. I'm stuck. Don't have the courage to back myself in."

"We went around the rivers and streams, old mining sites looking for gold, and it's funny, looking back, I believed my mate who kept telling me it was somewhere nearby, but when he found it, after all these years, that was when I doubted him."

"What world do you live in? I live in the world of beer. And you? I live in the world of chicks? And you? I live in the world of money? And me? I live in me parent's world. Geez, we live in the best possible worlds, don't we?!"

"Me best mate's a lawyer now. I'm a brikkie so we don't see each other much. I'm too busy. But it's funny you know. We used to play together all the time. Sport and stuff, you know. He told me last week that no one knows him. He's been in the game talking to people long enough, and they don't know him like I do."

"A friend of mine used to walk everywhere backwards. True. Said he was learning a lot about life, the way it was, the way it finishes. He walks forward now like everybody else. I think he works in the public service somewhere."

3. Spirits of the Night

Scene: In the living room. A Liberace man enters the party's living room from the kitchen and proceeds to walk the spectrum of voyeurs now settled in their positions, and then he makes the following announcement:

"Ladies and Gentlemen. Welcome to tonight's feature event - an exorcism. And we have with us four very special guests, the Family, AKA the Bad Clergy, the Toby Boys, etc, etc, who will judge on the proceedings, on account of them being the experts, them being Catholic and all that. So a big hand of applause for the Family."

The partygoers slowly clap, clap, 'n clap; and they throw in a few ironic jeers as well.

"OK, OK. It's time now to bring out the honoured possessed. Let's give a big hand to Jeanne D'Anges who has come all the way down from the Middles Ages to be here for just one special night. And to conduct the exorcism you have the honourable, Johnny Joe Surin, me! And I've come all the way from Rome just to be with you. So a big hand for us both."

Slow applause again.

A woman, and statistically, the gender most likely to be possessed, from superstitious times down to these times, enters the scene. She is dressed like a hippy nun wearing sandals, a tie-dyed dress and a psychedelic habit on her head. Why a woman, one might ask? The Family have never considered it. Why is it women are the possessed and men are the exorcists? Johnny Joe Surin follows the woman. An area in the lounge room has been cleared for the party goers. The Family sit on the lounge suite. Some music is put on. Kept low Tubular Bells establishes the scene.

Just then Muldoon in a mad fit gets up, grabs a party goer and takes the frightened individual to the bathroom. He slams the door and begins a manic rant. His fiery eyes penetrate the others' and in a high pitched voice peculiar to the castrati he speaks to the party goer thus:

156

"You my friend, like everybody else here are buggered up 'coz of the influence of evil spirits. By original sin we're all under the power of Him. The one from the time of Adam's cock-up 'as got hold of the universe of death by the cobblers, and we like to call him the Devil. And we're scared of death which makes us the Devil's porridge and no matter how many times the Big J, the Christ-Man redeems us all, we're in for the most violent temptations because our inner wrestlings aren't just about flesh and blood; it's against the chairman of the world of darkness, against the wickedest spirit who roams in high places, and he's got spawns of Demons, which as you should know from the Book get around, for them Demons attack our bodies through obsession, and they get in don't they, and possess us. Look into my bloodshot eyes. See how mad I am! Our souls are reckoned to be safe, 'coz we say we're sorry, but our minds, and the rest of us are real prey. The Devil is after us and God's the lifesaver. Listen to me galoot. (Muldoon's breath is hot and mildly putrid. His listener petrified). Our breath is the most likely symptom of life, it stops and we're dead; invisible and impalpable, our breath stands for the mystery behind us wot's going on. You see we've got this spirit within us all, living like, smart, an incorporeal being, big word that!, just like our soul, but it burns us, makes us vital; and it sits there between our minds and the gross needs of our bods. You know demonic possession is as old as black holes. But it gets real interestin' when the idea of it got into fear and loathing. And boy, from then on demonic possession gets real traction! Among the many miracles talked of, Demon casting gets a lot of word noise.

A real big show! Some bod with an unclean spirit gets it cast out in some synagogue by the big J, him who the God one anointed with the Holy Spook, who went about doing good, and healing them ones under the influence of the Devil. Man, were they troubled times! The big J spent a lot of his time casting out devils. So many bods possessed! So many! Nearly everybody I'd say. Sinners all of them and well out of their minds. Boy did devils screw them up. But the big J was up to it. And as he kicked out them 'orrible Demons he got pretty popular. Those who saw the Devil cast out couldn't get a grip. What thing is this, they said. What is this new style? We've gotta obey this bloke who kicks out unclean spirits, don't we. We gotta do as he tells us. Like I'm tellin' you to just listen. (The party goer tries to speak but Muldoon's tyre-fitter grip is incredibly tight). Here's a wonder man on a mission to save souls and break the power of Satan and His Demon henchmen determined to do them wrong. You might ask what control have they over themselves? Well I tell you, it is written that they had none whatsoever. They had the minds of monkeys. But the big J he saw everything that needed to be done. He was THE man. Sin was rampant and the big J was the One to do all the forgiving. Slaves to sin they were until he came along. They might have been sick but it was because an evil spirit had got in, and taken possession of them to control and direct the sickness and to speak through their vocal organs, or to tie their tongues. Those damned Demons somehow found a way in. Dumb, blind, crippled. It might have been natural. But a Demon might also be doing it. And wow! The big J would come along, say a few firm words, lay a hand on the body, and voila! the illness or disability disappeared. Bloody amazing! It was a Demon doing it all along. And the big J kicked it out. Bloody marvellous. And you'll be listening to me real close 'coz you look like scum. I'm only just getting hot under the dog collar!

Now you'd be thinking demonic possession is out back, away from this secular and enlightened society we live in. Think again. An exhibition's gonna happen real soon right before your magpie eyes And then you and your mates'll come running to us. You're full of Demons mate. Look at that tinnie in your hand. And that big spliff in your face. Full of bad spirits. I'm not joking mate. How do you reckon you lot lose control. And mate demonic possession is as thick and fast today as it was in them times. The big J's medicine show should be as big as ever. And just because you don't believe in them doesn't mean they're not around. OK the God one smiles on this great land of Oz where larrikins do nothing but conform. There's money, sun, space, a land of plenty, wide and long, girded by sea; its spine's a bit out of kilter, but hey, if you've got it good then the God one has cleared away the old Demon types the big J wrestled with. They just don't get around the way they used to, that's all. They're too sneaky for smart heads. We're here so that in big J's name specialist priests like Johnny Joe, all the way from Rome, can show you what happens when the likes of him cast out devils. And it's about time the big J and his Demon work got trendy. I mean it's boring isn't it? Nobody's running around like they're naturally possessed. It's drugs and booze that's doing it. False Demons they are. And the big J ain't got no power over them. You lot need to get obsessed with real Demons. And then the big J'll come running. And none of this artificial stuff. These party noises are in you man. And more are hanging around wanting to get inside. They want to control you. Take over your will. Only the big J can fix it when it happens. And it will happen. It's happened already. I betcha you don't like your dad. I betcha you don't like authority. I betcha you take the piss out of everything you see coz' it's funny. And if I tell you are possessed you'd better believe it. And if you tell me to piss off then all that tells me is that the Demon has really got in you and if you don't say so then you'll never get big J's help. You gotta repent man. You gotta say you're sorry. You gotta ask for forgiveness. You gotta allow the big J in your life. Don't worry about me. I'm gone. I'm a Demon. I really am. So are me brothers. It's too late for us. But look. I'll take my hand off your throat now, and we'll go arm in arm back to the action that's waiting on us to get back to so it can begin."

4. Commercial Break

The living room was dark when Muldoon and companion returned. And
no sooner had they found a place to sit than lighted spherical surfaces,
for which the source of their light had come from afar, and from the
wider to the narrower, began to appear. The density and strength of the
rays of light behind them in the narrower confines of the room has
created an illusion of more complex spherical surfaces, and as there is
now as much light in them, as against the dark room, the spherical
surfaces, becoming more compressed and dense, were now levitating
before the stunned punter's eyes. And like the power by which the Moon
seizes or holds the tides, and which, being corporeal, functions in the
manner of hands, images were now being emitting in burgeoning
patterns throughout the whole extent of the room. And like the
positioning of the Moon, the images revolve as with the body of the
Moon. And now the stunned punters begin to see corporeal imagery,
becoming strongly attenuated at a closer distance and without interval.
The density of the spheres have by now increased so much that they are
inverse to the pure light from which they first came. For these spheres,
having transcended a great distance, are now so reduced in size that they
are directed as though from a single source, to then become, in sound
and vision, the miracle of a television commercial on the far lounge-
room wall.

Scene 1

A handsome long-haired man wearing a flowing paisley robe descends
to Earth on a fluffy white cloud. The cloud lands in the middle of a
desert and he alights the cloud and walks in the desert with the camera
following. There are rapid scene changes as he is walking. Different
weathers, landscapes, cityscapes appear and finally he is shown walking
down a suburban street. He comes to an ordinary two story brick home,
opens the door with a golden key and steps inside.

Scene 2
The man is sitting comfortably at the kitchen table surrounded by
different objects, and he, with his hands clasped and smiling, is looking
directly into the camera. He then speaks with a countenance as
penetrating as the Marlboro Man.

160

"Hello my name is Jesus Christ and I want to talk to you today about a new project for my Holy Catholic Church to implement on my behalf.

Have you ever wondered why I said thou art Peter, and upon this rock I will build my Church; and the gates of Hell shall not prevail against it? Well, I'm here today to tell you all about the new spiritual possibilities my wonderful Holy Catholic Church is going to offer you. And of course no great corporation like the Catholic Church could have survived for so long unless it has had great leaders. Fortunately I have had many Peters follow in my footsteps, great men all. And now we have sitting on my throne John Paul, the number 2, soon to become a saint I might add. So far he has been great for my Holy Catholic Church and I'm very proud of him.

Now what makes my Holy Catholic Church truly great and unique is not only its sacramental aspects of the spiritual which gives me, its creator, true meaning, but also the sacramental objects such as what I have here on this kitchen table. These are the relics of my living self brought by me down from Heaven. You see before you genuine reproductions of my shroud, my cross, my foreskin (I do have the power to duplicate my flesh you know), images of my dead face, images of my risen face, the bloodied nibs from my crown of thorns, pieces of the cross upon which I died. All authenticated by yours truly."

Jesus shows each of the relics to the camera while speaking about them.

"These are very important for people who need a miraculous boost to their lives. In many cases I have healed sick people through these. How wonderful it is that my Holy Catholic Church infers in its teachings that the spiritual is the true cause of healing. I am very proud of my Church for selling this most important idea. In fact, and while I have your attention, I should say that down the years my Holy Catholic Church is truly the best at reinventing itself. There has been no greater seller of salvation and mercy. Heaven wouldn't be where it is today without my Church's insistence upon its existence. How else would I have got here!

One does not need to be a member of my Holy Catholic Church to benefit from relics. There have been many unwitting unbelievers who

have been healed by me through relics. Fortunately my Holy Catholic
Church approves wholeheartedly the honouring of relics which
it considers authentic. And those which seem highly improbable
shouldn't be dismissed in case my Holy Catholic Church should err
and toss out something which is truly a relic. There are some things I
need put my trust in.

You know I've always loved the way my body had been venerated. I
was given a special tomb for my well-wrapped body to rest. Beautiful
women anointed my body with oils and spices, and with their tears.
And I've loved how my Christian martyrs have been venerated. How
the living take up the bones, which are more valuable than precious
stones and finer than refined gold, and lay them in a suitable place,
where I permit secret gatherings, in gladness and in joy, to celebrate
the sacred remnants of martyrdom. After all, it is only through me
that there is a perfect kind of healing.

Now I'm banging on a bit here to use the local dialect, and I can see
you're getting bored. But wait, this is a very important infomercial
and I'm getting close to the point of my conversation with you out
there in TV land. People always say they want to touch something
of me, Jesus, because they're sick. There are so many prayers sent
to me every second of the day I simply cannot answer them all. And
often they are repeats, and repeats, and repeats. And ever since I've
left your material world, to my surprise I find it beset with afflictions,
despite my promises! My eyes have been opened. It makes me very
sad indeed. I thought my work on Earth would have done enough.
But I was quite wrong. See. Even I can get it wrong.

So today I am announcing that I am authorising my Holy Catholic
Church, which by the way never turns the wrong way, to market
these sacred relics on my behalf. I have directed The Vatican and its
Curia to draw from Heaven my relics and to distribute them through
the authorised retail outlets of Catholic Churches and selected
supermarkets. Pope John Paul number 2 will personally take charge.
So when you next go aisle shopping in the selected supermarket you
will see beside the sweets section a section called Authorized Healing
Relics. There you will be able to buy specially prepared packets and
jars of relics. Instructions on how to use them will be clearly printed.

162

The origins of them will be clearly labelled. And trust there will be nothing manufactured in them. No chemicals, sprays or artificial colourings.

My Catholic Church has my absolute trust in its ability to sell these authorised relics. I can assure you that its priests will not be tempted into producing fakes for private gain. Not that I wouldn't notice, eh boys! Only the Church has the authority to pronounce these relics as being Heaven sent. Indeed these relics are like Heaven where your healed bodies will get their final rest. And my angels always keep Heaven spotlessly clean. And so on behalf of my earthly but most spiritual corporation, and remember, there WILL BE NO FAKES, I urge you to buy these authorised relics. Know that you WILL be spiritually healed, and perhaps even your body if you are really lucky.

Remember all relics will be quality controlled. And to ensure this I have created an eleventh commandment - NO authorised or unauthorised holy relics shall be marketed by Protestants.

And when you buy a relic after Sunday mass you will get a 10 percent discount. So make sure you bring your money with you! May God, that's me folks, bless you all."

Scene 3

Jesus gets up from the kitchen table and gathers the table's relics into a red carry bag topped by white frothing. He is then shown walking to a fireplace. He steps into the hearth and shoots up the chimney.

Scene 4

Jesus is seen flying up into the sky carrying the red bag and if one can listen very hard one can just hear "hey hey, hey, it's been a relic kind of a day".

5. What, Another Bloody Commercial Break!

An ad for a sponge called The Grime Exorcist.

Brief scenes are shown of a beautiful young woman working down a
mine, on an oil rig, mucking out horse stables and as a car mechanic.
Her face is glum before the filth, and smiling after the filth is gone.
A suggestive male voice is heard marvelling over how the grime and
filth was expertly removed, restoring the young woman's skin back
to perfection. The scene changes to a light and airy bathroom. Cue
to a man dressed in black, holding a white sponge by his side and
standing over the discreetly naked body of the same woman lying in
a bath and covered in dirt and grime. The strains of Tubular Bells can
be heard in the audio.

Cue the man in black raising the white sponge over the woman's
body and saying "behold the white sponge of cleanliness". Then he
touches her neck. Then he asks her name. She says "I'm dirty" in a
low, guttural voice. She begins to roll her eyes, and she pokes out
her tongue. Her face is contorting, and her body goes into fits of
animation. The man in black stands over her with the white sponge
firmly fixed on her face. The man in black then shouts the command
that all the dirt and grime from her day's work leave her body
and enter the white sponge. She fiercely rejects the command and
continues her jerky movements. The man in black says a quiet prayer
over her, and then he lightly touches her forehead with the sponge.
Miraculously the sponge begins to change its colour. Imperceptibly
at first but soon the colour turns from a pure white to a light grey.
The sponge holder continues working the sponge over her body while
the woman continues to violently resist. The sponge changes colour
from grey to a green-grey and then to a deep, blue violet. While
this happens the woman's body becomes calmer and a veil of peace
descends upon her face. The bathwater is clear. Then the man in
black stands up holding the filthy sponge and walks to the side of the
bath. The naked woman discreetly gets out of the bath goes behind
the bath screen and soon walks out in cotton tiger print pyjamas
and runs to the side of the man in black. They are both smiling and
give a hint of romance to the viewer. She is standing by the man in
black and she is glowing. The camera pans over the parts of her body

suitable for a family TV audience to demonstrate to the viewer how clean she is. The camera then pans over the sponge which now sits trembling on a small bathroom table.

The camera cuts away to a blank screen and a new voice says "If you and your family are dissatisfied with the performance of your soaps and sponges try The Grime Exorcist. The results speak for themselves. And it is guaranteed to work on all smooth surfaces or your money back. Available at all major pharmacies and supermarkets. Just ask for the magic sponge and a shop assistant will happily do the rest."

6. Editions of Her

Liberace Man AKA Johnny Joe Surin speaks. "Commercial's over ladies and gentlemen and of course the Bad Clergy. Let the show commence. But first I'll sermonise on tonight's exclusively Catholic exorcism."

He motions for the audience to become silent. Jeanne D'Anges sits cross-legged on the floor with her eyes closed, concentrating.

"Now during the exorcism the evil may emerge in slow stages or with sudden explosions. The Devil does not want to show himself. He will be angry and he is strong. Once, during an exorcism I saw a boy child of 7 held down by four strong men. The child threw the men aside with ease. Afterwards I felt the muscles in the boy's arms. He could not have done it on his own. He had the strength of the Devil inside him.

No two cases are the same. Some patients have to be tied down on a bed. They spit. They vomit. They piss. They defecate. They will do anything to keep me away. Oh how Demons hate me! You could be in for a real treat tonight folks. At first the Demon will try to demoralise me, then it will try to terrify me saying something like 'Tonight I'm going to put a serpent between your sheets. Tomorrow I'm going to eat your heart. And the next day I'm going to put a sock full of black spiders in your mouth. And the day after I'm going to insert a corkscrew into the eye of your penis.' And so forth. Yeah, yeah, bring it on Demon. Bring it on.

Normally I do these in a Church, because it is a sacred place, and I want proximity to the Blessed Sacrament. And we have more control in a Church. We can lock the doors. There's more protection. Once the Demon knows it's in the Church all it wants to do is get out as quickly as it can. Me, the team, the possessed and her family meet in a circle in an area of the Church where there's a lot of space. If we need to get the possessed to lie on the floor, they do. I bless the whole group with holy water, the possessed, the team and her family. Then we would lay out these pre-exorcism prayers which give glory to God, and which acknowledge that God is in charge. The Demon is told in no uncertain terms what it can and cannot do. All those steps are taken before the formal exorcism begins. What it all does is to tell the Demon who is in charge. And that I have the power of the Lord Jesus Christ, the same one you saw earlier in the commercial, which is very important for me to say, even though the Demon may not recognize it.

Now you might think that I am frightened. Especially that I am here in this Syndey suburban living-room and out of my comfort zone. After all we are dealing with a most powerful spirit, one among millions of Demons which cause humans so much misery. I'll be honest. I'm not immune to them, even though I carry the spirit of Christ as ordained by the most Holy Catholic Church. Demons are so powerful. But I am never frightened. I have faith to steel my courage you see. I laugh at the Demon and say to it, 'I've got the Madonna on my side. I am called Gabriel. Go fight the Archangel Gabriel if you will.' That usually shuts them up. You see the secret is to find the Demon's weak spot. Some Demons cannot bear to have the Sign of the Cross traced with a stole on an aching part of the body; some cannot stand a puff of breath on the face; others resist with all their strength against blessing with holy water.

Relief for the patient is always possible, as you will see tonight, but completely ridding some people of their Demons may take many exorcisms over many years. When a Demon leaves a body and goes back to Hell it will be dead forever completely losing the ability to molest people. It will express its final desperation by saying: 'I am dying, I am dying. You are killing me; you have won. All priests are murderers'. Sadly another will come and take its place. We must all remain in a state of grace otherwise any of us are prone to be infected by Demon evil.

There is so much wickedness of the world. And believe it or not, most active Demons are manifest in the woman. Jeanne here doesn't know why. They come into her as they please and they go when I exorcise her, with all the help of Our Lord Jesus Christ the Saviour of the world. And we priests do not know why it is the woman to whom Demons mostly come. They may be more vulnerable because, as a rule, more women than men are interested in the occult. Or it may be the Devil's way of getting at men, just as he got to Adam through Eve. What we do know is that the problem is getting worse. The Devil is gaining ground. We are living in an age when faith is diminishing. If you abandon God, the Devil will take his place.

Demon-hunting is not that fashionable in the more conservative Church circles. The Catholic establishment is happier talking about 'the spirit of evil' instead of evil spirits. The Vatican has rules on exorcism which I don't really like. They say we cannot perform an exorcism unless we know for certain that the Evil One is present. This is ridiculous. It is only through exorcism that Demons reveal themselves. An unnecessary exorcism never hurts anybody. This is why exorcists like me are working outside of Church authority. We know what's going on and the Church establishment is turning a blind eye to it. If we could do more work the Church might demonstrate to a cynical world something useful instead of what it appears to be.

The Holy Father does know that the Devil is very much alive and active in the world. He has seen exorcisms. He knows what they can do. The work we exorcists do is to relieve suffering, to free souls from torment, to bring them closer to God. But remember, when we jeer at the Devil and tell ourselves that it does not exist, that is when it is happiest. We cannot be complacent. I myself wrestle with the Devil day in day out, ever since I confessed for the first time my wrongdoings to the Lord as a seven year old. And it doesn't get any easier with experience.

My role model Jesus performed fantastic exorcisms. He cast out monstrous Demons. He freed bodies from demonic possession and from Him the Church has received the power and office of exorcism. He helps me decide on the grades of possession. The Devil does not like to be seen, so there are people who are possessed who manage to conceal it. There are other cases where the person possessed is in acute physical pain, in such agony that they cannot move. And it is essential not to confuse demonic possession with ordinary illness. The symptoms of possession often include violent headaches and stomach cramps, but you must always go to the doctor before you go to the exorcist. I have people come to me who are not possessed at all. They are suffering from epilepsy or schizophrenia or other mental problems. The key method of telling whether there is a Demon present is by its aversion to the sacrament and all things sacred."

And to demonstrate this he flashes his cross at Jeanne who quickly shies away hissing and cursing.

"If the possessed get blessed they become furious. Or if confronted with the crucifix, they are subdued. There are ways Catholic exorcists sort out real possessions from the phoney ones. We look into their eyes. As part of the exorcism, at specific times during the prayers, by holding two fingers on the patient's eyes we then raise the eyelids. Almost always, in cases of evil presence, the eyes look completely empty. Even with the help of both hands, we can barely discern whether the pupils are hidden above the top or the bottom of the eye. If we find, when we lift the eyelids that the pupils are looking up, the possessing Demon behaves like a cornered Funnel Web spider. If looking down, the behaviour is like a hooked Great White. I'm giving the idea of exorcism an Aussie feel to help you understand what I'm talking about. I'm giving you an insight into what exorcists are likely to confront.

Let me finish this short sermon by saying that as faith diminishes, superstition increases. And as faith diminishes, darkness increases. We're all spiritual beings, we're all searching for meaning; and if we don't find meaning in ways the Church promotes, we'll go searching for ourselves. And because of our flawed nature, oftentimes we're drawn to things that, down the road, can do more harm than good. Even though you all here are Godless you can still see my point. The Bad Clergy do so. While there is evil in the world the Devil is most assuredly doing it."

7. May the Force Be with You

Johnny Joe Surin cuts a wink at the audience while lifting his right leg.

On cue Jeanne D'Anges jumps up from her sitting position before dropping back to the lounge room floor. She begins to writhe about, shouting obscenities at Johnny Joe, who stands to the side of her commanding in a low voice:

"I cast you out, unclean spirit, along with every Satanic power of the enemy, every spectre from Hell, and all your foul companions; in the name of our Lord Jesus Christ. Begone and stay far from this beautiful creature of God. For it is He who commands you. He who has flung you headlong from the heights of Heaven into the depths of Hell. He who once stilled the sea and the wind and the storm. Hearken, therefore, and tremble in fear, Satan, you scabrous enemy of the faith, you ferocious foe of the human race, you begetter of death, you robber of life, you corrupter of justice, you root of all evil and vice; seducer of men, betrayer of the nations, instigator of envy, font of avarice, fomenter of discord, author of pain and sorrow. Why, then, do you stand and resist, knowing as you must that Christ the Lord always brings your plans to nothing? Fear Him, who in Isaac was offered in sacrifice, in Joseph sold into bondage, slain as the paschal lamb, crucified as man, yet triumphed over the powers of Hell. Begone, then, in the name of the Father, and of the Son, and of the Holy Spirit. (Johnny Joe makes three signs of the cross in the air). Give place to the Holy Spirit by this sign of the holy cross of our Lord Jesus Christ, who lives and reigns with the Father and the Holy Spirit, God, forever and ever."

There is silence for a time and the Jeanne gives Johnny Joe a suggestive look, kicking her legs at him like she was vaudeville.

"Well that didn't work" mutters Johnny Joe to himself.

"God, Creator and defender of the human race, who made man in your own image, look down in pity on this your poor servant, Jeanne, now in the chains of this unclean spirit, now caught up in the fearsome threats of man's most ancient enemy, sworn foe of our human race, who befuddles

170

and stupefies the human mind, who throws it into terror, overwhelms it with fear and panic. (Johnny Joe opens a Bible). Repel, O Lord, the Devil's power, break asunder his snares and traps, put the unholy tempter to flight. By the sign of your name, let your servant be protected in mind and body. Keep watch over the inmost recesses of her heart; rule over her emotions; strengthen her will. Let vanish from her soul the tempting of this mighty adversary. Graciously grant, O Lord, as we call on your holy name, that the evil spirit, who hitherto terrorizes over us, itself retreat in terror and defeat, so that this servant of yours Jeanne may sincerely and steadfastly render you the service which is your due; through Christ our Lord."

Jeanne is thrashing and tumbling about swearing and uttering
obscenities. She motions to squat on the floor then lifts her dress
and a glass bowl Johnny Joe had by sleight of hand slid beneath her
is now full of red liquid. Johnny Joe snatches back the bowl and
exclaims: "This is the Devil's blood. See it looks and smells like piss
but it is the colour of blood. See." The audience aren't impressed.
"Tough gig" Johnny Joe again mutters to himself.

"I adjure you, ancient serpent, by the judge of the living and the dead, by your Creator, by the Creator of the whole universe, by Him who has the power to consign you to Hell, to depart forthwith in fear, along with your savage minions, from this servant of God, Jeanne, who seeks refuge in the fold of the Church. I adjure you again (Johnny Joe has got Jeanne's toe, who then twists and shouts) not by my weakness but by the might of the Holy Spirit, to depart from this servant of God, Jeanne, whom almighty God has made in His feminine image. Yield, therefore, yield not to my own person but to me a minister of Christ. For it is the power of Christ which compels you, who holds you low by His cross. Tremble before that mighty arm which broke asunder your dark prison walls and led souls forth to light. May the trembling that afflicts this human frame (he runs the Bible over her leg) the fear that afflicts this child of God, descend on you. Make no resistance nor delay in departing from this woman, for it pleases Christ that he dwell, in her. Do not think of despising my command just because you know I am a great sinner. It is God Himself who commands you through me; the majestic Christ who commands you. God the Father commands you; God the Son commands you; God the Holy Spirit commands you. The mystery of the cross commands you. The faith of the holy apostles Peter and Paul and of all the saints commands you. The blood of the martyrs commands you. The continence of the confessors commands you. The devout prayers of all holy men and women command you. The saving mysteries of our Catholic faith command you."

Jeanne suddenly howls like Bruce Lee in kung fu motion.

"Therefore, I adjure you, profligate dragon, in the name of the spotless Lamb, who has trodden down the asp and the basilisk, and overcome the lion and the dragon, to depart from this woman, to depart from this Church in Suburbia (signing the audience). Tremble and flee, as we call on the name of the Lord, before whom the denizens of Hell cower, to whom the Heavenly Virtues and Powers and Dominations are subject, whom the Cherubim and Seraphim praise with unending cries as they sing: Holy, holy, holy, Lord God of Saboath. The Word made flesh commands you; the Virgin's Son commands you; Jesus of Nazareth commands you, who once, when you despised His disciples, forced you to flee in shameful defeat from man; and when He had cast you out you did not even dare, except by His leave, to enter into a herd of swine. And now as I adjure you in His name, begone from this woman who is His creature. It is futile to resist His will. Through him I make it harder for you to kick against us vulnerable pricks. The longer you delay, the heavier your punishment shall be; for it is not men you are condemning, but rather Him who rules the living and the dead, who is coming to judge both the living and the dead and the world by fire."

Jeanne's arms are folded and she's dancing an Irish jig.

"The God of Heaven and Earth, God of the angels and archangels, God of the prophets and apostles, God of the martyrs and virgins, God who has power to bestow life after death and rest after toil; for there is no other God than Him, nor can there be another true God beside Him, the Creator of Heaven and Earth, who is truly a King, whose kingdom is without end; I humbly entreat His glorious majesty to deliver this simple servant of His from this unclean spirit; through Christ our Lord."

Jeanne lifts her skirt showing pink pantaloons, and she bends over in front of the audience displaying a group photo of a smiling ABBA on

172

her behind. And in unison all recoil in horror.

"Therefore, I condemn you and every unclean spirit, every spectre from Hell, every satanic power, in the name of Jesus Christ of Nazareth, who was led into the desert after His baptism by John to vanquish you to your citadel, to cease your assaults against humanity whom He has formed from the slime of the Earth for His own honour and glory; to quail now before this wretched woman, and see in her the image of almighty God, rather than her state of human frailty. Yield then to God, who by His servant, Moses, cast you and your malice, in the person of Pharaoh and his army, into the depths of the sea. Yield to God, who, by the singing of holy canticles on the part of David, His faithful servant, banished you from the heart of King Saul. Yield to God, who condemned you in the person of Judas Iscariot, the traitor. For He now flails you with His divine scourges, He in whose sight you and your legions cried out: "What have we to do with you, Jesus, Son of the Most High God? Have you come to torture us before our time?" Now He is driving you back into the everlasting fire, He who at the end of time will say to the wicked: "Depart from me, you accursed, into the everlasting fire which has been prepared for the devil and his angels." For you, 0 evil one, and for your followers there will be worms to eat you which never die. An unquenchable fire stands ready for you and for your minions, you prince of accursed murderers, father of lechery, instigator of sacrileges, model of vileness, promoter of heresies, inventor of every obscenity."

Jeanne pokes out her tongue and puts her hands to her ears making Devil's horns.

"Begone now! Begone seducer! Your place is in solitude; your abode is in the nest of serpents; get down and crawl with them. This matter brooks no delay; for see, the Lord, the ruler comes quickly, kindling fire before Him, and it will run on ahead of Him and encompass His enemies in flames. You might delude humanity, but God you cannot mock. It is He who casts you out, from whose sight nothing is hidden. It is He who repels you, to whose might all things are subject. It is He who expels you, He who has prepared everlasting Hellfire for you and your angels, from whose mouth shall come a sharp sword, who is coming to judge both the living and the dead and the world by fire."

Muldoon:
Saw something just as good on Countdown once.

Clancy:
William Shakespeare?

Muldoon;
Yeah, that's him.

Suddenly the room is quiet. Johnny Joe has stopped and Jeanne
moves to stand by him just like Cher used to do with Sonny on the
Sonny and Cher Show.

8. Veni, Vidi, Vici

Johnny Joe Surin: "The show ain't over until it's over folks. I'll now hand proceedings over to Jeanne D'Anges who will tell her side of the story. Over to you Jeanne."

"Thanks Johnny Joe. Well folks I'm very willing to say I am possessed, which means I am controlled by improper suggestions which enter me from outside and which also come from within. And then I will say that Revealed Truth is really a lie and the lie which is endlessly repeated becomes truth and I go into a truth hysteria which I can't get out of. And I will then lose myself in a Demon's revealed truth until I am exorcised, and then I am exhausted from the pain of love I have for this priest who saves me. I will continue to think of my badness, my 'furor uterinus', and therefore I will come out of any exorcism worse.

The spirit of evil blows around whenever and wherever it chooses. And me it regularly chooses. And when Johnny Joe, my team leader assumes it has, my rapport with him is as intimate as any relationship between the vulnerable and the powerful. We play together like actors on stage, the words and scenes well rehearsed.

Ain't that so Johnny Joe."

"In my thoughts right here right now, sweet Jeanne."

"When I am possessed by Demons I tick the great boxes of my transforming behaviour. I am me no more. I can speak in Latin. I can speak in Aramaic. Glossolalia really does work. Mumbles and gibberish. Babble gabble and other songs of hate Catholic exorcists really like. This from a simple girl who went into a convent. I can be as strong as your Andre the Giant. Nothing can hold me down. I can kick like the Unicorn. The weak priests stay away. I scream like burning witches. I hate the Church. And when the Bible speaks I go into a violent rage. How the Bible's words are like haloes of flies buzzing around my ears. Unbelievable words! When constrained the Demon always makes me tell the truth. I'll lift myself from the ground. And the Demon in me says 'Look, see how I can fly!'

I'm a prophetess.
I've seen buildings burn and fall
I've seen venerable reputations fall
I've seen memorials of mystical poets fall
I've seen love bombing at street marches
I've seen public niceties disappear
I've seen trolls.
I see my energy, my Demons
They come from everywhere
They come into me
And I am possessed.

Ain't that so Johnny Joe."

"Surely is, sweetheart Jeanne. Do give us the Devil's naughty prayer,
darling."

"The martyr who lived on Earth
Exploited be his name
His kingdom never was
YOUR will is to be done
On Earth, as there is no Heaven.
Help those in need with their daily bread
As it is, here and now
And fear not your weaknesses
Examine those who seek trespass against you
May you know your own temptations
And judge yourself your deeds
And reflect on those gone wrong."

Mahone:
The Devil's good, darn good!

Clancy:
Godsploitation, I like that!

Mahone:
The nice and the good.

176

Kelly:
If Thommo don't get ya Satan will!

Muldoon:
She stole that prayer from us!

Kelly:
Nah, I told her that one when she was in the kitchen.

Muldoon:
I'm up for second helpings. But you could've told us. Those words
are supposed to be exclusive.

Kelly:
No time bruvs, they dimmed the lights too quick.

"As a female I am vulnerable to the beguiling Devil who is the
master of pleasure and pain which plague me. He is spawned from
repression agitating in my unconscious. I leave open the door for the
Devil to help me do these things. I am of such a fickle nature. Moody
and emotionally unstable. I feel like I've always got my period.
The Devil must be male, he who possesses me, caresses me with
his masculine words, telling me I'm doing nothing for anybody and
everything for myself.

This evil spirit unites with me while I'm conscious and I go about
things carrying two beings as one. Both beings do their battling
within. One diabolical, the other God inspired. I'm at peace with
myself as much as I am overwhelmed by rage. And I loathe God and
disbelieve in him, separating myself from him. And I'll wail and cry
and feel absolute misery. I am damned, pierced by despair. But I am
always rescued by my benevolent side-man Johnny Joe right here
calling for me, making light of my dark utterances. But still I cry out
in a sound like a she-wolf growling. And I don't know whether I am
in a state of joy or frenzy. But as they are one of the same they create
energy. And when Johnny Joe finally runs his cross over my body I
shudder at his touch, feeling as though I want to sexually embrace it
and then cast it tumescent into Hell."

Muldoon:
That's what De Sade reckons.

Kelly:
Them two and them Devils are a mighty bunch!

Muldoon:
Blow out the candles and let us concentrate our minds.

"I feel joy when I'm with the Devil. I am turned against everything. But how do I love myself so enveloped in sin! I take as myself the conversion and heart to the Devil and its desire to do with me what it wishes."

Jeanne suddenly claps her hands together crying out in such a way that was horrible to the stoned Family, twisting and jerking, shouting, "set me free set me free", in a hoarse voice, and she's retching and farting, putting out her tongue like an elephant's trunk, arching and bending, her fetid breath airing the room gagging some, head banging, sobbing and throbbing, she lies on the carpet arms outstretched, feet crossed, her head lolled to one side, dribble running from the corner of her mouth, mumbling, her eyes rolling back into her head, laughing and crying, jerking as though she is receiving blows to her wrists and feet, then up she jumps, "I'm resurrected" she yells, and she stands erect and still with a terrible look in her eyes, her arms stretch down her sides to her ankles, then she folds them entwining them as though a fisherman's knot, she brings up one foot after the other touching her forehead, all awhile her stare is fixed, her eyes enflamed, her mouth grinning, then she brings both her legs to her forehead and suddenly she levitates to the ceiling and she stays there, her hair spread around the ceiling, her legs dangling, her arms punching the air, then she goes into a spin and comes down like a spinning top, then she is running on the spot and gives a wave to Johnny Joe, who marvels at her stamina.

To the Family she is possessed by the Devil who is stronger than everything equal to God, and who is in every mind that has been, is now, and who will be, healthy, premature, stillborn, handicapped, the Devil being God's only guest, the one who cannot leave parties, gatherings, massacres, epidemics.

Jeanne is skipping in and out of the audience, kissing man and woman, avoiding the Bad Clergy, she cannot kiss her own, avoiding Johnny Joe, he's for love.

The Devil is every personality's lover, God is perfection, there is no perfection, there is the Devil, who was there at the first misunderstandings, the first lies, the first deceptions, the first confusions, the first breaches of trust, God lost all control, the Devil exists in God and all else alike.

Jeanne cries shrilly, and giddy she falls to the floor and goes into convulsions, "Funnel Web spiders are running out of my orifices" she cries, she contorts her body twisting this way and that, her eyes roll about, she is tearing at her clothing and her hair, and she's throwing herself around the room, knocking over anything in her path, attacking the voyeurs, she screams abuse, uttering vile profanities and subversions, she laughs manically, her whole self in a frenzy, then she's suddenly limp except for her legs crossing and uncrossing in a frenetic manner, she turns her arms backwards as though twisted, her fingers extended, and then thrashing her body forwards and backwards, her head jerking from side to side, her face frightful, angry, eyes wide open, her lips parting and drawn together in opposite directions, her elephant's tongue dangling, her hands clench into fists and banging her forehead, she is now drawn and haggard, falls to the floor and curls up into a foetal position panting, appearing to lose consciousness Jeanne lies still. The voyeur audience have certainly got their cheap thrills tonight.

9. Fridee Night Fever

A future report of this spectacle written by a spy from the Gendarmerie Corps of the Vatican City State who, in order to blend with the party's culture wore a long hair's wig, hung a 10 inch joint from his mouth, was decked out like Hoges, and gagged in a strine so broad Muldoon couldn't understand a word he'd said in the bathroom just before.

She, this Jeanne D'Anges, had been invited to a suburban Syndey home expressly to tempt the men innocently drinking and talking, into sin. Surin the Exorcist soon turned up to put a stop to it. It appeared that this scenario was a demonstration of Surin's love for the possessed D'Anges. He gloried in her eyes, hair, body, voice and movement like an adoring fan. Like the men in the lounge room, he was obsessed by her to the point that the Devil nearly got on top. And that I saw. There was so much drama. So fixated was Surin on D'Anges' natural beauty and glamour that he almost lost control of the possession.

Surin tells us to fasten our seatbelts. It's going to be a bumpy night. The spectacle was a frightfully brutal jab at Devil work. It was magnificently demonstrated with finely drawn participants. Joe Surin and Jeanne D'Anges both earned the audience's praises for their spirited performances. The procedure was sharp and insightful. It's not hard to make an exorcism appear realistic. It's quite another for it to BE realistic. The exorcism was not only frightening but it was also thought provoking - and it had something strong to say about the machinations of the Devil.

The conclusion is particularly ingenious. The introduction of a disturbed character tells us all we need to know about the future of the Devil. Its basic point is never subtle, but there are so many intricacies in the way the Devil backs its point up that this spectacle became endless fodder for thought and debate. And the future witnessing of exorcisms like these are sure to be as entertaining and informative as this one was.

On the other hand the Bad Clergy thought it was mostly incoherent and nonsensical. I interviewed them soon after and Mahone said

180

that what started like a promising entry in the saga of Priests vs. Demons quickly degenerated into a total mess. The vast majority of the performance consisted of everybody creeping around the back wall on the trail of embarrassment. Not even World Championship Wrestling could match the camp action they all saw tonight.

According to Mahone the true 'plot', such as it was, involved a mysteriously possessed woman, some sort of a female Tarzan, who was at deadly odds with a priest of the Catholic tribe called Surin. Nobody knows why they wanted to thrill each other, but the Clergy knew which side to take. Priests are pretty much always against evil in these sorts of happenings. The possessed want nothing to do with them and the Demon doesn't like telling the truth. But Surin's motives, as eventually explained by the exorcism, are senseless. He wants to save the girl Jeanne, apparently, because she is not herself. As religious rituals go, this particular fiction of prayers and acrobatics meant there were two things to laugh at here. Firstly there are two separate versions of a woman, one from the neck up and the other from the way she wiggled her behind, which were too much unrelated and absurd. Secondly Surin's dialogue was wonderfully effete. Consider a scene where Surin is driving at the Devil, and his prayers are supposed to rid D'Anges of the Devil's spite. Surin says something like "depart with all your deceits" and the Devil spites on regardless. Where has Surin's power gone? The Devil is still in there causing mischief!

Another line of argument is just as inexplicable reckons Mahone. Surin comes back from creeping around the back side of D'Anges and asks: "To what purpose do you insolently resist? To what purpose do you brazenly refuse?" It's a joke. The Devil just ignores him!

And still other moments blatantly betray the lack of thought that went into this spectacle according to Mahone. For example, there is a scene where D'Anges is crawling on all fours on the floor, and she covers her tracks by breaking wind, before continuing on. Surin, just behind, loses the trail but spies her sneakers. "Dropping dirt," he says. "D'Anges knows all the tricks." Then he continues after her, undeterred!

Mahone said he didn't expect it to be boring. According to him this was a cheesy low-budget possession gig that was mind-numbingly banal, in which a good number of possession poses Surin missed. He was obviously too busy entertaining the audience. The exorcism was supposed to concern the evicting of a Demon from a poor possessed woman. From this it is assumed that she must house not only life but demonic life. But how do exorcists know? Mahone asks. There is only one way to find out, exorcists always say, and they go out looking for signs sans official Catholic Church sanctions. Though with hundreds of years of documented evidence behind them, exorcists to this day can still spend an inordinate amount of time running around, lying around, and sitting around before they happen upon a handful of possessed women yelling "Rrraaahhh, Rrraaahhh!", like D'Anges here!

Sure there are some nice action scenes, considering, says Mahone. But there's as much awkwardness in the performance which induced the Bad Clergy's nervous laughter. Jeanne D'Anges' evil laugh, contortions and levitations were more embarrassing than menacing. And the entertainment was very much in the same spirit. Some priest, a strong good guy, and a young damsel, go on an exorcism safari in search of the Devil in order to evict it until it comes back again in someone else, preferably female.

The Catholic Church is a broad Church and open minded to anything Catholically Christian and variations thereof. The Bad Clergy and Surin the Exorcist have their ways and the official Church welcomes that. The Church could not have survived without an evolving theology and a compassion for the weak and the needy. And sometimes extraordinary measures are required when orthodox remedies such as prayers and ablutions are tested.

The stroke of genius was to have Jeanne narrate her own thought processes and longings, which were then brought to life visually quite well. The human brain is a complicated thing. Every moment of our lives, we filter rogue thoughts and renegade urges before they manifest themselves as speech and action. But D'Anges narration allows us to peek behind the curtains, and the exorcism's complex

script shows us just how quirky a thing the mind is. Perhaps the
Bad Clergy were tired and missed it. Although Muldoon later said
he enjoyed this part of the spectacle. Reckons religious authenticity
is a truth which best relies on the phrase 'it by all means must be
believed, because it is absurd'.

Perhaps, even in a diluted sense of the term, this was a minor
masterpiece. An uncomfortable pantomime, with some unsettling
scenes depicting the horrors of helplessness. The whole scenario,
Surin, D'Anges the watchers, the Bad Clergy, was all about superior
people watching each other and looking out for inferiority; the
addictive instincts which prompts a kind of snooping on behaviour,
and the trouble it can cause if the watching is wrongly done. This is
why, when Church representatives witness a combination of people
such as these in an ordinary living room, and they see transformative
acts which make these people real and tangible, certain reportages are
required to arouse in the moral Church a strong interest in this kind
of behaviour. The Church permits itself a profound and intimate look
into the private side of people's lives, seeing facets of their characters
which are normally unseen, facets that the Church might need to see.
The people should really live their private lives with their windows
open for the Church to see, for the Church to become spiritually
intimate with them. Open windows of course are not the preferred
Catholic way of pronouncing judgments on behaviour. The preferred
intimacy is in the confessional. The modern Church has the difficult
talk of eradicating devilish behaviour; and though its investigations
are borne of an idealistic theology, its observations might on
occasion also need to include adult oriented TV.

10. The Jeanne Genie Speaks

"I ma nwonk sa EHT rerednals, EHT resucca, EHT rellet fo seil
The feich exposer fo rouy God's falsehoods, your God's rules
Your God's slanders nehw you go tuoba your ungodly behaviour
I was nrob doog in my nature tub made myself evil revo time
A ebab in innocence, and then I rejected my doG father
I appear as do angelic spirits, I am without ylidob substance
My chief failing is that I envy you who evah bodies
So much so it was I who brought death into the world
After Heaven's war I was cast to your quiet Earth.
How did I fall from Heaven having risen first in morning glory?
How had I fallen to the Earth, to wound whatever I spied?
And yet I will ascend again otni Heaven, to be enthroned above that
of God
I will sit in the mountain of the covenant, in the sides of the north
I will ascend above the height of the clouds, I will be like the most
High
But since I have come to Hell, into the depths of humanity and its
heat
I might as well make the most of it, and be responsible for ALL grief.

In myth I was the seal of benevolence, full of wisdom, and perfect in
beauty
I was in the pleasures of the paradise of God; every precious stone
covered me
The sardius, the topaz, and the jasper, the chrysolite, and the onyx,
the beryl
The sapphire, and the carbuncle, and the emerald; gold the work of
my beauty
And my glory was prepared on the day I was created, a cherub on
high
Set most comfortably on the holy mountain of God, in the midst of
stones of fire.
I was perfect in my being from the beginning, until iniquity was
found in me.
And then I became The Enemy.

I may not arouse so much in human souls but I do so in your minds
And which is more powerful, the human soul or the human mind?
And you, who are the living dead because of your sins
Wherein your dirty deeds accorded the course of this world
Suggested by me, the prince of the power of this air
Who works as the spirit which works through the belief in me!

Your minds are the Hell, a skullful of hollow, which accommodates
me
A dark and hidden place, the place of punishment for the living
damned
You, who are sunk in this hollow, seek your release in epoh or in
death
Naming it the abyss, the place of torments, the pool of fire, the
interior darkness
It is a place you know little of, but you are always trying to escape it
Yet the fire of Hell is eternal and unquenchable, you mustn't ignore
your genes
You are confirmed in troublesome thoughts, inspired by me, the
Disturbed One
You suffer from the loss of any moment of bliss, the intense pain of
emptiness
You subvert your desires for happiness with delusive pleasures
And your consciousness, on which you depend, is overwhelmed by
questions.

So, I am cast out, the unclean spirit, over and over again, but do I
really leave?
It is said Jesus of Nazareth himself, anointed with the power of the
Holy Ghost
Went about doing good, healing all who were possessed by me
And, as I am bound to tell the truth, he urged me out of him and her
and them
He spoke, he commanded, he wrestled, and sure enough out I went
Great miracles they were, impressing many, adding followers by the
score
And the force of his work carried him along, his divine mission
growing
But here I am, the conquered Devil, talking to you and nothing has

changed.
We have this pact Jesus and me, where we'd go in together and mess
with minds
And he'd come back and save all the possessed he could find
And their love for him became blind
He became their bind
Witnesses reckon he is master over me, and thus they must obey him
He delivers the likes of you from servitude to me to servitude to him
For, once my influence and restraint is removed, the malady then
goes
And I, who evilly speaks, am cast out, and the possessed are set free;
Apparently.

I've possessed sick people taken with various bodily diseases, and
torments
And lunatics, and those with the palsy, and I've been kicked out of
them all
Indeed in His name others cast out Devils; others shall speak with
new tongues
They shall fight serpents; and deadly things they shall not hurt them
They shall lay hands on the sick and they shall recover, and here I
remain!
You have to ignore the scoffers, who say His mind was filled with
delusion
You might think that I myself had got into His mind perhaps
For me He never corrected Himself, rather He encouraged this belief
in me
Nor did He deliberately give instructions that He knew were actually
false
Instructions that would mislead His followers, evidently calculated
To give them the impression He had something worthwhile to say!
For if He has lied, then I, the Devil, DO NOT EXIST!"

This exhortation was written on the reverse side of toilet paper
reserved for the exclusive use of the Angels of Heaven, or something
like that, and no apologies are given for the backwards words-
Speculator Theologinus, resident of Deckard, sister City of God, in
The Book of Questioning, chapter 7, passage 42.

11. The Ramp Up

Excerpts from a skit rejected by the producers of Laugh-In for not being funny enough.

Dick Martin:
Religion is the rule of dividing and conquering independent thought as the means of asserting its power. The religious presence is the material reconstruction of illusion. The illusory paradise representing a total denial of earthly life is not only projected into the Heavens, it is embedded in earthly life itself.

Dan Rowan:
Easy for you to say. However the indispensable embellishment of illusion has become a general articulation of religious rationales, and as an advanced system of imagineering it creates an ever-evolving worship through the illusionary spectacle of belief.

Dick Martin:
I didn't know that. Indeed the religious presence presents itself as a vast inaccessible reality which cannot be questioned. Its sole message is what appears is good; what is good appears. The passive acceptance it demands is already effectively imposed by its monopoly of authenticity, its manner of appearing without allowing an alternate reply.

Dan Rowan:
Easy for you to say. In a religious world in which reality has been turned upside down, the true is in the same moment as the false.

Dick Martin:
I didn't know that. Yet the spectacle of belief inherited by the weakness of the human spiritual concept, attempts to understand activity by means of the categories of supernatural vision, and it is based on the relentless development of the particular theological rationality which grew out of that thinking. The religious presence does not realize theology; it theologizes reality, reducing a believer's steady life to a universe of troubled speculation.

Dan Rowan:
Easy for you to say. The indirect character of the religious presence
stems from the fact that its means and ends are identical. It is the sun
which never sets over the ozone of modern passivity. It covers the
entire surface of the globe, endlessly basking in its own glory.

Dick Martin:
I didn't know that. Religion's triumph as an authorative power has
spelled its own doom, because the forces it has unleashed won't
eliminate an instinctual necessity to question. The necessity for
boundless religious growth has meant replacing the satisfaction of
primary human needs (now scarcely understood by religion) with
an incessant fabrication of pseudo-needs, driven by an authoritarian
need to further the reign of religion. And when religion loses all
connection with authentic needs, rebellion emerges from an ever
evolving social unconscious. Whatever is conscious will wear out,
while the unconscious is constantly threatening.

Dan Rowan:
Easy for you to say. And as long as necessity is dreamed of as fantasy,
dreaming will remain necessary. The religious presence is the bad
dream of societies bound by chains which express nothing more than
a wish for sleep. The religious presence is the overlord of fitful sleep.

Dick Martin:
I didn't know that. The religious presence is its advocate's nonstop
discourse about itself, its never-ending monologue of self-praise,
and a self-portrait of mental domination in all aspects of life.
The fetishism of the pure objectivity in religion conceals the true
character of these advocates relationship with their God and human
nature; a foreign nature, with their own inescapable laws to dominate
critical thinking. The religious presence, considered in the sense of
mass indoctrination, was never a neutral apparatus but rather a power
dynamic in desperate need for reverence.

Dan Rowan:
Easy for you to say. The consciousness of need and the need for
consciousness are the same projection, the projection in its negative

form which seeks to abolish incredulity and the way sceptics possess independent methods of how they see the everyday. The opposite of this projection is religion as illusion, where, for example, the advocate contemplates the holy relic's place in the world of Lego blocks.

Dick Martin:
I didn't know that. Also the religious presence cannot be abstractly added to concrete social activity. The religious presence which falsifies reality is sadly an accepted product of that reality. While lived reality is materially invaded by the speculation of the religious presence it ends up being absorbed by it and aligning itself with it. Subjective reality is present on both sides. Each of these seemingly fixed concepts has no other basis than its transformation into its opposite: reality emerges within the religious presence, and the religious presence is therefore real.

Dan Rowan:
Easy for you to say. The reigning religious system is a vicious circle of isolation. Its theologies are based on isolation, and they contribute to that same isolation. From miracles to relics, the 'goods' that this spectacular system produces serves as weapons for the constant reinforcing of the conditions which creates loneliness. With doctrinal concreteness the religious presence recreates its own threatened presuppositions.

Dick Martin:
I didn't know that. Indeed the concepts of the religious presence amalgamate, which explains a wide range of seemingly unconnected phenomena. The apparent diversities and contrasts of these phenomena stem from the prospect of appearances, whose essential nature must itself be recognized. Considered in its own terms, the religious presence is the origin of all theo-appearances and an identification of all human social life with such appearances.

Dan Rowan:
Easy for you to say. And the religious presence presents itself simultaneously as society itself, as a part of society, and as a means of unification. As a part of society, it believes itself to be the focal point of all thought and all consciousness. But due to the very fact

that this sector is separate, it is in reality the domain of delusion
and false consciousness: the unification it achieves is nothing but
an official language of universal speculation.

Dick Martin:
I didn't know that. Understood in its totality, the religious presence
is both the result and the project of the present mode of anxiety.
It is not a mere supplement or decoration added to the real world,
it is the heart of this real society's unreality. In all of its particular
manifestations - sacraments, theology, rituals, hierarchies - the
religious presence is the model of a prevailing way of life. It is the
omnipresent affirmation of the choices which have already been
made in the sphere of uncertainty and in the consumption implied by
it. In both form and content the religious presence serves as a total
justification of the conditions and goals of an authoritarian system.

Dan Rowan:
Easy for you to say. In order to describe the religious presence,
its formation, its functions, and the forces that work against it, it
is necessary to make some artificial distinctions. In analysing the
religious presence we are obliged to a certain extent to use the
religious presence's own language, in the sense that we have to
initiate a new methodological terrain for a society which needs to
freely express itself.

Dick Martin:
I didn't know that. The fact that the practical power of modern
religion has detached itself from ordinary society and established
an independent realm as a religious presence can be explained
only by the additional fact that its practice of power continues the
contradictions with itself.

Dan Rowan:
Easy for you to say. The non-believer's divorce from religiously
contemplated objects, within his or her unconscious activity,
works like this: the less he or she contemplates them, the more he
or she lives; the less they identify with the dominant images of
religious need, the more they understand their own life and desires.
The religious presence's estrangement from the acting subject is

expressed by the fact that the believing individual's gestures are
no longer their own; they are the gestures of someone else who
represents them to them. The believing individual does not feel at
home anywhere, because the religious presence is everywhere.

Dick Martin:
I didn't know that. The root of the religious presence is that of the
oldest of all social specializations, the specialization of power. The
religious presence plays the specialized role of speaking in the name
of all the other activities. It is hierarchical society's ambassador to
itself, delivering its messages at a court where no one else is allowed
to speak. The most modern aspect of the religious presence has also
become the most archaic.

Dan Rowan:
Easy for you to say. Also the religious presence's primary function is
the manufacture of alienation. Religion consists primarily of the
expansion of the sector of fear and worship, the cycle of alienation
from and yearned for closeness to a god. The growth is generated
by insecurity guilt developed for its own sake, which is nothing other
than a growth of the very alienation that was at its origin, emptiness.

Dick Martin:
I didn't know that. When religion is transformed into mere language,
mere language becomes a real being; figments which provide the
direct motivations for hypnotic behaviour. Since the religious
presence's purpose is to use various specialized meditations in order
to show a world they cannot be directly grasped, it naturally elevates
the sense of hearing to the special pre-eminence once occupied by
sight: the most abstract and easily deceived sense is the most readily
adaptable to the generalized abstraction of present-day society. But
the religious presence is not merely a matter of language, nor even
of language plus rhetoric. It is whatever escapes people's activity,
whatever eludes their practical reconsideration and correction. It
is the opposite of conversation. Wherever human representation
becomes independent, the religious presence will regenerate itself.

Dan Rowan:
Easy for you to say. Even the present stage, in which social life has

become completely occupied by an imbedded religious language, has brought about a general shift from appearing to having. What is done through having, must now derive its immediate prestige and its ultimate purpose from religious appearances. Individual reality is allowed to appear only insofar as it is not actually real unless it is expressed through religious language.

Dick Martin:
I didn't know that. In this world, at once present and absent, which the religious presence holds up to view, is a world of accumulated nervousness dominating all living experience. The world of nerves is thus shown for what it is, because its development is identical to people's haphazard estrangement from each other and from everything they produce.

Dan Rowan:
Easy for you to say. The religious presence was born from the world's loss of unity, and the immense expansion of the religious presence reveals the enormity of this loss. The extraction of individuality and the general abstractness of living are perfectly reflected in the religious presence, whose manner of being truthful is precisely abstraction. In the religious presence, a part of the world represents itself to the world and is superior to it.

Dick Martin:
I didn't know that. And the fetishism of anxiety, the domination of society by the unimaginable, attains its ultimate fulfilment in the religious presence, where the perceptible world is replaced by a selection of beliefs which is projected from within, succeeding in making itself the perceptible feeling par excellence. Sincere belief is a function of knowing how to believe.

Dan Rowan:
Easy for you to say. Again the religious presence is a permanent high designed to encourage people to equate happiness with its consumption and to equate dissatisfaction with denial which grows according to its own rules. If augmented, happiness never comes to a resolution, if there is no point where it might stop expanding, this is because it is itself stuck in the realm of depression. Happiness may

192

gild emptiness, but it cannot transcend it. In this way the religious
presence endures.

Dick Martin:
I didn't know that. Stimulation, which is both normal for modern
living and the epitome of its practice, obliges the religious presence
to resolve the following contradiction: the theologies which
objectively tend to eliminate critical thinking must at the same time
preserve want as a commodity, because theology is the surest creator
of speculative want. The only way to prevent stimulation from
speculating one's dead time is to encourage self actualisation.

Dan Rowan:
Easy for you to say. In the religious presence for any god to
objectively exist, each and every living person will hold in their
consciousness the same belief simultaneously at any given time.
It is the triumph of persuasion. All then, in a singular voice, are
free to ask of this god to declare its presence true through a simple
proclamation, I am therefore I am. But when an individual at any
time declares that they do not believe, for the rest this means their
crisis of faith must continue, to be resolved by its surest remedy,
death, believing in the hope there awaits for them a better life in
Heaven hereafter.

Dick Martin:
I didn't know that.

12. Before on the Road Again

On this final hour of tonight's Festival of Luna Park, the Bad Clergy, despite their low opinion of the performance just gone, nevertheless ask Johnny Joe Surin, "Where would you like us to meet and share with you Humble Pie?" To which Johnny Joe replies, "Let us go into the backyard shed and there we will do things together which makes us special."

The Bad Clergy and Johnny Joe Surin quietly leave the party 'backslang', as they would say. The weary Jeanne D'Anges was still signing autographs so no one noticed them leaving.

Johnny Joe Surin and the Bad Clergy sit down at a makeshift table and break the first cold pizza taken from the fridge and begin to eat it washing it down with the Fizzy Tar. The Clergy were eating quietly; they had a lot on their minds. They were worried because some in the party said Johnny Joe was a fraud and Jeanne D'Anges was his trick for the night.

Johnny Joe could see the Bad Clergy were uncomfortable. He said to them quietly, "I tell you the truth, one of you in here will betray me." The Bad Clergy looked at each other in mock shock, and Muldoon asked Johnny Joe, "It isn't me, is it Johnny Joe?"

He replied, "The one who dips his pizza into this glass of Fizzy Tar with me will betray me. I will disappear in smoke and be forever suspected a fraud, but the Bad Clergy who betrays me will feel sorry forever."

Then Kelly, with his head down, spoke quietly to Johnny Joe, "It isn't me, is it?" Johnny Joe answered, "Yes, you are the one." Kelly's head hung down lower, he had hoped that the other Bad Clergy had not heard what Johnny Joe said.

Luckily, they were paying more attention to Muldoon's violent mouth attack on another pizza slice.

Johnny Joe thanked Jeanne D'Anges for the pizza and shared it with the Bad Clergy and said, "Take this and eat it. This is my body which is given for you." Then he took a full schooner of Fizzy Tar, thanked Jeanne for it and said, "This is my blood, which will be poured out for many people and their scepticism will be forgiven." Then they all took a sip from the schooner.

The meal continued after this, and it was a long celebration. The Bad Clergy took their time, because they enjoyed talking with Johnny Joe who had many exorcism stories to tell.

After some time Johnny Joe got up from the table and went to a different part of the shed. He took off his exorcism clothes, and put a large beach towel around him, making himself look like a servant. After that, he poured the Fizzy Tar into a large bowl and began to wash the Bad Clergy's hands. Then Johnny Joe dried them with the towel that was wrapped around him. Underneath he wore a plain pair of tight blue swimming togs.

When it was Clancy's turn to have his hands cleaned he said to Johnny Joe, "Look mate, are you going to wash my hands as well?" Johnny Joe replied, "You don't understand what I am doing, but you will later."

"No," said Clancy, "you will never wash my hands." He said this because he didn't feel right having Johnny Joe wash his hands. He knew Johnny Joe was very special.

Johnny Joe replied back to him, "If I don't wash your hands, you cannot remember me."

"Then, Johnny Joe," Clancy replied, "don't just wash my hands but my feet and head too." Johnny Joe then explained that he only needed to wash his hands; and that would be enough to make his whole body feel sticky.

When Johnny Joe had finished washing the Bad Clergy's hands, he put his Liberace garb back on and returned to the table. "Do you understand what I have done for you?" Johnny Joe asked them. "You call me The Special One and that is who I am. And now that I have washed your hands, you can also wash everybody else's hands with the Fizzy Tar. And then everyone will feel sticky and they will remember me, Johnny Joe Surin, the greatest exorcist the world has ever seen, because you would have told them about me in spite of the one of you who will betray me."

FANTASY 5

DIVINITY

1. On the Road Again

It's three AM Saturdee morning dear reader. Another big night is
drawing to its banal end. The goosey two never made it to the party
but the Lag Motor knew where to find them. And sure enough there
they were. At the front gates of the Paddington Church of Christ
Kindergarten, on their knees and praying. In they got, nothing was
said, and back to the Granville crib did the Lag Motor head.

Clancy:
Not a bad night eh. Oliver's missed a bit.

Muldoon:
Betcha that Jeanne weren't no virgin. But boy could she dance!

Mahone:
I got a wink from her. As good as a tickle with a Marilyn in a jar of
flies I'd say.

Muldoon:
Ah you're easily pleased Mahone, just like any priest should be with
a soothing Marilyn.

Kelly:
What about that stigmata guy hey, at the Gag n' Throttle. Wonder if
the Callan Park Squad picked him up.

Clancy:
The highlight of the night for me. Not every day you see a Jesus guy
with stigmata all over him. Makes you wonder if he's the real deal.
If the Callan Park Squad did their thing when the Christ was around,
they would've spotted him and got him into a daisy coat quick smart.

Mahone:
They couldn't care less. We're all inmates to them.

Muldoon:
Find a picker, use a picker, throw it all away. Gimme some of that
there gossamer son, I could use it for today.

Mahone:
There goes Muldoon again. Into fairy-ness, exit wonderland.

Muldoon:
Hey, I was thinking about mother.

Kelly:
Which one? Yours or the one and only?

Muldoon:
Yer too straight to work it out deary.

Clancy:
But who's straight enough to work out how the three in one man
works? It's been bothering me. On this trip and th' others.

Mahone:
A spliff at three in the morning might help.

Muldoon:
Roll, inhale, and blow out big smoke. And there you have it. Three in
one.

Kelly:
Sky Padre's a spirit, the Holy Spirit's a spirit, and the Son got
spirited away. No way can you divide smoke.

Mahone:
Why's it bother you brother? Isn't there enough bothers in our
troubled lives to keep us going until we find redemption. Them
brisket beaters we speak to want it simple. Sin for us to show 'em the
way. It's easy for 'em. They can go off and bother with low lentils,
and other household rackets we don't need to bother with. Anyway
they probably don't do what they're been told by us to do. There's
vermin in that sermon Herman!

Clancy:
I'm as wide awake as when I first jumped over the stirrups from

The Virgin's pink canal. The weed's got me lucid all of a sudden. We should talk. It don't matter the Lag Motor's knows where it's goin'.

Muldoon:
Transubstantiation.

Kelly:
What's that brother?

Muldoon:
I dunno. But it's been swimmin' in my head all night.

Mahone:
Wafers and wine.

Kelly:
Oh that! Write scripture on the body and wash it down with a sip of claret. That stuff. The honourables like it. Did it for a prisoner once. Ever so grateful. Never did understand the words.

Clancy:
Got spoken about in the seminary.

Kelly:
I wasn't listening.

Clancy:
Funny how we all got through eh.

Muldoon:
Don't know about you but I cheated.

Clancy:
So did I.

Kelly:
Me too!

Mahone:
I'm with you brothers. *(looks at the goosey two)* No need to ask them.

Muldoon:
I was called so hard I'd do anything to get through. Didn't want to fail and end up a loser.

Clancy:
Nothin' worse than failing at something you burn to do.

Mahone:
Speaking of burning, look at that fire. One of them Redfern warehouses s'gone up again.

2. Three Persons in a Tub

Clancy indream. A recurring dream. A long dream. Like a film. He
remembers flash scenes of one he saw back in '57 as a kid. Three
in One. A portmanteau film with three distinct stories: 'A Load of
Father', 'The City Son' and 'Joe Wilson's Holy Ghost'. Somehow
they appeared together, simultaneously, like light, sky and air,
one essence, one substance. Somehow. And besides who was Joe
Wilson? And who was Henry Lawson? And what was the name of
the colt from Old Regret that got away? And why isn't Shaw Neilson
a household name?

"Rub a dub dub
Three ghosts in a tub
And who do you think they could be, Clancy?
The Father, the Son
The Holy Ghost?
And worship them together, spirits three in one."

So says Thomas the Rhymer indream to Clancy.

"There is no greater God than the one who is made up of three
They who address each other as you, I and me
One who is the universe, one who came and went, one who is the
breath of life
If they were gender roles, they would each be husband and wife
All three as one and thoroughly divine
Three persons they are, who would if they could, share the same
Spine.
There's a left and right and middle hand
Working together on mountains, in waters and on land
Three bodies conjoined in one dimension which stands and sits
Three dimensions conjoined in one body without the sexual bits
And the Father is no Father without the Son's wise speaking
And the Father is no Father without the Holy Spirit's soul seeking
And the Son is no Father
And the Holy Spirit is no Father
Without the presence of the Father
Who beget his only Son

202

The Holy Spirit the seed for the Son.
When tying the marriage knot there's a cord of three strands
Lovers united while holding each other's hands
And three ropes entwined produce a stronger cable
Whereby comes virtue, morality and love that is able."

Thomas the Rhymer brought in words from out of the rough
And now here's bush poetry for lovers of the right stuff
But back to the Trinity and what it entails
And the metaphor of a ship which uses three sails.

"In the unity of the Godhead there are three sails
And if one or another falls this ship never fails
In the words of the Athanasian Creed: The Father is God
The Son is God, The Holy Spirit is God
And yet there are not three Gods, but one God
Co-eternal and co-equal, the uncreated and omnipotent God
The foundation of all that is the Church's dogma
The one and only intoxicating soma
With consubstantiated natures, distinct but naturally the same
At whom the Devil constantly takes aim
God's essence, will and action are together as one
Clearly demonstrated by the life and death of the Son
The second person of the Trinity who is the word
The Son's life documented in ways needed to be absurd
And when one divine spine is shared so is the mind
So believers can imagine God as THE ONE of a kind.

It is by divine revelation that God is the Son
For he spoke to the faithful like he is THE son of a gun
Since his transient action is as perfect as perfect can be,
And those blinded by scoffing scepticism cannot see
How God breathes the Holy Ghost
And offers his blessed host
And the divine seal which secures God's presence.
Sinners keep on yearning, for they weep in God's absence
For they are not given love by which God loves himself
This love a mystery in theology and a truth in itself
Whereby no full knowledge of it is ever truly attainable

At best parables and scripture make the mystery sustainable.
Of all revealed truths the Trinity is the most impenetrable to reason
Such is the human mind, in which there is a permanent lesion
Wherein the God mind has a threefold theological persistence
A three way mind according to its three modes of existence.

And in the Gospels the evidence of this notion is given the nod
When Christ taught believers to recognise him as the Son of God
And in his place is the Holy Spirit, come after his resurrection
The first martyrs were the great and good's righteous insurrection
Against those who didn't believe Christ was God, and God was he
And what God his Father has given Christ is for all in eternity
Such has been written and repeated until every infidel gets it
Feed the truth, add it to human endeavour, bit by bit.

This is your job Clancy, to make believe the Trinity
The marvellous thing about it is its orthodox simplicity
Repeat, Glory to The Father, The Son, The Holy Ghost, repeat
Repeat, until thinking about it wearies you, it'll all be sweet
There's no point in fighting it, your papal commands have hissed
Every argument against it has been forcefully dismissed
First with the violence of words, and then with violence itself
Believe Clancy, like in THC, which you say is good for your health."

3. At the Jesus Transubstantiation Centre for Lost Souls - with tonight's guest Lecturer the Very Rev. Rev. Luther J Kramer

Muldoon:
Wake up Clance. If you free your mind your arse is gonna follow. The kingdom of Heaven is within. Though that won't suit dog, and ma.

Kelly:
Deep within. Ha ha. Deep in the gizzes. Right there in the penal colon!

Clancy:
Muldy, if you look to me for inspiration then the Trinity is all you need.

Muldoon:
Like I said I've got transubstantiation to muddle me complete.

Kelly:
We follow a special God don't we? The only one who invites everyone to eat him. Comes out as crap but confident he's still a God. That's the one I like!

Mahone:
You mock Kelly. You mock. But what about our brisket flock?

Muldoon:
Rhymin' speech. Not so flash. Wish I knew a flash phrase for transubstantiation.

Kelly:
Go gnaw a cracker on a tabernacle, and like make a story out of crumbs.

Muldoon:
Not bad. I'll paste them words behind the tabernacle with the rest.

Clancy:
Must have a good vocab brewing.

Muldoon:
Can never get enough of a flash language, Clance.

Mahone:
Hey Kels, where's the Lag Motor takin' us. This ain't Parramatta
Road. Looks like Concord Road.

Kelly:
You'd be right there matey. You know how the Lag Motor can go all
funny. Remember that time we ended up in the abattoirs.

Mahone:
Had to hear all that screamin' and moanin' like we were in Hell.

Clancy:
I know what it's like now. Them poor unrepentant sinners who died.
If only they understood. And we tell 'em don't we. Even added sound
effects for good measure. I can still hear them slaughter cows.

Muldoon:
This doesn't look good chappies. We might be headin' to Rhodes, the
golden centre for chemical manufacturing. More Hell. Haven't we
seen enough!

There's silence in the cabin as the Lag Motor finds its way to
Rhodes. It stops at Rhodes Point and the wharf. The Bad Clergy can
see from the cabin a red light which flashes like a lighthouse at the
wharf's end. The Lag Motor rumbles low before the Bad Clergy
including the goosey two alight. At the end of the wharf is a tentlike
structure, its canvas white, and with a doorway in the Gothic
tradition.

The Bad Clergy go inside where there are four chairs arranged in a
straight line across the floor. They take one each. The goosey two
meekly sit on the floor in front of the small low stage, their backs facing
the Bad Clergy. After a few minutes of silence a small, bald man with a
beaky nose and piercing eyes, wearing a safari suit, comes out from
behind a curtain and stands before them. And then he shouts "Let the

206

Lecture Begin". The soft sounds of K-Tel's Musical Journey of The Pan
Flute playing in Sensurround slowly increases in volume.

"So it is Bad Clergy. The Pan Flute is indeed the music of Heaven.
Now I'm pleased to meet you, hope you can guess my name. If you
cannot it is the Very Rev. Rev. Luther J Kramer at your service. Now
let us get down to business. Tonight I am going to talk to you about
the scepticism of atheists who question Jesus Christ's Resurrection.
I hope that after this lecture you will go away and Christfully apply
your new found knowledge.

Discord has long been created by sceptics in their rather peculiar
turn of thinking and argument. Every person of sound mind believes
the Resurrection to be idiosyncratic to the individual, distinguishing
one from another, but not from God's unique character; this belief
shared by us as the Holy Family under one Holy Church. However,
every lunatic atheist, and let's face it, they swarm around in droves,
bleats on about some religious thing irritating their scepticism, and
boy how they bother to share this bleating with every other damnable
atheist on this planet. Big on their agenda is their statement that the
Resurrection is completely untrue. Totally made up. An invented
fantasy contrived from some deep wish. The second biggest lie after
the lie of God's existence. How can our religion possibly be a lie
brothers? This would mean decay and disorder, wouldn't it? Imagine
if the world knew that Christianity is no better than any other moral
principle. Imagine if there was no objective truth. Then our 'Christian
truth' would have no meaning. And atheists love to argue that for
God to exist it must be outside the limits of the human imagination,
which they say contemptuously, has no limits. Preposterous! God IS
the human imagination! But it is not my intention brothers to discuss
further these splintered subversive theories. Instead I wish to exhibit
their prominent features, by which their insanity may be detected,
as far as such appearances seem worthy of remark, and which have
been the subject of my own observation. And I need not explain
that scepticism and atheism are of the same as I interchange theses
horrible words during my lecture.

In Christianity, the first attack of the sceptical disease was seldom
observed; and it might naturally be supposed, that there once existed

in Jerusalem traces of the incipient madness of scepticism. It is true, that all who, in history, have admitted to it, are assumed to be greatly afflicted with this disorder. Yet from the occasional relapses to a soundness of mind which insane sceptics are subject, we can theologically discern how they managed to do it, which I will soon speak about. However it would be improper, and even dangerous, to trust them at large in Christian society; and even those, who are curable, for a recurrence of the malady might still take place. Upon these occasions, there is an ample scope for observing the attacks of the disease under supervised and comprehensive physical and mental torture.

Atheist sceptics under the influence of anger and mania, exhibit a violent train of symptoms. Their countenance wears an anxious and fierce aspect, and they are little disposed to quietude. They boast in the company of those with whom they despise, and brag about their exclusive lives. Frequently they will keep their eyes fixed on the crucifix for hours and hours, hell-bent on finding vacuity in the object. They next become imaginative, and conceive a thousand fancies; often they return to some immoral act which they have committed, or imagine themselves innocent of atheist crimes. They proclaim that God never was, and, with mockery, await his so called punishment. Sometimes they become frustrated, and endeavour by their own hands to terminate a believer's existence, which appears to them an afflicting and hateful encumbrance. Ultimately this all is the Devil's work, though Atheism's remedy cannot be as simple as an Exorcism.

Atheist madmen do not always continue in the same furious state; the exhausted maniacal paroxysm does abate of its violence, and some beams of hope occasionally cheer the despondency crippling the melancholic. We have in the world some unfortunate persons, who need to be secured by straightjacket the greater part of their lives, who now and then become calm, and to a certain degree rational. Upon such occasions, they are allowed by Christians some movement, and are admitted to associate with priests such as yourselves. In some instances, the degree of rationality is more considerable; they conduct themselves with propriety, and a short conversation about the truth of the Resurrection will appear sensible

and coherent. Such remission however, expressed as a lucid interval,
is not to be trusted.

When higher priests are called upon to attend a council of atheist
lunacy, they always ask whether the heretic has had a lucid interval.
A term of such latitude as a lucid interval requires to be explained
in the most accurate manner. In common language, it signifies both
a moment and a number of years; consequently it does not comprise
of any stated time. The term lucid interval is therefore relative. I,
in my capacity as Lecturer define a lucid interval as a complete
recovery of the atheist's lost intellects, ascertained by repeated
examinations of his positive conversations about the Resurrection,
and by constant observation of his conduct, for a time sufficient to
enable the priests to form a correct judgment. Unthinking people
are frequently led to conclude, that if during a short conversation,
a person under confinement says nothing absurd or incorrect, the
person is therefore well, and will only complain about their the
incarceration. Even in common society, there are many persons
whom we never suspect, to be shallow minded; but, if we start a
conversation on the Resurrection, and wish to discuss it through all
its ramifications and dependencies, we find atheists incapable of
pursuing a connected chain of reasoning. In the same manner atheists
will often, for a short time, conduct themselves, both in conversation
and behaviour, with such propriety, that they appear to have control
of their faculties; but let the inquisitor protract any discordance
under torture until the atheist's favourite subject of the Resurrection
overwhelms his conversation, and then under further torture the
atheist will be convinced that the scepticism of the Resurrection is
terribly wrong. To those unaccustomed to atheists, a few coherent
sentences, or rational answers, would indicate a lucid interval,
because they discovered no madness; but he, who understands the
peculiar turn of the mad atheist's thoughts, might merely encourage
them to disclose them, and by a flick of the lash a correct conversation
will spontaneously break forth.

Let me give you an example of perverted atheist thinking which
came under my observation some years ago, and which is appropriate
to the subject. A young atheist had become insane from habitual
masturbation; and, during the violence of his disorder, had attempted

to destroy himself. Under a supposed imputation of having unnatural propensities, he had amputated his penis, with a view of precluding any future insinuations of that nature. For many months, after he was admitted into the hospital, he continued in a state which obliged him to be strictly confined, as he constantly meditated upon his own destruction. All of a sudden, he became apparently well, was highly sensible of the delusion under which he had laboured, and conversed, as any other person, upon the topic of the Resurrection which was the order of the day. There was, however, something in the reserve of his manner, and peculiarity of his look, which persuaded me he was not quite well, although no incoherence could be detected in his conversation. I had observed him for some days walking rather lame, and once or twice had noticed him sitting with his shoes off, rubbing his feet. On enquiring into the motives of his doing so, he replied that his feet were blistered, and wished that some remedy might be applied to remove the blistering. When I requested to look at his feet, he declined it, and prevaricated, saying that they were only tender and uncomfortable. In a few days afterwards, he assured me they were perfectly well. The next evening I observed him, unperceived, still rubbing his feet, and then I insisted on examining them. And indeed they were blistered. He now told me, with some embarrassment, that he wished much for a confidential friend, to whom he might impart a secret of importance; upon assuring him that he might trust me, he said, that the shoes in which he walked, (for they were made tight for his personal safety) were the root cause of his blisters. I now rest my case. As I have referred to before, atheists simply cannot be trusted.

A certain Luis Bunuel, a most unpleasant fellow, has on many occasions so completely masked his disorders with his films that I, his fiercest critic, almost believed he was actually well, when he was quite otherwise. He once came over here to especially challenge me. And he had not been in this country for many hours, before his derangement became quite discernible, but not to those who came to congratulate him on his films. His impetuosity and mischievous disposition was daily increasing, and I had him sent to the Callan Park mad-house; there being, at that time, no vacancy in the local hospital. Almost from the moment of his confinement he became tranquil, and orderly, but he remonstrated on the injustice of his seclusion. I became very suspicious and I was allowed to take charge of him.

It seemed deceiving to me that he wished that I respect him, and he assured me that he would submit to my determination that the Resurrection was true. My suspicions were aroused even more. I had taken care to be well prepared for our formal interview, by first obtaining an accurate account of the manner in which he had conducted himself. At our examination, he managed himself with admirable address. He spoke of the treatment he had received from the persons under whose care he was placed as most kind and matronly: he also expressed himself as particularly fortunate in being under my care, and bestowed many handsome compliments on my skill in explaining the Resurrection, and my reserve when perceiving the slightest tinges of insanity. When I wished him to explain certain parts of his conduct, and particularly some extravagant opinions on the Catholic Church, regarding certain clergy and truths including the Resurrection, he disclaimed all knowledge of such circumstances, and felt himself hurt, and that my mind had been poisoned. He displayed equal subtlety on three other occasions when I visited him; although by protracting the conversation, he let fall sufficient words to satisfy my mind that he was a madman. And not before long, his time with me became the subject of severe antagonism; he said he was treated with extreme cruelty; that he had been nearly starved, and eaten up by vermin of various descriptions. On enquiring of some other patients, I found (as I had suspected) that I was as much the subject of abuse, when absent, as any of his supposed enemies; although to my face his behaviour was courteous and respectful. More than a month had elapsed, since his admission into the mad-house before he pressed me for my opinion; confiding in his address to me, and hoping to deceive me. At length he appealed to my better judgement, and urged me to say how well he behaved as the argument for his liberation. But when I told him that he was indeed most suitable for the asylum, because of his attitude toward the Catholic Church, and in particular its dogmatic principles, he suddenly poured forth a torrent of abuse; talked in the most incoherent manner about it all being the greatest lie that's ever been told; ranted vengeance against my family and Catholic friends, and became so outrageous that it was necessary to order him to be strictly confined. He continued in a state of unceasing fury for more than six months. Eventually I was required to let him go since our ideas of truth were never going to meet anywhere in the universe, and besides, he had a new film to make.

Of the sense organs which are affected by insanity, the ear, most particularly suffers. It is certain that in people, more delusion is conveyed through the ear than the eye, or any of the other senses. Even those who are deaf say they hear voices in their heads. An insane person will believe that the Devil, through the ear, has commissioned him or her to make known his evil words to others, and to perform some horrible act, as a manifestation of his will and power. These devilish commissions generally bring human mischief and calamity, and instances are not infrequent, where such evil inspirations have urged these mad atheists to go and burn down Churches, to lemonade the Bible, to use your uncouth expression, and to ransack the Vatican and take its wealth and give it to the needy. From this source may be explained the numerous delusions of modern prophecies, which relate the gossiping of atheists producing hallucinations of a feverish repose.

In consequence of afflictions of the ear, the atheist, under the pain of torture, will insist that malicious Demons contrive to blow streams of infected air into this organ; and that by means of what they term hearkening wires and whiz-pipes, various obscenities and blasphemies are forced into their minds; and it is not unusual for those who, during torture, are in a greatly despondent condition like that of Bunuel, to assert that they distinctly hear voices telling them, and with no holding back, to go right ahead and debunk the Resurrection.

When a Catholic is in the purest state of a Catholic mind, the Catholic is more liable to be lead by the ear, than through the other senses, because of the power of God's words. An enhancement of faith shall cause the person so affected, to hear the coursing of words through the Holy Ghost, the ringing of Church bells, or the sounds of choirs. And on some occasions, although the relation seems tinged with superstition, men of undeviating veracity and of the highest attainments, have asserted, that they have heard themselves

being called. Ring a bell Bad Clergy? That is hearing one's name
pronounced by the voice of an unknowable being at a great distance,
far beyond the possibility of being reached by any sound uttered by
the human mouth. This phenomenon is, I think, as wonderful as any
other mysterious fact, which many people are very slow to believe, or
rather, indeed, reject with an obstinate contempt. And it is this I say
to you Bad Clergy. Hear the voice of your calling, and the mystery of
the Resurrection is a mystery no more, provided you allow into your
mind the voice of God every second of your life."

4. Something About Mary

Transfixed by the power of LJK's voice the Bad Clergy were unable
to move from their seats. They remained seated and simply stared
into the now vacant stage. The other two just looked goosey. An
announcement comes over the intercom. "For the benefit of the
Bad Clergy the Jesus Transubstantiation Centre for Lost Souls
management has, for their ongoing entertainment, a part broadcasting
of the manifesto concerning the true condition of the Virgin Mary.
Broadcasted daily to packed audiences in the Vatican in many
languages the cult of the Virgin Mary is a reminder to all Catholics
of her fundamental importance in all Catholic life. As this broadcast
is normally in Latin there will be a delay of a few seconds after each
sentence, sorry for the hissing sound, before the English translation
is presented, ably compiled and narrated by the very reverend Father
John Gilroy." And in a breathy voice inspired by the virginal Abigail
of Number 96 fame, Father Gilroy speaks eternally thus:

But while in the most Blessed Virgin the Church has already reached
perfection without spot or wrinkle, so virginal and pure, the faithful must
still strive to conquer sin and increase their holiness. !!!!!!!!!!!!!!!!!!!!!!!
And they turn their eyes to the Blessed Mary who shines forth to the
whole community as the exquisite model of virtues. !!!!!!!!!!!!!!!!!!!!!!!
Devoutly meditating on her and contemplating her in the light of the
Word made man, the Church reverently penetrates deeper into the great
mystery of the Incarnation and thus is becoming more like her loyal
spouse. !!!!!!!!!!!!!!!!!!!!! Having entered deeply into the history of
salvation, Mary, unites in her person Catholics and re-echoes the most
important doctrines of the Faith: and when she is the subject of
preaching and worship she prompts the faithful to come; her son, in his
sacrifice and by the love of the Father. !!!!!!!!!!!!!!!!!!!!! Seeking after
the glory of Christ, the Church becomes more like her ideal self, and
continues to progress in faith, hope and charity, seeking and doing the
will of God in all things. !!!!!!!!!!!!!!!!!!!!!! The Church, therefore, in her
apostolic work too, rightly looks to her who gave birth to Christ, who
was thus conceived of the Holy Spirit and born of a virgin, in order that
through the Church he is born and reborn and increase in the hearts of
the faithful. !!!!!!!!!!!!!!!!!!!!!!! In her life the Virgin was a model of
perfect motherly love by which all who join in the Church's apostolic

214

mission for the regeneration of mankind should be animated. !!!!!!!!!!!!!!!!!!!!! Mary has by grace been exalted above all angels and men to a place second only to her Son, as the most holy Mother of God who was involved in the mysteries of Christ: she is rightly honoured by a special cult in the Church.

And there's more !!!!!!!!!!!!!!!!!!!! From the earliest times the Blessed Virgin is honoured under the title of Mother of God, whose protection the faithful take refuge together in prayer in all their perils and needs. !!!!!!!!!!!!!!!!!!!! Accordingly, following the Council of Ephesus, there was a remarkable growth in the cult of the people of God towards Mary, in veneration and love, in invocation and imitation, according to her own prophetic words: "All generations shall call me Blessed, because he that is mighty hath done great things to me." !!!!!!!!!!!!!!!!!!!! It is fitting to consider her place in the mystery of the Church. !!!!!!!!!!!!!!!!!!!! The Virgin Mary is acknowledged and honoured as being truly the Mother of God and of the redeemer. !!!!!!!!!!!!!!!!!!!! She is clearly the mother of the followers of Christ since she has by her charity joined in bringing about the birth of believers in the Church, who are members of its corpus delicatus. !!!!!!!!!!!!!!!!!!!! Mary's role in the Church is inseparable from her virginal union with God and Christ and flows directly from it. !!!!!!!!!!!!!!!!!!!! Thus the Blessed Virgin advances in her pilgrimage of faith, and faithfully perseveres in her union with her Son unto the cross. !!!!!!!!!!!!!!!!!!!! There she stood, in keeping with the divine plan, enduring with her only begotten Son the intensity of his suffering, joining herself with his sacrifice in her mother's heart, and lovingly consenting to the immolation of this victim, born of her: to be given, by the same Christ Jesus dying on the cross, as a mother to his disciple. !!!!!!!!!!!!!!!!!!!! After her Son's Ascension, Mary aided the beginnings of the Church by her constant prayers. !!!!!!!!!!!!!!!!!!!! In her association with the apostles and several women, Mary by her prayers implored the gift of the Spirit. !!!!!!!!!!!!!!!!!!!! The Immaculate Virgin, preserved free from all stain of original sin, when the course of her earthly life was finished, was taken up body and soul into Heavenly glory, and exalted by the Lord as Queen over all things, so that she might be the more fully conformed to her Son, the Lord of lords and conqueror of sin and death. !!!!!!!!!!!!!!!!!!!! In giving birth she kept her virginity !!!!!!!!!!!!!!!!!!!! She conceived the living God and, by her prayers, will deliver Catholic souls from death. !!!!!!!!!!!!!!!!!!!! By her complete adherence to the Father's will, to his Son's redemptive work, and to every prompting of the Holy Spirit, the Virgin Mary is the Church's model of faith and charity. !!!!!!!!!!!!!!!!!!!!! Thus she is a pre-eminent and wholly unique member of the Church, indeed she is the exemplary realization of the Church. !!!!!!!!!!!!!!!!!!!! Her role in relation to the Church and to all humanity goes as far as God himself. !!!!!!!!!!!!!!!!!!!!!! In a wholly singular way she cooperated by her obedience, faith, hope, and burning charity in the Saviour's work of restoring supernatural life to souls. !!!!!!!!!!!!!!!!!!!!! For this reason she is a mother to all Catholics in the order of grace.

So much more !!!!!!!!!!!!!!!!!!!!!! She is Queen of the entire human race faithful to the exact meaning of her name, who is exalted above all things save only God himself. !!!!!!!!!!!!!!!!!!!!! Mary is Queen who is always vigilant to intercede with the king whom she bore. !!!!!!!!!!!!!!!!!!!! Because the Virgin Mary was raised to such a lofty dignity as to be the mother of the King of kings, it is deservedly and by every right that the Church has honoured her with such a title as Queen of Heaven where the seraphim wait upon her and the ranks of the Heavenly army bow before her. !!!!!!!!!!!!!!!!!!!!! Art, which is based upon Catholic principles and is animated by its spirit as something faithfully interpreting the sincere and freely expressed devotion of the faithful, should portray Mary as Queen and Empress seated upon a royal throne adorned with royal insignia, crowned with the royal diadem and surrounded by the host of angels and saints in Heaven, and ruling not only over nature and its powers but also over the machinations of the dastardly Satan. !!!!!!!!!!!!!!!!!!!!! She is a Queen, since she bore a son who, at the very moment of His conception, because of the hypostatic union of the human nature with the Word, was also born as man King and Lord of all things. !!!!!!!!!!!!!!!!!!!! God has willed her to have an exceptional role in the work of our eternal salvation. !!!!!!!!!!!!!!!!!!!!!!

All this is for your own good !!!!!!!!!!!!!!!!!!!!! Let all try to approach with greater trust the throne of grace and mercy of the Queen and Mother, and beg for strength in adversity, light in darkness, consolation in sorrow. !!!!!!!!!!!!!!!!!!!!! Let all strive to free themselves from the slavery of sin and offer an unceasing homage, filled with filial loyalty, to their Queenly Mother. !!!!!!!!!!!!!!!!!!!!! Let her Churches be cleaved by the faithful, her feast-days honoured. !!!!!!!!!!!!!!!!!!!!! May the beads of the Rosary be in the hands of all, even those who are unfortunately limbless. !!!!!!!!!!!!!!!!!!! May Catholics and future Catholics gather, in small numbers and large, to sing her praises in Churches, in homes, in hospitals, in prisons, at sports stadiums. !!!!!!!!!!!!!!!!!!!!!! May Mary's name be held in highest reverence, a name sweeter than honey and more precious than jewels. !!!!!!!!!!!!!!!!!!!!! May none utter blasphemous words, the sign of a defiled soul, against that name graced with such dignity and revered for its motherly goodness. !!!!!!!!!!!!!!!!!!!!! Let no one be so bold as to speak a syllable which lacks the respect due to her name. !!!!!!!!!!!!!!!!!!! It should come about that all Catholics, in honouring and imitating their sublime Queen and Mother, will realize they are truly brothers and sisters, and with all envy and avarice thrust aside, will promote love of each other, respect the rights of the weak, and cherish peace. !!!!!!!!!!!!!!!!!!!! No one should think himself or herself a son or daughter of Mary, worthy of being received under her powerful protection, unless, like her, he or she is just, gentle and pure, and shows a sincere desire for true brotherhood and sisterhood, not harming or injuring but rather helping and comforting others. !!!!!!!!!!!!!!!!!!!!! May the powerful Queen of creation, whose radiant glance banishes storms and tempests and brings back cloudless skies, look upon innocent and tormented children with eyes of mercy. !!!!!!!!!!!!!!!!!!!!!! May the Virgin, who is able to subdue violence beneath her foot, grant to the persecuted Church in this year of 1980 the rightful freedom to practice openly, so that, while serving the cause of the Gospel, it may also contribute to the strength and progress of nations by its harmonious co-operation, by the practice of its extraordinary virtues which are a glowing example in the midst of moral turmoil. !!!!!!!!!!!!!!!!!!!!! It's the Virgin's dearest wish that you get it Bad Clergy.

Clancy:
Hola. Bad dreams are made of these.

Muldoon:
(delirious) I might as well have been watching sad iguanas polluting sandpits during a Jacques Tati dress rehearsal and be stumbling over a mood swing like I was channelling my afflictions and then I'd be finding myself co-depending with nuff nuffs and them like pious necromancers who alter their egos for Sunday Mass. And then what would they do to me when they catch me. I'm in civvies and there's

no forgiveness. No more eternity. Not until Monday!

The goosey two think in unison: Not in the willy willy never-never!!!

Kelly:
I'll scream for the Lag Motor. That was too bloody intense. I just
want a quiet life.

Mahone:
(crying) I never knew the Virgin was so beautiful. She's more than
everything. I'm a small priest who's got a lot smaller.

Kelly:
Laaaaaaaaaaaag Motor rumble yea gizzards and turbine and spirit us
away.

Suddenly the Motor bursts through the tent's gothic doorway with its
doors open and it sucks the Bad Clergy and the goosey two in. Kelly
gets behind the wheel and reverses halfway down Concord Rd. Then
the Lag Motor does a huge burnout before it gets back into the left
lane. Not long after, the police pull them over. While one remains in
the car, the other slowly walks over to Kelly.

Constable Blue: Evenin' brethrens. *(casts his eye into the cabin)*
Looks like you boys just seen the Devil. Ha Ha. Have your license
please. Father Kelly eh! You're drivin's a bit reckless. You haven't
been on the grass have you? 'Ere blow into this. Hmmn dodgy
reading. I like your beast. Great duco. Father Kelly, eh. I could
book you, you know that. But I'm a sinful Catholic, and you know
that too. So's Constable White over there. We're friendly you see.
Still like the look of someone, like you lot, and let 'em off. Give
'em a warning. I see your motor doesn't have a license plate. Better
get a couple. You can get 'em personalised these days. How about
Christone or maybe Devilone. That'll suit. Give us a blessing
wontcha. Got troubling with me guilt. Been messin' with my wife's
ex off duty. We're mates like, but sometimes I like to smell his
armpits. Know what I mean. Bloke stuff. Bonding like them convicts
did back in them rough colonial days. It was Hell back then. Then
you'd know all about Hell. Warning us sinners like you know what

you're talking about. And still the best in the business I might add. My buddy's into Kings Cross Whispers and that sort of stuff. I tell him to get a lady or two but he won't listen. Loves the guilt he says. He gets rid of it in confession knowing it'll come back as soon as he leaves. Forgiveness eh! Works a treat! Do you think we're cynical? I reckon he needs a helping hand. The stain always remains the same. Forgive me fathers. Please forgive me. Then I've got temporary relief. Roadside gifts don't do it for me anymore. Been his buddy for too long. Got to know each other like. We're a team and the station lads leave us alone. As long as we keep our bookings up. Help out in traffic. Give us a blessing won'tcha. *(Kelly does the sign of the cross, mumbles a few venerate words about the Cloying Pitch, and then silently let's out trouser incense from beneath the seat of his Buster Keaton pants.)*

It is not long before the Lag Motor is back on Parramatta Road. The Bad Clergy haven't spoken a word. Not until the Lag Motor parks itself outside the abattoirs.

5. Sympathy for the Beast

*A brief history of the Homebush Abattoir and something of the
slaughter process.*

The Homebush Abattoirs were officially opened in 1913, however,
processing did not commence fully for a further 12 months. By
1923 the Homebush Abattoir was the biggest of its kind in the
Commonwealth and employed up to 1600 men. It had a killing
capacity of 18000 to 20000 sheep, 1500 cattle, 2000 pigs and 1300
calves per day. By-products of the works included tallow, dripping,
fertiliser, oil, sinews, hoofs, hair, glue pieces, bones and horns,
all of which were sold at profit. Maintenance of the facility was a
constant problem for the Abattoir administrators and following the
Second World War, the State opted to decentralise slaughterhouses
and a number of new abattoirs were established in country areas. In
the 1960s at the commencement of meat exports, the facilities were
modernised. This modernisation program between 1965 and 1976
saw the fitting of new machinery into old buildings and the patching
and repair of degraded structures. In 1979, the facilities were
assessed and found to be near the end of their economic life and all
renovation work was ceased. The constant repair of aged buildings
was stopped and export licenses were relinquished in 1980.

Upon arrival at the abattoir (either the day before or on the day of
slaughter), animals are provided with water, shade, shelter and feed
as appropriate. Sick or injured animals are segregated and given
appropriate treatment or humanely euthanized.

Within 24 hours before slaughter, animals are checked by a meat
safety inspector to ensure they are healthy and their meat therefore
likely to be suitable for human consumption.

Just prior to slaughter, animals are walked up a raceway into the
abattoir where they enter the stunning box. This box separates
the animal off from the rest of the animals in the raceway. Within
seconds of entering this box, an operator stuns the animal. With
sheep or pigs, this may be an electrical stun. With cattle, this may
be a captive bolt. Both devices are aimed at the brain. Pigs may also

be stunned using carbon dioxide. This stunning process ensures the animal is unconscious and insensible to pain before being bled out.

As soon as the animal is stunned, it is shackled by a hind leg and then, within seconds, the large blood vessels are severed to induce bleeding (a process known as 'sticking'). Because the animal has been stunned, it is unconscious and does not feel or experience the shackling or sticking process. The animal does not regain consciousness or sensibility before dying due to loss of blood.

After slaughter, the meat safety inspector examines the carcass to determine whether it is suitable for human consumption or whether the carcass is best used for pet food, pharmaceutical material or should be condemned.

The abattoir workers manage animals before and during the slaughtering process. They remove hides and internal organs and split the carcasses using saws. They trim, bone and slice carcasses so they are ready for sale or further processing. They may package meat products and they may also be involved with processing hides and by-products, as well as loading meat into trucks.

Within two hours of the animal being stunned and slaughtered, the carcass is placed in a refrigerator for chilling or freezing. The process of slaughtering and further processing is designed to either destroy pathogens or prevent pathogenic growth, and to produce edible meat. In Australia, the killing of animals for food, fibre and other animal products (referred to as 'slaughter') is underpinned by the Australian standard for the hygienic production and transport of meat and meat products for human consumption. As the word suggests, the main objective of the standard is to ensure food safety, however, it also includes an animal welfare component.

6. Blazwaorden

Kelly's indream.

When he is starving for vegetables, and after the Bad Clergy's first
ever visit to the Homebush Abattoirs, Kelly often sleeps fitfully in his
sparse bedroom in the Granville Crib, pondering the transmuting of
the slaughterful cattle and imagining himself as cattle eating himself
and naturally he is very afraid.

Indream he hears the abattoir cattle speaking as one like humans do
when praying in church:

Great are we, and great is the work of the slaughtermen transmuting us
from flesh to meat and their slaughtering heat which is cooled by vast
refrigerators, and great is our number, for our flesh is infinite. And it is
the slaughtermen who are the ordained to transmute us from blood and
muscle into meat; men, who are humble particles of their inspiration
above; men who bear about them something immortal, men who are
witnesses to Edens of meat irresistible: and so it is that slaughtermen
transmute us. We must awaken to the delights in their transmuting; for
we are made for immaculate consumption, and our hearts are very
restless, until we are given in slaughter. Grant any meat eater to know
and to understand which is first, to eat us raw or to transmute us. And
again, grant them an attempt to get to know us before they eat us. We
were flesh and blood and now we are meat. Vegetarians cannot know us,
because they do not eat our flesh. Those who do not eat meat try to tell
of us as being other than what we really are. Or, it is rather, that
carnivores know us that they may also love us. But how do carnivores
know when the spiritual reason for our slaughter is not believed? Yea all
should believe by listening to the true words of the meat preacher. For all
who seek our flesh shall enjoy it: for all who seek meat shall find it and
they shall enjoy it. For all who eat us know that we are fully transmuted
from flesh to meat. They will seek us, by asking for meat at the butchery;
and they will know us, believing in meat; for to carnivores, flesh must be
eaten. All who hunger shall want meat, which the supermarket gladly
gives to them for a special price, and where the taste inspires them to
cook meat in a variety of ways, through the ministry of the television
chef.

222

And how shall meat eaters call to use carrots? Since, when they call for them, they shall be calling them to empty bellies. And what room is there within them, whither other vegetables can also come into them? How can potatoes come into them, potatoes made of starch? Is there, indeed, enough room in meat eater bellies to contain both meat AND vegetables. Will meat AND vegetables, which they dream to transmute together, and wherein has made them, sustain them? Or because everything which exists could not exist without meat, does therefore what exists be meat? Since meat eaters must exist, why do they desire that meat should enter into them, which is not a part of them? Why? Because they are afraid to go without it; for meat is more than being just for the taking. And because they cannot eat their own flesh or other human flesh. When meat eaters go to a meat restaurant, they expect meat to be on the menu. By transmutation meat eaters could themselves be meat, for meat is in them and of them; and they are meat, which is of all things, by which are all things, in which are all things. Therefore why do meat eaters call for meat, since they are also meat? How should meat enter into them? For where else can meat eaters go beyond the butcher and the supermarket, so that meat should come into them and fill them from the gullet to the anus? When they cannot get meat should they eat themselves? Are meat eaters as wholesome as the meat which lives outside of them? And how can vegetables be eaten on their own? And why is fish meat?

And more questions! Are the butcher and the supermarket also made of meat, since meat always brightens the displays? Or does meat fill them to overflow, since they cannot contain all meat? And where, when the butcher and supermarket are filled, does the remainder meat go? Or does meat, which contains all things, fill everything else by containing itself? And when meat is thrust out onto humanity, it is not cast down, but uplifts; meat is not to be dissipated, but to gather all meat eaters, and closet cannibals, and all who dare to eat meat, including subversive vegetarians. But does meat, which fills all things, also fill everything with its whole self? Or, since all things cannot contain meat wholly, do they contain remnants of it such as memory and feelings? And is all meat eaten at once the same part of the whole? Or is each its own part, the greater more, the smaller less? And is there a part of one part of meat greater, another less? Or, is meat wholly everywhere, while nothing wholly contains meat? So many questions.

7. After the Sun

Kelly:
'tis queer we're back here yet again. I thought I told the Lag Motor
one Hell in a night is enough.

Muldoon:
The abattoir's in sleep down. Not hearin' much cattle ghosting noise
and fright tonight.

Clancy:
'Tis folly calling them from their humble abodes. Then I suppose,
they are the spirits of the unhappy dead.

Mahone:
Let us pray.
O Adorable pasture lands
Cast upon the cattle your weatherful glance.
Look at these souls which you fed
And who suffer far from you in unutterable grief.
Look at these poor servants of the dinner plate
They know little of how they are to be done.

For the sake of our glorious Virgin
Legendary mother of the Christ
And the Bad Clergy's mother too!
Please alleviate the sufferings of these meaty souls;
And to these which labour in the miserable life
Grant them the bliss of eternal grazing.

We are the best sinners
But in obedience to your command mighty Jesus
We dare to intercede for our captive brethren.
Deign by your Holy Sacrifice
To transform transubstantiation
And put your body in their place.

O gentle Heart of Jesus
Ever present in the Blessed Sacrament
Ever consumed with burning love
For the poor captive souls in Homebush

Have a plan for them.

Be not severe in your judgments
But let some drops of Your Precious Blood
Fall upon the devouring flames
Of the boners and cutters
So they be blind to their movements.

And, Merciful Saviour
Send your angels to conduct them
To a place of refreshment
Grass and peace.

We demented souls
As ones sometimes devoted to animal rights
We promise never to forget them
And continually to pray for their release.
We beseech the Christ to respond to this dilemma
Which we make to you
And to obtain for us from God
With whom you are so powerful on behalf of the living
That they be free from the dangers of spit roasts and BBQ's.

We beg both for themselves
And for their relations and pigs
Friends and fellow grazers
Safety in their lives
And the grace of perseverance in good
Whereby you may save their hides.
Obtain for them peace of heart;
Assist them in protest actions;
Succour animal rights needs;
Console and defend them from dangers.

Muldoon:
How marvellous it is that prayers are like burning Churches which
illuminate the darkest of nights.

Clancy:
Burning witches did it better.

8. Once there were No Facts

15 minutes of silence followed before the Family got back into the
Lag Motor for the journey back to the Granville Crib. And then out
of the blue Mahone began to talk trance-like and in priest speak about
the Immaculate Conception.

Mahone:
By the grace granted by God, and in view of the merits of Jesus
Christ, the Saviour of humanity, Mary is exempt from all stain of
original sin.

Clancy:
Tranced I says she was made exempt from all stain of original sin at
the first moment of her liveliness, and sanctifying grace was given to
her before sin could have taken effect in her soul.

Muldoon:
Don't leave me bruvvers! The immunity from original sin was given to
Mary by a singular exemption from a universal law through the same
merits of Christ, by which other men are cleansed from sin by baptism.

Mahone:
Mary needed the redeeming Saviour to obtain this exemption, and to
be delivered from the universal necessity and debt of being subject to
original sin.

Muldoon:
I'll raise you Mahone. The person of Mary, in consequence of her
origin from the First Bloke, should have been subject to sin, but,
being the new Eve who was to be the mother of the new Bloke,
she was, by the eternal counsel of God and by the merits of Christ,
withdrawn from the general law of original sin.

Kelly:
Raise you again me Muldy. Her redemption was the very masterpiece
of Christ's redeeming wisdom. He is the redeemer who paid the
greatest debt so that it may not be incurred by us who have fallen and
for the Redeemer to recoup through his love and forgiveness.

226

Muldoon:
Not enough Kels. She, full of grace demonstrates a unique abundance of grace, a supernatural, Godlike state of soul, which finds its explanation only in the Immaculate Conception of Mary.

Kelly:
Beat this. Mary is all fair, O our love, and there is not a spot on her. She is exempt from defilement and corruption, worthy only of God, immaculate of the immaculate, most complete sanctity, perfect justice, neither deceived by the persuasion of the serpent, nor infected with his poisonous breathings, created in a condition more sublime and glorious than all them other natures.

Muldoon:
You've got me goin' Kels. Most holy Lady, Mother of God, alone most pure in soul and bod, alone exceeding all perfection of purity, alone made in your entirety the home of all the graces of the Most Holy Spirit, and hence exceeding beyond all compare even the angelic virtues in purity and sanctity of soul and bod. Lady most holy, all-pure, all-immaculate, all-stainless, all-undefiled, all-incorrupt, all-inviolate, spotless robe of Him who clothes Himself with light as with a garment, flower unfading, purple woven by God, alone most immaculate.

Kelly:
That's a tough get. Fortunate we are the men who are the best at discussing the most holy bod of the Virgin. Father Gilroy must've got to us, eh bruvs!

Mahone:
She's as pure as air for no ordinary man can see it. And her voice.

Muldoon:
That was Gilroy's. But it'll do.

Kelly:
And we thank Her for giving us a powerful concupiscent imagination.

Clancy:
Our Mother of the Redeemer was made free from the power of sin
and from the first moment of her existence. God could give her this
privilege, because He can, and therefore He gave it to her.

Muldoon:
Ah my dears, thinking about her, us alone in our ragged beds is
gonna help us get our bit of rest at night, won't it!

Kelly:
Which stick am I meant to use to change gear? Ha ha.

Clancy:
The Lag always knows Kelly, just in case you crack a stiffy from all
this talk.

Muldoon:
Sometimes indream I catch the Virgin in flagrante delicto. I'm her
special observer of her toilette routine just in case word gets out she
was a made up character, and I can defend her and say, no way!

Kelly:
No priest has EVER been accused of being a pervert Muldy. You're
not the only priest who indreams this way.

Mahone:
Who dare say we're perverts. We're theologians who look after The
Redeemer's intimate bits, and the Virgin's!

9. Living After Death

Muldoon:
Eh, what's that galloot over there *(pointing from the back seat)*
doin'?

The Family stop and look across the Parramatta Road to see a bloke
wearing a black bowler hat and a two piece black and white striped
costume, white gloves, yellow suspenders and hobnail type boots;
and who was moving strangely and slowly underneath a bright lamp
post situated in front of a fish and chip shop.

The Lag Motor pulls over and out gets Muldoon still dapper in his
Buster Keaton togs and walks over to the man. His face is covered in
white paint, with thick black eyeliner and teardrops down the cheeks,
his eyebrows are painted jet black, his kiss lips dark red lipstick.

Muldoon:
What's goin' on here Mr Mime?

The Mime:
I've been called to entertain you at this ungodly hour with a mime
rendition of the Stations of the Cross.

Muldoon:
Oh yeah, you takin' the piss? Hey bruvs *(he shouts)* this guy's doin'
the Stations of the Cross for us.

The Family rest and the goosey two get out of the Lag Motor and
join Muldoon. They surround the mime who continues his slow
movements.

Muldoon:
Show us what it's about then.

And without any further speaking the mime begins to move and
gesture.

Don't remember the order, do you Mahone?

Mahone:
I'll interpret eh! *(the mime begins his show)*

See how this bloke's got half his face covered with his hand, and the other one is shaking and he's kind of squatting, that's when Jesus was in the Garden of Gethsemane, and look his face is sorrowful and he's waving his body like he's been accosted like when the Big J is betrayed by Judas and arrested, now he's upright and gripping the post and see how he's trying to climb it as well, that's when the big J is condemned by the Sanhedrin, now he's rapidly passing his hands across his face, that's when the big J is denied by Peter *(looks at Kelly)*, now see how he's pushing air with his hands away from his body, that's obviously when he's been judged by Pilate, now look how our mime is bent over doubled and hiding and protecting his body when the big J is being scourged, O fantastic, this is great look how the mime is frantically whacking his head and it looks like he's planting something on it and his face is in agony, well that's when the big J gets his crown of thorns, and now he's bent double and he can barely stand like when the big J got his cross, and he's walking on the same spot, the big J doesn't want to go anywhere, and he's walking bent, and see how he's standing straighter and his face is in incredible agony, well that's when Simon helps the big J carry his cross, O this is weird, what's the mime doing? looks like he's puffing his chest, and thrusting his hips, did the big J really do that when he met the women of Jerusalem?, might be a bit of poetic license here, now this is the easy bit, see how he's standing upright and his arms are outstretched, and he's jerking once, twice, three times, and now he's not moving, and his head is lolling to one side, that's when the big J is crucified, have to wait awhile now bruvs, not much happens until, wait for it, there he goes a big jerk, that's when the big J cops a lance in his side, now the mime is looking over and mouthing words, that's when the big J promises his kingdom to the repentant thief hanging on the cross next to him, and now he's looking down and smiling moving his head slowly left to right and back again, now that's when the big J entrusts Mary and John to each other so's they can maintain the faith, now get ready for it, here it comes, the cry of anguish, the angry face, the big gasp and then his head flopping for one last time which is of course is

when the big J dies on the cross, now I reckon we'll have to wait around
for a couple of minutes bruvs.

Kelly:
Why's that?

Mahone:
Well they've got to make sure the big J is dead before he's laid in
his tomb, the final drama, and as I speak the mime here is slowly
dropping to the ground, and see how he's rolling around now, like
he's being covered with something, and now he's still. It's all over
folks, that is until the really big surprise happens.

Muldoon:
Let me guess, the Resurrection.

Kelly:
We're not gonna wait around for that, are we?

Muldoon:
Nah *(and heads across the road to the Lag Motor)*

The Family rest and the goosey two soon follow without a thank you
and the mime remains lying down on the footpath. As the Lag Motor
pulls out the mime begins to levitate and it's Clancy who happens
to look back and sees the mime levitating past the shop front's
windows, then the roof, and into the sky, Clancy's eyes following
the mime higher and higher until the mime is out of Clancy's sight.
Clancy doesn't say a word in case it was real and not a hallucination.

Indream the big J once spoke to Clancy about his Resurrection. On
recalling it Clancy was a bit suspicious as to whether it really was the
big J because the voice sounded a lot like Gomez Addams.

"In a nutshell Clancy, resurrection is the rising again from the
dead, the resumption of life. To elaborate, all people Clancy, all
people, including you and your fellow Bad Clergy, who are not
unreformable, even at this late stage, will rise again with their own
bodies which they now go about in: but youthful and in perfect

health. For those that sleep in the dust of the Earth, they shall awake unto life everlasting, dead men shall arise and live, the slain shall rise again, the Earth shall disclose her blood, and she shall cover her slain no more. Know Clancy that I live, and on the last day even you and the Family rest shall rise out of the Earth. I did preach there is everlasting life for each and all, remember, despite your scepticism, and that I rose from the dead, and in doing so I have shown you the way. What you must do Clancy is believe, believe with every fibre of your body, which, by the way is soon to die.

As the soul is naturally of the body, its perpetual separation from the body is unnatural. As the soul is the partner of the body's crimes, what they are is a matter of conscience, the companion of all virtues, and my justice demands that the body shares in the soul's punishment and its rewards. As the soul separates from the body upon death it is naturally imperfect, the consummation of its happiness, filled with every good, demands the resurrection of the body. Look at my life Clancy and you will see. And there have been plenty of other documented examples as you should be aware. Jonah in the whale's belly, the three children in the fiery furnace, Daniel in the lions' den, the carrying away of Henoch and Elias, the raising of the dead, the blossoming of Aaron's rod. And in nature you see the grain of seed dying and springing up again, the egg, the season of the year, the succession of day and night.

All shall rise from the dead in their own, in their entirety, and as immortal bodies; but the good shall rise to the resurrection of life, the wicked to the resurrection of judgment. It would destroy the very idea of resurrection, if the dead were to rise in bodies not their own. So keep your eye on Kelly, Clancy. Again, my Resurrection, like the creation, is perhaps my main work; hence, since the creation all things are perfect from my hand, so the resurrection of all things must be perfectly restored by my same omnipotent hand, provided Clancy, you've done your bit to my satisfaction. But remember, there is a difference between the earthly and the risen body; for the risen bodies of both saints and sinners shall be invested with immortality. This admirable restoration of nature is the result of my glorious triumph over death. But while the just shall enjoy an endless joy in their entirety in order that they know forgiveness, the wicked shall

232

seek death, and they shall not find it, desiring to die, and death shall fly from them. And their souls will burn eternally in the fires of Hell. And they will yearn for me and I will not listen and I will ignore them, for they did not do what they were told on Earth and repent and seek my forgiveness.

Three characteristics, identity, entirety, and immortality, will be common to the risen bodies of both the just and the wicked. But the bodies of the just shall be distinguished by four transcendent endowments, often called qualities. The first is impassibility, which shall place them beyond the reach of pain and inconvenience. Meanwhile the bodies of the damned will undie; they shall be subject to heat and cold, and all manner of pain. The next quality is the glory of the eternally good which shall sparkle like a jewel. Some will have the glory of the Sun, others the glory of the Moon, others the glory of the stars, depending upon their merits. The third quality is that of agility by which the body shall be freed from its slowness of motion, and endowed with the capability of moving with the utmost facility and quickness wherever the soul pleases. The fourth quality is subtlety, by which the body becomes subject to the absolute dominion of the soul. The body participates in the soul's more perfect and spiritual life to such an extent that it becomes itself like a spirit which was demonstrated when I passed from one life to another.

So you see Clancy there is much to look forward to in your resurrection. Being clergy you are halfway there and of course much more is expected of you. You have the word incarnate within you and technically you should know better. But as you know I am forgiving, and very tolerant, and you'd be surprised to know how much I understand the difficulties you face in this secular world of 1980. So too this Church of mine which has certainly not gone to script since I left this mortal coil."

And this indream haunts Clancy again as the Lag Motor gently rumbles along an almost empty Parramatta Road.

10. A Single Motor Vehicle Accident

But first.

*Lyrics to a lost song called Word into Flesh written by Placates and
meant for Buffalo's Volcanic Rock.*

And the Word was made into flesh
And the weak man is naturally flesh
Then God emptied himself into man
And without sin God became a man.

Human and divine, one of the same
And they found out Jesus was his name
A union of two natures in one lad
God the Father being also his dad.

They said he was an individual completely rational.
And no other person has ever come before.
His appearance in Jerusalem was sensational.
In no time at all his death was becoming lore.

Of human nature and then some
He did what no human has done
Christ had natures mostly human
Him the perfection of perfect man.

The Word hadn't actually changed
It was Flesh which was rearranged
In the womb of the Blessed Mother
With God the obvious Father.

They said he was an individual completely rational.
And no other person has ever come before.
His appearance in Jerusalem was sensational.
In no time at all his death was becoming lore.

The Body of Christ will suffer pain
It was sin which took not its gain
Jesus was known never to be sick
Freeing him to heal the sadly sick.

Jesus was destined never to be old
He was handsome, kindly and bold
Noble in bearing and a lovely form
Never cold and always warm.

They said he was an individual completely rational.
And no other person has ever come before.
His appearance in Jerusalem was sensational.
In no time at all his death was becoming lore.

In sinlessness Jesus gave himself
A wonderfully fleshy selfless self
Without sin Jesus is willing to save
This sick world so likely to deprave.

When he tasted, he wouldn't drink
To depravity he wouldn't sink
In joy he would endure the cross
His death was just a temporary loss.

They said he was an individual completely rational.
And no other person has ever come before.
His appearance in Jerusalem was sensational.
In no time at all his death was becoming lore.

The Humanity of Christ was holy
Not partly but always totally
There was his sanctifying grace
His work rate took up the pace.

His effective grace shone through
There was nothing he couldn't do
He abounds in supernatural powers
His golden heart parried the howlers.

They said he was an individual completely rational.
And no other person has ever come before.
His appearance in Jerusalem was sensational.
In no time at all his death was becoming lore.

In one person was the man-God
His divinity showed he was God
His human nature made him man
As one person he was God-man.

There is no-one better to adore
Even the clothes Jesus wore
Adore the sacred heart of Jesus
Who had come just to please us.

They said he was an individual completely rational.
And no other person has ever come before.
His appearance in Jerusalem was sensational.
In no time at all his death was becoming lore.

...Or so the wannabe rocker Placates wrote while listening to the record one night in his suburban bedroom. The lyrics went nowhere and Placates fell into despair. And from despair there arose a new vision of himself, as Persecutor.

While this diversion was taking place there is a single motor vehicle accident not far out of Clyde. A car appears to have veered off the road and crashed into a telegraph pole, causing it to snap in two. The occupants are two men and a woman. The men have been flung from the car and the woman is trapped in the mangled wreck. There are neither police nor ambulance when the Lag Motor arrives at the scene.

Muldoon:
Looks like these two blokes have gone to the afterlife. Not much the body can do with faces like that! What's in the car Kelly?

Kelly:
A Marilyn. Her body's all twisted and looks like her chest's impaled on the steering column. She's dead alright. The funny thing is I swear she looks like the barmaid we met at the Gag 'n Throttle.

Muldoon:
What, the Virgin Mary herself, allow me to cast my reverence over her wreck.

236

And with a gaze one blink short of a leer Muldoon looks into the cabin where the woman lies motionless and bleeding. Suddenly Muldoon lets out an anguished cry.

Muldoon:
It is true. She's the Virgin right here, her dead eyes still open, and dead before my eyes, how can this be, how can this be?

Kelly:
Are you sure Muldy? I'll get the Family rest over and we'll verify.

Muldoon:
No need Kelly, no need. No time anyway. They would be upset, even them two might show a bit of regret. It's time. Kelly, it's time to get a remembrance of her, to have her in the crib, our own special relic we can worship any God's time we choose.

Kelly:
You mean get something of her?

Muldoon:
Hopefully. Let me search her body. She's a mess for sure but let's see what flesh relic I can remove without much violation.

Kelly:
Hola, a memorial of the departed Mary, before her Annunciation into Heaven. What a way to bring to an end a great night. The Family rest'll get a relicious surprise when we get back to the Motor. Get something off her body. Her gear's ordinary, and I bet her panties'll be stained with you know what!

Muldoon:
I'll do me best Kels.

And with that Muldoon gets in the cabin, quickly removes the woman's broken seatbelt, gently pulls her body off the steering column, undresses her, runs his hands over her flesh and upon findings that her genitals have been severely lacerated *(which Muldoon had feared)*, he gently lifts her onto the passenger seat,

and puts her head and upper body over the rim of the passenger's
door which was framed by broken glass, and Muldoon, positioning
himself and leaning into the front cabin, blood splattered everywhere,
spreads open the woman's thighs, and upon bringing his face direct
to her genitals, Muldoon takes from his pocket a small flick-knife
and cuts hair from her mound of Venus, and quickly puts the hair
into a snotty rag, kisses her exposed labia, wipes his face, and then he
dresses her and gently places her body back onto the steering column.

Muldoon:
It is done Kels.

Kelly:
Hola! It's time for true worship. The Family'll be sanctified yet! And
Muldy, pin down a couple of miracles with it and they'll make you a
saint!

And as the Lag Motor quietly rumbles away from the scene, the
Police arrive at the scene, and the Lag Motor passes by unseen,
leaving behind the accident nice and clean, as though they had never
been.

Kelly:
We didn't give her the unctions Muldy.

Muldoon:
No need. She's too pure for us. Only She is annunciated. And we
merely tremble in her wake.

Clancy:
I give you the rules Muldy. Them holy bods of holy martyrs and of
others whose bods were the living members of Christ and the temple
of the Spirit Man, and which by Him are raised to eternal life and
glorified, are worshipped by the faithful, and us Muldy. And there'll
be none if there's useless honouring by the faithful, and vain visiting
of relic places to snaffle their aid; so that every superstition's got to
be removed and all filthy lucre abolished. Can't pervert the meaning
of relics. Oh no. And no new miracles of relics are good to go unless
our bishop whacks his seal on it.

Muldoon:
What he don't know won't hurt him eh!

Mahone:
I heard the Bish say in private that us Clergy shouldn't be so
stupidly incredulous to dismiss miracles not happening, even a
snotty handkerchief and a dirty apron of some saint which touches
a diseased body can cure it, and who's to say the Christ's bod itself
didn't get itself up from the canvas!

Muldoon:
Couldn't agree more!

Kelly:
When we see her locks floatin' in the venerable vegemite jar there'll
be no horror. Looking at her we'll see her sanctified and a blessing.
She'll be a great and unique offering. And as for touching her, if
that should be the Family's happiness, and it will, only we who have
experienced it and who have had our wish gratified can know how
much this is desirable and how worthy an aid it is to our aspiring
prayerfulness.

Muldoon:
She'll be solemnly transposed from that place of death to our place of
life, our heroic sanctity of her remembrance which any fair dinkum
worshipper would instantly understand and desire to be a part of.

Kelly:
Hola. Here here.

11. Sky Riot

Indream Satan returns again to Pope John Paul number 2. Satan is as usual bleeding everywhere. It holds out two beating hearts in its clawed hands. It is naked except for a pair of Bonds briefs (imported) girding its loins. And Satan tells the Pope it is as usual real happy with the Catholic Church. And in fact, after all these centuries of Papal visitations, it is its Church now. The frightened Pope asks Satan how it was so. Satan said it was no use to that Jesus bloke anymore, it being full of hypocrisy, corruption, sanctimony and the like. But that's your fault the Pope screamed. Satan laughs and says the Vatican City is Hell's Vegas on Earth and it is a perfect place for it to live in. And as it always needs Demons, the Pope and his mates are welcome to stay. All they have to do is keep up their 'good work'. The Pope screams and said he would rather abandon the Vatican City and move with his Curia to a little favela in Brazil and start again. Suit yourself said Satan. And good luck. You'll need it. Ha Ha. Satan then tells the Pope that the time of its takeover of the Vatican remains an uncertainty. The Pope asks why. It must be prophesised. Then Satan flew back into the Pope's amygdala. The heat in there is really hot.

Clancy:
No weed and I'm as wide minded as Oliver up there. And as straight as the spine of Jesus on the cross. Think I'm back into proper Clergy-speak. Like we do on Sundays, weddings and funerals.

Mahone:
Me too. Guess it's time for another Catholic did you know. Like did you know that strictly speaking prophecy means the foreknowledge of future events, divinely revealed, though it can apply to past events of which there is no memory, and to present hidden things which cannot be known by the natural light of reason.

Clancy:
Well bugger me. Really!

Mahone:
Prophecy consists of knowledge and is supernatural and infused by

240

God because it concerns things beyond the natural power of created intelligence. And the knowledge must be manifested either by words or signs, because the gift of prophecy is given primarily for the good of others, and therefore needs to be manifested in Divine light by which God reveals things concerning the unknown future and by which these things are in some way represented to the mind of the prophet, whose duty it is to manifest them to others.

Clancy:
Is that why Islam's prophet is giant?

Mahone:
The biggest that's ever lived.

Clancy:
By reason of the illumination of the mind prophecy may be either perfect or imperfect. It is perfect when not only the thing revealed, but the revelation itself, is made known it is perfect, and the prophet then knows it is God who speaks.

Mahone:
The prophecy is imperfect when the recipient does not know clearly or sufficiently from whom the revelation proceeds, or whether it is the prophetic or individual spirit that speaks. This is why Christianity has so many prophets. Some of them are likely to get it wrong.

Clancy:
Christian prophecy relies on foreknowledge, which takes place when God reveals future events which depend upon created free will which he sees present from eternity. They have reference to life and death, to wars and dynasties, to the affairs of Church and State, as well as to the affairs of individual life.

Mahone:
So this is why Christianity and Islam are kith and kin.

Clancy:
Both share the prophecy of predestination which takes place when God reveals what He alone will do, and what he sees present in

eternity and in His absolute decree. This includes not only the secret of predestination to grace and to glory, but also those things which God has absolutely decreed to do by His own supreme power, and which will infallibly come to pass.

Clancy:
So when things which are beyond the power of the mind are not in themselves knowable because their truth is not yet determined, the future of contingent things must then depend entirely upon the use of free will. This is regarded as the most perfect object of prophecy, because it is the most general and embraces all events which are in themselves unknowable.

Mahone:
Funny you should say that. I've heard a rumour on the Catholic grapevine that Satan keeps visiting His-Nibs in a dream telling him the Church is its greatest asset and that it will soon take over the Vatican to use as its earthly palace, and that His-Nibs and his Curia mates are more than welcome to stay on as Devils.

Clancy:
Really! When's that going to happen?

Mahone:
It supposed to be prophesised like the miracle of the second coming.

Clancy:
Reckon we'll be right for a job for awhile yet.

The others have dozed off just as The Lag Motor rumbles to a halt back at the Granville Crib and the weary Family fall out into the fibro house and into bed with their Flash clothes on and not saying a word to each other. Muldoon takes from his spotless rag the Virgin's hair and places it in a vegemite jar filled with fetid holy water. And to his bed he goes. Neither he nor the Family rest will see the pubic hair illuminate like Oliver above and peering through the kitchen window; and in the purest water that ever was, before the glow disappears forever at first light, when Oliver has also gone to bed.

12. Sleep Nevertheless

The Virgin Birth - How Is It So?

Placates speculates that a vaporous breath (The Holy Ghost) entered Mary's vagina restoring her virginity as it passed through her birth canal and into her womb, where the Holy Ghost supernaturally seeded the Jesus egg with sperm like no other, for it was shaped like a crucifix, fusing with the Jesus egg on the cusp of menstruation. After nine months the baby Jesus passed through Mary's birth canal restoring her virginity along the way; and screaming and bloody he entered the world as Christ Redeemer the Saviour of the World.

It is the dogma of the Catholic Church which teaches that the Blessed Mother of Jesus Christ was a virgin, before, during, and after the conception and birth of her Divine Son.

The Immaculate Conception.

Dogma. The virginity of the Blessed Lady was determined in the third canon of the Lateran Council held in the time of Pope Martin I in 649 AD. The Nicene-Constantinopolitan Creed, as recited in the Mass, expresses belief in Christ incarnate by the Holy Ghost of the Virgin Mary. The Apostles' Creed professes that Jesus Christ was conceived by the Holy Ghost, born of the Virgin Mary showing that the body of Jesus Christ was not sent down from Heaven, nor taken from Earth as was that of Adam, but that its human matter was given by Mary who partook in the creation of Jesus Christ's body as all mothers do in pregnancy, since Jesus Christ could not have been born of Mary in the same way Eve was born of Adam; that the embryo in whose development and growth into the infant Jesus Mary nurtured, was seeded not by male sexual action, but by the Divine power attributed to the Holy Ghost; that the supernatural influence of the Holy Ghost extended to the birth of Jesus Christ, not only to preserve Mary's integrity, but also reflecting Jesus Christ's birth as gift from the Eternal Father to the world, in that the Light from Light proceeded from Mary's womb as a light shed on the world; that the power of the Most High passed through the laws of nature without interfering with them; that the body of the Word formed by the Holy Ghost penetrated Mary's body after the manner of spirits.

The Virgin Birth.

Dogma. There can be no doubt as to the Church's truthful teaching regarding the perpetual virginity of the Blessed Virgin Mary and the virgin birth of Jesus Christ. The mystery of the virginal conception is furthermore taught by the third Gospel and confirmed by the first. According to St. Luke (1:34-35), "Mary said to the angel: How shall this be done, because I know not man?" And the angel answering, said to her: "The Holy Ghost shall come upon thee, and the power of the most High shall overshadow thee. And therefore also the Holy which shall be born of thee shall be called the Son of God." The sexual intercourse of a man is excluded in the conception of the Blessed Lord. According to St. Matthew, Mary's husband Joseph, when perplexed by the pregnancy of Mary, is told by the angel: "Fear not to take unto thee Mary thy wife, for that which is conceived in her, is of the Holy Ghost."

Perpetual Virginity.

Dogma. In the Constitution Ineffabilis Deus of 8 December, 1854, Pius IX pronounced and defined that the Blessed Virgin Mary, in the first instance of her conception and pregnancy, by a singular privilege and grace granted by God, in view of the merits of Jesus Christ, the Saviour of the human race, was made exempt from all stain of original sin at the moment of the creation of her soul and its infusion into her body. The essence of original sin was not removed from her soul, as it is removed from others by baptism. It was excluded, and was never in her soul, and simultaneously with the exclusion of sin. The state of original sanctity, innocence, and love, as opposed to original sin, was conferred upon her, by which gift every stain and fault, all depraved emotions, passions, and disabilities, essentially pertaining to original sin, were excluded. She was the perfect mother though she was not made exempt from the temporal penalties created by the sins of Adam - from sorrow, sickness, and death. The immunity from original sin was given to Mary as was given to Jesus Christ, by which other humans are best cleansed from sin by baptism. Mary needed the redeeming Saviour to obtain this exemption, and to be delivered from the universal necessity and debt of being subject to original sin. The person of Mary, in consequence of her origin from Adam, should have been subject to sin, but, being the new Eve who was to be the mother of the new Adam, she was, by the eternal counsel of God and by the merits of Christ, withdrawn from the general law of original sin. Her redemption was the very masterpiece of Christ's redeeming wisdom. Mary was born pure and she died pure and she ascended into Heaven pure. There is no holier simile for purity than virginity. Thus is Mary a virgin, now and forever.

And as always early on Saturday mornings after their big night out Pope John Paul Number 2 enters indream with the Bad Clergy in REM sleep, as well as the goosey two. And the sermon is always the same.

"You as Catholic priests have Christ for your foundation, and although you can fall away from union with Him, you and your depraved life, it is good that our Church promises your re-directed faith by which our Christ as your foundation will suffice to deliver you every time from the guilt of the continuance of your depravity, your so-called knapping dues, though it be with loss, since these things you like to do smoulder like unquenchable fires. I often ask God if priests who say they have faith, and yet have not the works, can have faith alone to save them. And shall the particularly depraved among you be saved? But as your habits are within Church, the true Church of God, your faith is expected to save you, and you shall rejoin our Christ through your repentant union with our Church.

Let us together ascertain how you are saved while your fires still smoulder. And this we may very readily learn from the image itself. In a building the foundation is first. Whoever has our Christ in their hearts, so that no earthly or temporal thing, not even the most dear and enjoyable are preferred over Him, they also have our Christ as their foundation. But when you prefer to do these things, and though you have the appearance of faith, our Christ might not appear to be your spiritual foundation. And when you, in contempt of wholesome precepts, seek forbidden gratifications, you are then clearly convicted of putting our Christ not first but last, since you have despised Him as your ruler, and have preferred to fulfil your own wicked lusts, in contempt of our Christ's commands and allowances. Accordingly, if any priest loves a child, and, attaching himself to the child, becomes one body, he does not have our Christ for his foundation. But since all priests unconditionally love the Virgin, and believe in the Virgin Birth, and love her as our Christ would love her, who can doubt that a priest also ultimately has our Christ for a foundation. And when a priest who loves the Virgin but who also carnally loves a child he knows not, his forgiveness is allowed because the act is by the Virgin loving priest, and the Church allows this carnal act as a venial fault. And therefore even among the worst of you are such who have our Christ for your foundation.

For though you do not prefer such affection for our Christ, He remains your foundation, although He also builds it with combustible materials; and therefore you are saved as if by fire. The fire of affliction shall burn such luxurious pleasures and earthly loves, and they are not damnable, because they are enjoyed as in spiritual wedlock. And of this fire the fuel is sorrow, and all the associated calamities which then consume these joys. Consequently the Church superstructure is agonized by its loss because of the things which you priests have found pleasure in. But by this fire you shall be saved through the virtue of the Church's foundation, and even if a legal prosecutor demands whether the Church would retain Christ or allow these things, the Church will unhesitatingly say Christ.

A fire shall try every priest's pastoral work whatever sort it is. If a priest's work abides, for a priest cares for the things of the Lord, and how he may please the Lord, which he has built thereupon, he shall receive a reward, that is, he shall reap the fruit of his pastoral care. But if a priest's work is also burned, he suffers loss, and for what he loved is not retained. But nevertheless he himself shall be saved, for no tribulation shall move him from his stable foundation, even if he's lost the sweetness of pure love. Here, then, we have a fire which destroys neither, but enriches the one, brings loss to the other, proving both as foundation for the love of our Christ.

The fire of which our Christ speaks is one where deeds on the side of right as well as those on the side of wrong are cast into it. For this fire is to try both, since Christ has declared that the final reckoning shall be revealed by fire, and the fire shall try every priest's work whatever sort it is. And therefore, the fire shall try both in order that a priest's work abides, and he may receive a reward, and that though his work is burned and he suffers loss, he can be certain that

246

this fire is not the eternal fire itself. It is only into eternal fire that those unrepentant shall be cast and with a final and everlasting sense of doom. And so it proves that when the Church burns it will not disappear because it has been built with Christ as the foundation, and for priests it proves in a similar fashion, for things burn what has been built up, and causes them to suffer loss, but they themselves are saved because they have retained Christ, who was laid as their sure foundation, and have loved Him and the Virgin above all. And saved they certainly stand on the side of right, and shall inherit the kingdom prepared for them. Those who do not love Christ and the Virgin shall not be saved from eternal fire, and they shall all go away into eternal punishment, where their tormenting worms shall not die, nor their fire be quenched, in which they shall suffer day and night forever.

In the interval of time between the death of your body and that last day of judgment and retribution which shall follow the resurrection, your body shall be exposed to a fire of a cleansing nature because your pleasures and pursuits the Church considers venial, and they shall be consumed in the fire of tribulation either here only, or here and hereafter both, or here that it may not be hereafter. For even the death of your body is itself a part of this tribulation, for it results from the first transgression, so that the time which follows death takes its colour in each case from the nature of your pleasure building. In general the guilty pleasures of bad Catholics of all kinds creates suffering through the fire of tribulation, and the eternal fire will consume them if the love of Christ and the Virgin is not found in them. While bad priests have fires which consume them without suffering, because Christ and the love of the Virgin is found in them, they are saved, though with some arbitrary loss. How many edifices shall there be, of love and wealth, built on the best foundation Christ Jesus, by which fire shall prove its worth, bringing joy to some, loss to others, but without destroying either sort? God only knows. Because of the Church's stable foundation there is only one true edifice for all to go to, one which is before and one which is after forever. And know Bad Clergy that you 'ex gratia et ad majorem gloriam Dei in perpetua' as such remain on this journey."